Also by Emily Kerr

Duvet Day

Meet Me Under the Northern Lights

TAKE A CHANCE ON GREECE

EMILY KERR

One More Chapter
a division of HarperCollins*Publishers* Ltd
1 London Bridge Street
London SE1 9GF
www.harpercollins.co.uk
HarperCollins*Publishers*
1st Floor, Watermarque Building, Ringsend Road
Dublin 4, Ireland

This paperback edition 2022
1
First published in Great Britain in ebook format
by HarperCollins*Publishers* 2022

A catalogue record of this book is available from the British Library

ISBN: 978-0-00-854301-3

Printed and bound in the UK using 100% Renewable Electricity
by CPI Group (UK) Ltd

To my parents who first introduced me to Greece, and to the teachers who inspired my love of its language

Chapter One

If I'm being completely honest, I think I was still a little drunk when we got on the airport shuttle bus, which could have been something to do with the ouzo Kat had persuaded us to down as we rushed to get packed. She'd claimed it was pretty much the same as mouthwash and would help freshen our morning-after-the-night-before breath. I'm not sure the shot delivered on Kat's promise, but the aniseed-tasting liquid had certainly cleared my sinuses as it burned its way down my throat, leaving my lips feeling weirdly numb.

'Hurry up, Lydia, you're keeping everyone waiting,' Amira called across the bus as I stumbled my way down the aisle, feeling strangely queasy and floaty at the same time. Was this what a hangover was like? If so, why did people subject themselves to it on a regular basis? It had been a big mistake to go beyond my usual personal limit of a glass of wine with a meal, but the girls had accused me of letting the side down – especially as I was the reason we'd flown out to Kefalonia for this trip in the first place – and I'd allowed myself to be peer-pressured into becoming the life and soul of the party. At least, I think that's what happened, but my memory of last night was more than a little patchy. I read in the newspaper once that even after only a few drinks, the brain can stop forming new memories, so perhaps here I was demonstrating that scientific study in practice. I didn't feel great about it. I remembered getting ready at the hotel, the three of us playfully squabbling over mirror space in our cramped room and posing for pictures on the balcony before we set off. I remembered enjoying our meal in the coastal town of Sami, especially the delicious honey-oozing pastries which the waiter presented us with when we'd paid the bill. And I also remembered Amira leading us along a seemingly endless street between tavernas, promising that there was an amazing bar at the end of it, while Kat and I tried to keep each other upright as our heels wobbled on the uneven surface. But after that, mostly nothing, until I was woken this morning by Kat chucking a glass of water on the back of my head as I lay face down on the bed, still clothed in last night's outfit. We'd been in too much of a packing rush to compare notes on the evening, but hopefully when it wasn't ridiculous o'clock in the morning, my brain would crank into gear and I'd be able to fill in the blanks.

The slight unease about not being able to account for every minute was adding to the booze-induced churning in my stomach and I was worried it might tip me over the edge. Despite letting their hair down just as much as I had, this morning Kat and Amira looked healthy and put together, whereas I felt like acid was swirling around my insides while tiny creatures held band practice in my skull. But then again, as the girls kept reminding me when they were nagging me about this holiday, they're far better at letting loose than I am, so maybe they'd built up a hangover immunity.

Even thinking about the word 'hangover' made me feel sick. A bubble of bile threatened to make its way up my oesophagus and I paused to take a few deep breaths, clutching the back of a complete stranger's seat so I didn't end up slumping onto their lap instead. This was mortifying. Why had I allowed myself to be talked into coming on this trip when I could have had a nice, quiet few days at home instead, ticking things off my to-do list while bingeing episodes of *Bake Off* and secretly imagining what it would be like to be one of the contestants? Actually, thinking about *Bake Off* and all the creamy, sugary concoctions they create was a seriously bad idea. I gulped.

'Uh-oh, she's turning green,' Kat announced to the entire bus as she thrust a sunhat under my chin. 'If you're going to vom, aim for that. We'll miss our flight if we get chucked off this thing.'

I forced myself to swallow as my cheeks glowed with embarrassment. I'm not sure what was worse, the effects of the hangover, or the humiliation of my fellow travellers judging me for my terrible state. We'd had to hustle hard to make the transfer bus, and I'd not even had time to change or check my appearance in the mirror before leaving, which was probably a good thing, because I had a horrible feeling that the remnants of last night's mascara had gone full panda eyes on me. It was also horribly obvious that I was still dressed in last night's going-out clothes, and while the girls would probably argue that my version of going-out garb was still pretty understated compared to their fabulous efforts, my attire of sparkly top, which was now rather crumpled, and too-tight-to-be-comfortable denim shorts, made me feel like I was doing the walk of shame down the bus aisle. The one thing I had managed to achieve before setting off was dowsing myself in perfume, but such was my delicate state at the moment, the flowery scent was making my eyes water.

I wanted to assure the other passengers that, despite appearances, normally I was a perfectly respectable human being who held down a sensible job and everything, but I wasn't sure I was capable of stringing the words together in the right order.

'All good,' I said, shakily, 'I'm definitely not going to throw up.' I hoped that saying the words out loud would make them come true.

Kat shoved the hat back on her head. 'Excellent. If you'd ruined my favourite hat, it would have sorely tested our friendship. Besides, I'm not sure it would have made a very good bucket, being made of straw and all. Smile for the camera.'

Before I could process her words, she'd whipped out her

phone and snapped a shot, which I knew was far too close up to be flattering.

'Jim is going to love this, his beautiful bride-to-be in all her hen-do glory.'

'Give me that.' I tried to grab the phone, hoping to delete the horrible picture, but also thinking that there might be some images on it which could fill in my memory blanks, but my dexterity and reaction speeds were not up to their usual standards. Yet another reason why I shouldn't have had those extra drinks last night. Kat slipped the phone out of my reach and winked at me. I silently prayed she wouldn't immediately upload the photo to Instagram as was her usual habit. Jim didn't really bother posting to social media, but he always seemed to be amazingly across what was on there, and that picture would definitely not fit into the guidelines of acceptable professional behaviour at the firm which he ran and I worked for. He was so diligent about not being seen to give preferential treatment to me, that he would be bound to make a point of speaking to me about it, regardless of what his boyfriend perspective on the picture might be. Actually, his boyfriend perspective would probably be similarly unimpressed. He wasn't keen on either of us making a spectacle of ourselves in any context.

'And I'm not a bride-to-be,' I added, for what felt like the hundredth time. I was beginning to think Kat was doing it deliberately to make a point. 'I don't know why you keep insisting on calling this my hen-do. Jim and I are just moving in together, we're not getting married.'

Kat pulled a face. 'Oh yeah, I forgot. He's decided not to

propose until he's done a full analysis to decide whether the costs of a wedding are offset by the tax benefits of marriage.' Her tone made it very clear that she did not agree with his logic.

'It makes sense. There's no point in being saddled with tons of debt for the rest of our lives.' I automatically defended Jim, even though I secretly still felt rather affronted by his pragmatic approach to our relationship. If there was one area to throw caution to the wind and go with the heart rather than the head, it was this. And then I felt disloyal for thinking that way. Jim had always been steady and dependable, I knew exactly where I was with him, and that was why he was so good for me, as he always reminded me.

'Careful consideration of decisions leads to no unexpected surprises.' I recited our mantra.

'Typical accountants,' muttered Amira. She was one to talk. As a doctor who spent most of her life picking up the pieces from other people's mistakes, she was nearly as risk-averse as Jim and I, but perhaps the holiday spirit had got to her too.

The bus lurched forwards as the driver decided he'd had enough of waiting for me to sit down and turned the engine on. Hot, petrol-scented fumes started pumping from the air-conditioning vents and the speakers crackled into life, blasting out a Greek pop song at full, painful, volume. It was a ridiculously cheesy tune, the kind of ditty which insinuates itself into your brain and remains playing on repeat for hours, even if you have no idea what the lyrics mean. It was definitely not hangover-appropriate. I fumbled in my handbag, trying to find my earplugs, but then the music changed key and the briefest flash of a memory sparked in my head as the singer crooned a high note. For a moment, the disgusting sensation of ickiness disappeared, to be replaced with something else altogether. It was more a recollection of a feeling of happiness and joy, rather than an image of an actual event, but that impression of utter contentment helped make my insides settle down a bit. I knew it was silly to rely on intuition rather than cold, hard facts, but I suddenly had a strong sense that last night's blank spaces had been filled with good experiences rather than bad.

That was enough to give me the strength to stagger the last few steps, reach up and stow my hand luggage in the overhead shelf. The girls had both bagged themselves window seats, so I was left with a choice of who to sit next to.

'Finally,' Kat said, moving her handbag so there was room for me. 'I thought you were going to spend the whole journey walking down the aisle. I suppose you've got to make the most of it for now until Jim pulls his finger out and puts a ring on it.'

I refused to rise to the bait, knowing there was nothing Kat enjoyed more than teasing people. I turned my back on her, plonking myself down next to Amira instead. In fact, I must have plonked a bit too heavily because I got a sharp pain in the small of my back when I landed on the chair.

'Ouch,' I winced, pulling the seat belt slack so I could

turn around to see if there was something sticking out of the seat. I ran my hand over the worn fabric, but couldn't feel anything sharp enough to have hurt me. Deciding I must have imagined it, I leaned back, but the pain started again.

I reached around and placed my hand against my back. Yes, it was definitely feeling tender and tight, as if I'd grazed it against something. I untucked my top and tried to feel my skin, but my fingers met with a layer of plastic which appeared to be stuck over the sore patch with some kind of tape.

'What the heck?' I muttered, trying to pick at the tape. I'd felt pretty grotty leaving the hotel without washing – 'No time for showers,' Kat had said – but now I felt even more grim, knowing that I'd managed to come out with some kind of makeshift plaster stuck to my lower back. This was not like me at all. The bus went over a pothole on a hairpin bend, making my nails slip and land in the centre of the painful bit. I winced and decided to stop pulling at the plastic and instead try to find out how I managed to get an injury. I closed my eyes and concentrated hard, trying to visualise the town we'd spent the evening in, focusing on different senses in case any of them ignited a memory. I could feel the rough stone of the buildings I'd brushed my fingers along as we'd made our way down the road between the pools of light from the streetlamps. I could hear the tinny sound of pop music mixed with the hubbub of different languages, voices raised over each other in a bid to be heard. And I could smell the scent of the sea in the air, and something else, something vaguely spicy, warm and comforting, closely followed by the tang of antiseptic. But try as I might to sharpen these flashes of sensation into something more tangible, the memories remained frustratingly elusive.

'My back's stinging. Did I scrape myself last night or fall over or something?' I asked Amira, lowering my voice in the hopes that Kat wouldn't overhear my question. I'd never live it down if she realised that the previous evening was pretty much a blackout for me. It was mortifying enough to have to ask in the first place.

Thankfully Amira looked concerned rather than amused.

'Not when you were with us. Are you OK, babe?'

I turned to face her square on. 'What do you mean, not when I was with you? Wasn't I with you all night?'

It was as if my stomach had fallen out of my body, leaving a horrible sense of dread behind in its place. I knew that statistically Kefalonia had a very low crime rate – it was one of the reasons I'd agreed to it as a destination – and I'd never felt anything but safe during our brief holiday here, but anything could have happened in my drunken state. I did another quick body scan, but thankfully the soreness on my back was the only niggle. I checked my purse, but my cash and cards were still safely in place. I reminded myself of the memory of a flash of happiness. Surely if anything terrible had happened, it would have overridden that?

Amira shrugged. 'I'll be honest, my memory is a tad patchy too, but there were definitely a few hours in the bar when we weren't all dancing together. You said you wanted to chill out at the hotel because your feet were sore. Maybe you bashed your back then.'

'But what about girl code? Never leave anyone behind,' I said indignantly. 'You know I'm a lightweight compared to you guys.'

'Sorry, Lyds, but you did insist you'd be fine sitting out for a bit and the hotel was only over the road and we watched you walk across to make sure you'd got there OK. If a bruise on your back is your biggest concern, then nothing really bad happened, did it?'

Kat cleared her throat from across the aisle.

'I hate to interrupt the heart-to-heart, ladies, but I've got a very important question to ask.' She paused and looked me squarely in the face. 'Lydia Evans, who is Andreas, what makes him awesome, and why do you now have his name tattooed on your lower back?'

Chapter Two

'What the actual f...flip are you talking about?' I said, as an uncomfortable hollowness settled in the pit of my stomach and slowly spread to the rest of my body.

'Gosh, Lydia, I thought you were going to break the habit of a lifetime and swear,' laughed Kat.

'I do swear, but internally – I just choose not to vocalise it,' I retorted. 'Jim doesn't like women swearing. And that's really not the point. Why are you trying to freak me out by saying I've got a tattoo? If this is your idea of a joke, it's really not funny. You know I'm scared of needles. Why on earth would I have a tattoo?'

Kat's eyes were sparkling with amusement, but I thought her attempt at a joke was anything but funny. I wished she'd stop messing around and allow me to nurse my hangover in peace.

'Turn round and let me get a photo of that lovely

inscription saying "Awesome Andreas" which is scrawled on your lower back and you can see it for yourself.'

She sounded so sure of herself that I did as instructed, despite the fact that her words made absolutely no sense to me. She rolled my top up and I heard the snap of the shutter before she handed her phone across to me. As she was doing so, the coach went over another bump in the road and the phone nearly fell out of her grasp. She juggled it around in a rather showy way until she'd got hold of it again properly, another thing which made me suspect that this was one of her silly pranks. After making a great display of checking she hadn't broken it, she finally handed the phone across, by which time of course the screen had locked so I couldn't even see the picture.

'Nice try,' I said, typing in her passcode with fingers which were rather trembly, whether from nerves or excess alcohol, I couldn't tell you.

The image was slightly blurry and distorted because of the reflection of the flash on the plastic covering, but beneath it there was definitely something there. I zoomed in to take a closer look. I couldn't swear to it saying 'Awesome Andreas' but it did look like some kind of swirly writing, the type of fancy cursive script you'd see on a wedding invitation. Only, wedding invitations normally had a much smaller font. This writing must have been at least half an inch high. I stared at it, not wanting to believe what was in front of me. The photo was time-stamped from just a minute ago, so I knew it wasn't one that Kat had prepared earlier. I zoomed in even closer, trying to detect how she'd worked the trick.

'OK, very funny. I'm guessing this is some kind of non-hen-do mickey take. How did you do it? Did you stick a transfer on my back while I was asleep? Or draw it on in pen? Because you've been a bit heavy-handed about it. I'm probably allergic to whatever it is you've used because my back is really sore.'

'I remember that from my first tattoo,' said Kat, sitting back in her seat casually. 'I don't know why I was so surprised by the pain. I had after all been repeatedly stabbed by a tiny needle pricking ink deep enough into my dermis to make a permanent mark. Don't worry, hon, it'll stop stinging soon. You won't even remember the pain. You'll probably go back for more. Maybe a "Breathtaking Barry" or a "Corr-blimey Colin". What would Jim be? "Jolly Jim"? No that's not really right. "Jobsworth Jim" is probably more accurate.'

She started laughing at her own bad joke, gurgling away without a care in the world. I'd never been so close to wanting to lash out at my oldest friend. Her rude, rambling nonsense was totally infuriating. This prank had gone too far. Was I the only grown-up around here?

'Kat, be serious, please. There's having a joke, and then there's just being mean. And drawing a fake tattoo on my back and then being offensive about my boyfriend is very much the latter. I've had enough. Tell me how you did it, or...'

My words faded as I saw the expression in Kat's eyes. Beneath the amusement, there was definitely a flash of something that looked like pity, and that made me very nervous. Sure enough, a few seconds later, she'd managed to rein in the laughter and was looking properly sympathetic, head slightly tilted to one side, regarding me as if I were a fragile glass object that was teetering on the edge of a shelf. Amira, meanwhile, grabbed my shoulder and held on tight as if she expected me to make a run for it off the bus.

'No, no, no, please, Kat, tell me it's not true,' I begged, my voice getting rather high-pitched with panic. 'Amira, tell me, what's going on? You're more sensible than she is, I know you'll be honest with me and won't string this farce along.' But I knew what the response would be before she even opened her mouth. However much I wanted to tell myself that my friends were playing a mean joke on me, I knew in my heart of hearts that they would never be so cruel and push things to this extreme when I was obviously in distress about it. Which left the question, how had I ended up with a tattoo and no memory of asking for it? Who the heck was Andreas? And why did I think he was so awesome? I wanted to hide away with the utter shame and horror of it. I was never going to touch a drop of alcohol ever again. I cursed myself with all the names under the sun, feeling like a first-class fool. And then the guilt kicked in. Here I was, just about to move in with my long-term boyfriend, and I'd gone and got the name of some random other bloke etched into my skin. What would Jim think of me? Would he even still want to be with me after this? How could I have done something so hurtful and awful?

I bit the inside of my mouth, trying to distract myself from the tears which were forming. I didn't have time to cry. I needed to think, to come up with a plan and sort out this nightmare situation, but my body had other ideas. I've never been one of those people who could cry delicately. The minute the waterworks start, my nose always wants to join in the party. I'd lost enough dignity without turning into a snotty mess on top of everything else. I sniffed hard, and tried through misty eyes to find a packet of tissues in my handbag, my movements clumsy with distress.

Amira reached over and squeezed my hand which didn't help me in my increasingly desperate search for the tissues. 'Oh, babe, what have you done?' she said, her voice so gentle and kind that it made me blub even more. Kat took my other hand and squeezed too. She quietly apologised for laughing at my predicament, explaining it was her startled reaction to the shock of spotting the inking. Normally I'd have taken strength from my two best friends, but their compassion made me feel even more alone in my misfortune.

I snivelled until my runny nose made it necessary for me to let go of Amira and Kat's hands and find that tissue. By this time, fellow passengers were becoming aware of my distress, despite my best efforts to cry quietly.

'He's not worth it, darling,' said one, assuming I was going through a break-up. *Not yet*, I thought. She passed me a bottle of water and a piece of chocolate. 'It's good for shock,' she promised. Although consuming anything was the last thing I felt like doing, I took a small sip from the bottle and swallowed the chocolate to be polite.

'You keep it,' she said, as I offered her the bottle back. 'When it's meant to be, you'll find Mr Right. And until then, enjoy your freedom to be answerable only to yourself.'

Her words, while kindly meant, only made me feel worse, hammering home all over again that my actions had the power to hurt someone very dear to me. As if on cue, the *Doctor Who* theme tune started blaring from my handbag. Jim had assigned it as his personal ringtone before we set off on holiday so I'd always know that it was him ringing me. Or at least, that's what he claimed was the reason, but we both knew it was really a bid to get me to answer the phone more quickly because I was so embarrassed by the loud tune. 'I know you'll be having fun with the girls, but there's no one who knows the filing system better than you,' he'd said, a glowing compliment, if not quite the one I'd have liked my boyfriend to give as his primary reason for needing to get hold of me during my vacation.

This time, the mild humiliation of the ringtone making the other bus passengers laugh was preferable to speaking to Jim. I knew he'd be able to tell the second I answered that something was wrong, and I wasn't ready to have that conversation yet. To be fair, I wasn't sure I would ever be ready to have that conversation. I waited for the phone to ring out – he'd be bound to notice if I rejected the call and ask me about it – then I switched it off, hoping that he would assume there was a bad signal rather than that I was deliberating swerving him. Then I turned my attention back to the matter in hand. Time to assess the damage properly and come up with a plan of action. I fixed my friends with as stern a look as I could muster.

'I need to know exactly what I'm dealing with. Tell me honestly, how bad is it? And does it really say "Awesome Andreas"? I mean, it sounds like something I'd say if I actually knew someone called Andreas who I thought highly of, but I really hope you've made a mistake. I think I could deal with a surprise tattoo of almost anything else, just so long as it didn't say a random man's name.'

Kat opened her mouth, clearly about to suggest a load of other inappropriate tattoos which I could have got, but I shot her a steely glare and she wisely decided that this was not the moment to try out a new stand-up routine.

This time it was Amira who examined my back. She squirted some anti-bac gel on her hands, then carefully peeled off the plastic covering with clinical efficiency.

The hubbub of our fellow tourists faded into noisy nothingness as I waited for Amira's verdict. After what seemed like a lifetime of scrutiny, I felt her putting the plastic covering back in place and pressing on the tape to make sure it stuck to my skin properly.

'Well, Lydia, the good news is that it's cleanly done. It's rather swollen at the moment, but that's to be expected. The skin doesn't look overly irritated, and there's no sign of infection or anything bad around the area.' It was a relief, even though the thought of getting an infection hadn't even occurred to me. 'And the script is really quite beautiful,' she continued. 'Trust me, I've seen much worse. Whoever did it was obviously talented and took care to do a proper job.'

What did I care how beautifully the words were written? What mattered was that they were words which it was no exaggeration to say had the capacity to ruin my entire life. Now that I was no longer able to deny the existence of the tattoo, the anger took over.

'Yep, definitely showing great care and diligence in agreeing to give a tattoo to someone who was quite clearly drunk.'

Kat and Amira exchanged glances.

'What?' I snapped, then immediately regretted it. 'Sorry, I shouldn't take it out on you guys. I just don't understand how this could have happened.'

What I really meant was I couldn't understand how this could have happened to me. It was just the kind of impulsive thing Kat would end up doing on a night out, but I normally never made any decisions without thinking at least five steps ahead to assess the consequences and calculate whether it was worth taking the risk. Boring it may sound, but that kind of careful consideration of circumstances had always kept me on the straight and narrow and prevented any disasters happening. Until now.

Amira knew exactly what I was really getting at. She smiled sympathetically.

'The thing is, babe, you are the most sober-seeming drunk person we know. To be fair to whoever it was who did this, you probably appeared to be pretty normal, just another tourist wanting something special to commemorate their trip.'

'But I don't want a tattoo as a souvenir,' I gulped, feeling thoroughly sorry for myself. 'I don't want a tattoo full stop. Especially not one with the name of someone who isn't my fiancé.'

Kat cleared her throat. I glared at her. 'If you dare be a complete pedant at this crisis moment in my life and point out that Jim isn't yet my fiancé, I will never speak to you again. You know exactly what I'm getting at.'

Kat held her hands up in surrender, although I could tell from the sparkle in her eyes that it was precisely what she had been about to do. 'I didn't say a thing and I'd never be so insensitive.' Her voice grew more serious. 'But speaking of Jim, what are you going to tell him?'

That of course was the question which was making my already-delicate stomach churn even more. What on earth could I tell him? Where would I even start? In self-help books, the experts always say that the foundation of a good relationship is honesty. But how could I sit down and have an open and honest conversation with Jim about how I'd somehow acquired a tattoo when I wouldn't be able to answer the first question he'd inevitably ask? Who was the mysterious Andreas, and what was it about him that had inspired Drunk Me to get his name tattooed on my skin for the rest of eternity? Having the name of another man on my back was not a good look, and certainly not something I could easily explain to Jim when I couldn't even explain it to myself. I could protest all I liked that it didn't mean anything, but if I were in Jim's position, would I believe me? No, in this situation I felt strongly that honesty was not the best policy.

'I'll get it covered up before he can even see it,' I said determinedly. There were loads of programmes on television which featured people getting cover-ups for dodgy tattoos, and while I'd never thought I'd require that kind of service, it was reassuring to know that there was generally a solution for even the biggest, most misguided of tattoo errors. Perhaps I could get a bunch of flowers inked there instead, I thought wildly. Or a cute dog. Frankly, I'd even accept the option of a plain rectangle of ink if it concealed the dreadful phrase before Jim saw it.

This time it was Amira who cleared her throat to signal another obstacle to my crazy plans.

'Oh, just say it, before our fellow passengers feel obliged to offer cough sweets to the pair of you with all the throat clearing you're doing,' I sighed. 'Let me guess, you're about to dash my last hopes? In which case, please can you get on with it. I'm not sure I can cope with any more horrible revelations.'

'I'm sorry to be the bearer of worse news, but you can't get it covered up just like that, Lyds. It's got to heal properly first. You don't want to end up with scarring.'

'But how long is that going to take?' I asked, the panic rising still further.

Kat pursed her lips. 'Longer than you want it to. Put it this way, it's not a plan that's going to be possible before you next see Jim, unless you pretend you've got some contagious disease and have to go into quarantine for a prolonged period.'

I mentally crossed the cover-up option off the list. But before I could vocalise my next suggestion, the bus pulled up at the airport, and all the other passengers stood up in a hurry to be the first ones at the check-in desks. I didn't even bother undoing my seat belt.

Amira and Kat watched me closely, a look of surprise on their faces.

'Aren't you going to join the masses charging for the departure lounge?' asked Amira.

'We're all getting on the same plane. I don't mind letting them go first,' I said.

'Who are you and what have you done with our friend Lydia? Getting a tattoo was out of character, but not caring about potentially being late? That's even more unlike you. Are you unwell?'

Kat touched the back of her hand to my forehead in mock concern.

'Stop teasing me. Why would I be in a hurry to get on a plane back home and face the disaster that will be trying to explain this tattoo to Jim? I can't tell him, I just can't. What if he thinks I've cheated on him? It would destroy him. We're moving in together. Like literally moving in as soon as I get back from this trip. This is meant to be the start of our happy ever after, and I've completely messed everything up.' I was actually wailing by now. A couple of stragglers who were still making their way off the bus turned to stare at me, which made me feel even more like wanting to curl up in a ball and die.

Kat put on her best bracing voice. 'Everything's going to be fine. Let's get into the airport, grab a drink, and we'll come up with a plan.'

I shrank against my seat, which once again set my back stinging.

'Oh no, I am never drinking again. This whole situation happened because you two talked me into having more than my limit. Jim's right. You are a bad influence on me. I wish we'd never come on this holiday. I think I prefer the option of staying on the bus and hoping this will all turn out to be a horrible nightmare.'

I actually pinched myself in a last-ditch hope that I really was asleep and dreaming this whole bizarre situation.

'I meant a coffee, not booze,' said Kat. 'And I'm afraid you are very much awake. We didn't hold you down and force the liquid down your throat. Whatever Jim thinks, you are a grown woman and perfectly capable of making your own choices and decisions.' Her tone softened. 'Look, I know you don't mean it and you're really upset right now, but this isn't the best way of handling it. While we'd all love to check out of reality and continue our Greek holiday, we have lives we need to get back to. Besides, I don't think the driver would take too kindly to you living on his bus for the rest of time.' She laughed. 'Bloody hell, it's a sorry state of affairs when I'm turning into the voice of reason. Come on now, things will look better once you've had a proper breakfast.'

Begrudgingly, I allowed myself to be led off the bus and into the terminal building. I felt vulnerable among the crowds, wary of someone bumping into me and making my back sting. Everyone seemed to be talking at once, no, not talking, shouting, which set my head throbbing again. I'd have been grateful for the noise if it had distracted me from my tattoo-induced terror, but it just made me feel even worse. Even though my newly acquired skin art was hidden beneath my clothing, I was so conscious of its presence that I feared everyone around me must be aware of it too, as if there was a giant arrow pointing at it. Every time someone smiled, I cringed, convinced that they were laughing at my situation.

I could barely concentrate as we went through the process of the security checks, and my dazed manner must have made me appear suspicious because I got selected for an extra pat down by a guard who ignored my pleas to be gentle when she reached my back. I supposed I should have been grateful that it didn't extend into a strip search. The fewer people who saw my stupid new tattoo, the better.

Chapter Three

Despite Kat's promise that breakfast would solve everything, funnily enough, the spinach and feta miniature pie which I managed to force down did not bring with it the answer to all my problems, although it did make me feel slightly more human. Amira and Kat tried to help me to remember the inspiration behind the inking, but I still drew a blank. For all I knew, the 'Andreas' could be the name of the tattooist himself. Or perhaps it could be nobody in particular. Maybe I had pointed at a stock image in my drunken state. I still couldn't understand why I would have done such a thing.

We managed to switch seats on the aircraft and sit together, but despite our collective brainpower, the best solution we could come up with for my predicament was covering the tattoo with a bandage and hoping for the best. It didn't exactly fill me with confidence. My face must have said as much because Kat offered another of her nuggets of wisdom.

'Don't overthink it, Lydia. Tell him you caught your back on the swimming pool wall, and if he asks more questions, distract him with some sexy lingerie and he'll forget he ever noticed the bandage,' she said. 'You'd be amazed at the number of times a good pair of pants have got me out of a pickle, trust me. Besides, you're moving in with him. Sexy knickers will help keep the magic alive when you've been bickering over whose turn it is to put the bins out.'

Privately, I thought Jim would be more startled by me suddenly starting to wear sexy lingerie than he would by the appearance of a bandage wrapped around my torso. But at this stage I was willing to give anything a try, so when we landed back in the UK, I did a detour to the duty-free shop on my way to the baggage collection and picked out a couple of sets of extremely uncomfortable-looking lacy concoctions. I felt like a massive imposter in the shop, as if all the other customers could tell that I was at heart more of a comfy pants kind of girl, but I told myself that if I could get a spontaneous tattoo, then surely I could have the gumption to style out a red push-up bra and French knickers.

Amira utilised her many years of medical training to make sure the bandage was firmly fixed over the offending inking, and then I stood in the baggage hall and listened to a pep talk from my friends in which they promised over and over again that everything would be absolutely fine, while having absolutely no basis for their assertions.

I was starting to wonder whether I could be like the Tom Hanks character in *The Terminal* and live out the rest of my days in the baggage reclaim when my phone bleeped. My stomach flipped as I read the message.

'Oh my goodness, Jim's here. He's come to pick us up so we don't have to find a taxi or get the bus back.'

Normally I would have been touched by his thoughtful gesture and relieved to avoid the immediate post-holiday low of having to scrabble for transport home, but I had been relying on the journey to give me extra thinking time.

'He can be a sweetie sometimes,' said Kat.

I felt even more guilty at the secret I was nursing.

The phone bleeped again.

'He's not gone into the short-stay car park because they've started charging for it, and he's in a layby over the road, so he says we need to get a wiggle on, or he might get a fine.'

I set off at the quickest pace I could muster while dragging my rather heavy suitcase. I'd gone a bit overboard buying presents for Jim from Kefalonia airport in a bid to assuage my conscience.

Kat and Amira scurried in my wake, grumbling between themselves as if I was out of hearing.

'And lo, normality returns, a classic Jim move,' muttered Kat. 'How does he think we're going to get our suitcases across the dual carriageway? And I bet you the short-stay car park will only be about three quid, and he wouldn't think twice about paying that for a coffee, so why can't he pay out now? Typical stingy so-and-so.'

'Come on, Kat, it'll be easier than fighting for public transport,' replied Amira quietly. 'And we can give Lydia some moral support. Knowing her, she'll blurt out about the tattoo the second she sees him. You know how she is with him. At least we can be on hand to pick up the pieces.'

Determined to prove my friends wrong, I started rehearsing my greeting to Jim in my head so that I didn't fall into the trap which they thought I would. Jim and I had been together long enough to know all of each other's little habits, and just like I could tell from the way he put his key in my door that he'd stopped for a pint with his mates on his way to see me, he would probably know the instant I walked up to him that I was trying to keep something from him. And although it went against my every instinct to even consider lying to my partner, I told myself it was out of consideration for his feelings, and therefore for the greater good.

It was only later that I wondered what exactly Amira had meant when she'd talked about the way I behave around Jim.

'Alright, Liddy-Lou, good holiday?' Jim was waiting by the open boot of his car, ready to take hold of our luggage. 'You look like you caught the sun. Was that factor fifty I got you not up to scratch?'

He kissed my cheek and I cringed as his hand rested on my back, mere millimetres from where the offending tattoo was lurking beneath its bandage. I only just managed to stop myself from flinching.

'It was very good, but I probably wasn't as diligent about applying the sunscreen as I should have been,' I confessed.

Jim shook his head. 'That's a shame. You should be careful, sweets.' His concern for my wellbeing made me feel even worse. 'The sun can be terribly ageing for women,' he added.

I caught Kat rolling her eyes.

'But let me guess, as a bloke, you're miraculously untouched by such concerns?' she said. I shot her a glance. Now was not the time to go on a feminist rant to Jim, even if I agreed with the sentiment.

Jim laughed. 'Duly noted. Right, hurry up, girls. I think that might be a police car on the other carriageway, and I don't fancy getting a talking to from some jumped-up plod because I've parked here for all of five minutes.'

As if to emphasise his point, he jumped into the driver's seat while we finished packing the car. Naturally I sat in the front passenger seat, but wished I was in the back with my friends, because my guilt and anxiety were growing every second I was spending next to Jim. How I was going to stand this long term, I had no idea.

Amira and Kat played their parts well, keeping up a stream of merry chatter about the holiday, which Jim pretended to listen to, although I knew from the mutterings under his breath that he was actually wondering if the guy in the Fiat Punto in front of us was going to hurry up and travel at the speed limit any time soon.

We dropped Amira off at her place first, then it was round to Kat's new house share. I'd never seen it in the light, and, when we drew up outside, I had serious misgivings about whether it was safe to leave her there.

'Are you sure you'll be alright?' I asked, looking at the boarded-up front window and noting the rather offensive graffiti on the side of the building. Kat, of course, misinterpreted my genuine concern as a ploy to put off the moment of being alone with Jim.

'Best get it over and done with,' she hissed in my ear as I helped get her suitcase out of the boot. 'Like ripping off a plaster. Only for God's sake, don't rip that bandage from your back. Or at least, don't do it unless Amira or I are around to intervene…or to watch the fallout.'

She winked at me, and went merrily into the house, leaving me alone with Jim. I sat back in the passenger seat and stared out of the window, wondering what to say next. Even if I didn't have the sword of Damocles hanging over my head in the form of a dodgy tattoo, I think this journey would still have felt a bit strange. Jim and I had been together for yonks, and of course we'd spent lots of time at each other's places, but this was the first time I was heading to his for an extended period. In fact, I really should stop thinking of it as *his* place, and start referring to it as *ours*. It was going to be my home now, and once I'd got my own key and my things unpacked there, it would be bound to feel more like I belonged. Jim was obviously thinking along the same lines too.

'What shall we have for tea?' was his first comment after I'd got back in the car. 'I thought we could swing by Tesco for a few bits on our way back to mine.' He paused. 'Sorry, I should say back to ours, of course, even though you haven't got round to signing that tenancy agreement with the landlord yet. You need to hurry up and do that. Got to get things off on a proper legal footing.'

'You and your paperwork,' I sighed, then kicked myself for saying something which could start a disagreement. 'You're right, of course. I'll make it a priority.'

Before the tattoo drama had taken over my mind, I'd been harbouring tender dreams of Jim picking me up and carrying me over the threshold into the house the first time we arrived back there as an officially co-habiting couple. Yes, I knew that was what you were meant to do when you'd actually got married, but moving in together was the first step in that process, and it would have been a romantic gesture to make, a symbol of our commitment to each other and our hopes for the future. But now that I had a fresh, slightly sore, tattoo to consider, I was rather glad that Jim wasn't one for romantic gestures. Besides, he probably would have struggled to lift me with the added weight of guilt I was carrying.

'Isn't there anything in the house we can eat?' I said. The late night and the emotional stress of the last few hours were starting to catch up with me and I wanted nothing more than to go straight home and crash out on the sofa, my back safely hidden among the cushions.

'Ah, well the lads came round last night and you know what they're like. They've eaten me out of house and home. We could probably do with a complete restock. Tell you what, I'll let you finish work a bit earlier tomorrow and you can do it on your way home, and we'll just get the basics today. And it's a good time to pop in. They'll have put the discount items out by now.'

Stopping off at Tesco to pick up some bargain pizza and salad felt like a pleasingly normal thing to be doing with Jim.

'The usual?' I asked. 'Don't worry, I'll zip round extra fast, it's hardly worth you coming in.'

It would give me the perfect opportunity to get some extra bandages. I could also have a quick look at the cosmetics counter and see if they had any makeup which might be suitable for using as a cover-up once the tattoo had healed.

I grabbed the first pizzas I could find so I had more time to seek out my other necessities. I'd tell Jim they were from the bargain section and he'd be happy at that. Then I caught myself. Just because I was telling one lie by omission, it didn't mean I should start adding other untruths to it.

When I got back to the car, Jim was deep in conversation on the phone. He gestured an apology to me and rolled his eyes as if exasperated by the other caller, but I could tell from the way he was chuckling that he was really enjoying the conversation.

I sat and stared out of the window for the rest of his call, trying to pretend that everything was alright, while simultaneously torturing myself by rehearsing how I would try to lessen Jim's devastation when the inevitable truth emerged.

'Sorry, sweets, that was Dan, as you probably guessed,' said Jim as he eventually hung up. 'He was wondering if I was watching the match tonight.'

What he really meant was Dan was wondering if Jim fancied watching the match with him.

'It's our first evening in as a proper couple,' I said, unable to conceal my disappointment. This couldn't be further from the dreamy night I'm imagined, where we'd have a candlelit dinner and he'd gaze lovingly into my eyes and be most un-Jim-like by starting to talk about ring shopping then and there. But then I remembered that I had no right to be upset about something so trivial. In fact, wouldn't it be better if Jim did go out to see Dan? It would at least delay the dreaded moment when he'd spot the bandage and start asking awkward questions.

'How about a compromise? We'll enjoy the pizzas together, and then you head out to watch the match down the pub with Dan,' I suggested.

'Compromise, the secret to all good relationships,' said Jim. 'And you can get on with unpacking your bits and bobs without me getting in your way. I've cleared out a couple of drawers for you, and there are a few spare hangers. I thought maybe we could pop to B&Q at the weekend and pick up some extra storage. I don't think I realised quite how much junk you were bringing with you. Do you really need so many books? I've no idea where we're going to find room for them.'

'Ha ha, very funny. It's not all junk. So that's how you entertained yourself in my absence? Going through my things. I hope you'll return the favour.'

Jim grinned. 'I am an open book. What you see is what you get. In fact, that's what I've always liked about you, Liddy-Lou. You're nice and straightforward, aside from the tendency to get carried away by silly romance novels which have no bearing on real life, of course.'

Yep, that was me, nice and straightforward, with no terrible skeletons in the closet. I was so guilt-ridden that I didn't even pick him up on his insult of my favourite books. The silence stretched out between us. Jim turned the car into the drive. As we came to a halt, he leaned across and lightly patted me on the knee.

'Are you sure you're OK after that holiday, sweets? Normally you jump on me for insulting your precious books.'

I pulled myself together. 'As I should have done. Don't worry, now we're practically married, I'll bring you round to my way of thinking sooner or later.' I forced a laugh.

'We'll see,' said Jim. I couldn't decide whether he was referring to the marriage comment or my threat to get him reading romances.

'Anyway, now that we're back at our home—' despite everything, I still got a small thrill out of saying that '—

where's that key which you've been promising me for ages?'

Jim looked shifty.

'Sorry, I knew there was something I'd forgotten. I haven't got round to getting yours cut yet. We'll have to manage with this one until I sort it.'

I told myself the tattoo meant I had no right to feel the disappointment I did. But I couldn't help feeling hurt that he'd not bothered. A key was such a small object, but it meant everything. I tried to keep my voice level.

'That's a shame. Perhaps you could ask Dan, doesn't he have a spare key?'

It had always felt rather unfair that Jim's best mate had been given a privilege which had so far been withheld from me, but then again, they had been friends as long as Kat and I had.

'But what if we get locked out? We'd be in trouble then,' said Jim, as if it was the most sensible, logical thing in the world.

'But we wouldn't be locked out, because I'd have a key.'

'Maybe,' he replied distractedly, glancing down at his phone. I got out of the car before I said something I regretted. As I heaved my suitcase out of the boot and struggled indoors with it and the shopping, I decided not to pursue the issue. It was probably better not to get wound up about silly things for the moment.

We were both studiously polite to each other as we prepared the meal. It wasn't like it was the first time we'd cooked together, but somehow knowing that us being in the same house together didn't have an expiry time on it anymore made us act a bit differently. Or maybe I was imagining it because the tattoo spectre was clouding my judgement. I really wanted to enjoy every moment of this new stage, savouring our living-together firsts, establishing the patterns which would become our routines. But instead, I found myself overthinking my every move and worrying that Jim was about to find out my secret. At one point, I couldn't stop myself wincing when he accidentally brushed my back as he was reaching past me to get a drink out of the fridge, but I managed to turn it into a sneeze.

'I hope you've not picked up something from the flight,' said Jim. 'I've always thought airplane cabins were full of nasties circulating around everybody on board.'

'It's nothing, maybe it was some dust.' I said the first thing that came to mind.

'I'll have to show you where the vacuum cleaner is then,' he retorted, and I knew I'd offended him by my inadvertent suggestion that the house wasn't clean. Why was I making things worse?

Thankfully we both started to relax as we ate the pizzas, and Jim more than filled the conversational gaps that I left, telling me about a new project he needed me to start at work, and speculating how quickly the council tax would go up now he no longer qualified for the single resident discount.

'You'll have to show me your holiday snaps when I get back from Dan's,' said Jim, casually. 'Kat's Instagram only gives part of the story, I'm sure.'

I nearly choked on my mouthful of salad.

'Kat's Instagram?' It came out as more of a squeak. She hadn't put up the awful photo of me on the bus, had she? And what if the snap of the tattoo had somehow wound its way onto her feed? Was this his way of trying to get a confession out of me? Was it a test?

I watched Jim's features carefully, but his expression was as open as always.

'Yes, it was nice to see you girls having fun.'

The tension in my shoulders eased slightly, but I felt like the skin on my back was starting to throb in a psychosomatic reaction to my nerves.

'Maybe we should take a trip away somewhere,' he suggested.

'I'd love to go back to Greece, it was gorgeous,' I said, rapidly considering how I could get away with wearing a wetsuit to conceal the tattoo. 'You've not taken any holiday for ages, and I know I've still got some leave left.'

'Maybe,' he said, 'but I was thinking closer to home so we could still keep an eye on things in the office. We'll have to look into it one day.' He checked his watch. 'Goodness, is that the time? Better go, don't want to miss kick off.'

I flinched as he gave me a squeeze goodbye, but thankfully he didn't notice.

I FaceTimed Kat almost as soon as I heard Jim's car reverse off the drive and go around the corner. She picked up on the first ring.

'Is everything OK? What did he say? Hold right where

you are, I'm coming over,' she said breathlessly, not even letting me say hello.

'It's fine, Kat, I've managed to keep it from him, and he's gone out to watch the footy.'

She rolled her eyes. 'On your first night together as loved-up cohabiters? The man's mad. You should be christening each room of the house and annoying the neighbours with your sexual antics. Tell me you at least flashed your sexy new knickers at him.'

I turned my phone around and gestured at my still unpacked luggage.

'I'm saving them for a special occasion.' My stomach flipped over. This was ludicrous. It wasn't a matter of if he noticed the tattoo, it was when. 'Oh Kat, I feel so terrible about this whole situation. Who am I kidding that I'll be able to keep this from him? Maybe I am better off telling him after all.'

Kat settled back on her sofa.

'Have you worked out who Awesome Andreas was yet?' she asked. Her face slipped out of view for a second. 'Sorry, just trying to prop this thing up on the cushions. My arm is going to start aching if I hold it at this angle for much longer.'

'Well, no, of course I haven't.'

'Then if you take my advice, you'll keep quiet about it for as long as possible. I know you didn't have a holiday fling, and you know that, but the tat is bound to make him suspicious, and you don't want that coming between you at such a delicate stage in your relationship. Wait until you've unpacked your stuff properly, and then see how you feel.'

'You're probably right.' I sighed. 'I guess I should wait until I at least have my own key. I don't want him to lock me out because of it.' I made a lame attempt at a joke, but I could tell from Kat's expression that she was not taking it as one.

'The bastard's not given you a key yet? Sorry, he's not a bastard, he's a very lovely man, I know. But why hasn't he given you a key? It's pretty selfish at best, and controlling at worst.'

'It's not a big deal, he's been busy at work, especially as he'd have had to pick up my stuff while we were off on holiday. And work is another reason why I'd really rather he didn't find out about the tattoo. If I damage his trust in our relationship setting, it'll also damage his trust in the work environment. I know it's way down on the priority list compared to our relationship, but I don't want to spoil my promotion chances.'

'You're sleeping with the boss. If he's not given you a promotion yet, then I'm not sure what more you can do,' she retorted.

I stuck my tongue out at her and she laughed.

'Seriously though, you're damn good at your job, Lydia. You're overdue a promotion. I know you say he's holding you to higher standards because he doesn't want to be accused of favouritism, but it's really holding you back. Have you thought about looking for a job at another firm? You guys are going to be spending a lot of time working together and living together now. It might do you good to spread your wings and let Jim see that you're in demand elsewhere too.'

I shrugged my shoulders. She made it sound so easy, but to me it felt like a daunting prospect. I'd worked at Jim's firm for years now, even before we started dating, and I couldn't really imagine going anywhere else. It was comfortable and familiar and safe, and I didn't fancy the upheaval which going to another company would involve. Besides, wasn't there a danger that Jim would interpret any move to another firm as a personal affront? I knew how much it meant to him having my support in the professional domain as well as in his personal life.

'Promise me you'll think about it,' said Kat, as we ended the call. 'You can do far more than you let yourself believe.'

Chapter Four

The next morning, I woke with a start as the alarm clock went off. Jim leaped out of bed and turned the lights on, swearing with irritation that we would be behind schedule if I didn't hurry up.

'People will think I've lost focus now you've moved in,' he said. 'And that audit is due by close of play. We can't afford to waste a minute.'

'Let them think what they like,' I said. 'And we've still got plenty of time.'

'Not if you carry on languishing in bed like that we haven't.'

There went my plan of hiding under the covers until he left the room. I slid out of bed and moved sideways, trying to appear nonchalant as I attempted to keep my back against the wall.

'Weren't you roasting in that get up?' he asked, nodding towards the voluminous flannel pyjamas I'd donned last night as part of my plan to keep him from discovering my terrible secret. Thankfully he'd fallen for my feigned deep sleep when he'd arrived back after the footy, which had given me another few hours' grace.

'I felt really cold. I think I've become acclimatised to the warm temperatures in Kefalonia,' I answered, rather appalled at how quickly and frequently the lies were now slipping off my tongue.

Of course, this would have been the perfect opportunity for Jim to make a comment about being able to warm me up, and then for him to follow through on his suggestion, but I guess the thoughts of the audit had driven any idea of that kind of thing from his head. I quickly launched into further diversionary tactics, just to be on the safe side.

'Good match last night?' I asked as I grabbed an appropriate work outfit and started my attempt at changing in a way which wouldn't give him a glimpse of my back while simultaneously not giving the impression that I'd suddenly developed the modesty of a nun.

Thankfully Jim launched into a lengthy blow-by-blow account of the game, including an in-depth analysis of all the referee's apparently dubious decision-making abilities. By the time we'd arrived at the office, he was nearly hoarse from his enthusiastic description of the action and I felt like I'd watched the entire match. He pulled up the handbrake and looked carefully around the car park to check that none of our colleagues were around, then he leaned across and squeezed my knee.

'I think the break has done you good, Liddy-Lou. We've

had a lovely chat this morning. I could get used to this living together malarkey.'

What a romantic way to describe the start of the rest of our lives together. I would have been irritated by the fact he seemed unaware that I hadn't managed to get a word in edgeways, if I wasn't so relieved that I'd got away with my deception. As soon as we got out of the car, he stepped away from me, determined to keep an appropriate distance apart now that we were on work premises. Normally I would have teased him by attempting to loop my arm through his or by slipping my hand up his jacket, but today it felt safer to keep physical contact to a minimum.

I settled myself at my desk to go through my inbox. It was brimming with emails after my trip, and, as I waded through them, the holiday quickly faded away as if it had never happened. I say that, but there was one reminder which kept making its presence felt to make sure I didn't quite forget about my Kefalonian stay. Today the tattoo had started itching. Not the occasional irritation that I could ignore, but a persistent prickliness that made me want to stand in the doorway and rub my back up and down the frame like a bear until the itchiness went away. I tried to concentrate on my spreadsheets, but I felt unsettled and out of sorts, so I kept on making silly mistakes. At lunchtime, I decided getting away from my desk was the best option. I knocked on Jim's door and went in.

'Do you want to grab a sandwich? Perhaps we can get that key cut while we're at it?'

Jim frowned over his monitor.

'What did you want? I'm in the middle of something.'

I was rather taken aback. 'I'm sorry for disturbing you, *sir*,' I couldn't help retorting. Guilt-ridden I may be, but I wasn't going to allow Jim to speak to me like that. He may be my boss as well as my boyfriend, but that didn't give him the right to be so short with me. My obvious sarcasm shook him out of his number-induced reverie.

'Sorry, sweets, that was unnecessary.' He pinched the bridge of his nose in the way he does when he's got a headache developing. 'These figures have been driving me up the wall all morning. I'd love to go to lunch with you, but I'm not going to have time with the deadline this evening.'

He looked so deflated that I instantly forgave him for his rudeness. I made a move towards him, intending to massage his hunched-up shoulders, then stopped myself. Instigating any kind of physical contact was not a good idea at the present time. I offered the next best thing instead.

'Do you want me to take a look? Sometimes it can help to have a fresh pair of eyes checking things over.'

Jim perked up right away. 'Would you? That would be fantastic.'

His genial grin set my guilty conscience clanging all over again. How could I be brazenly smiling back at him when the etching of another man's name was making its itchy presence felt on my back?

'Tell you what, you settle yourself down in here, and I'll bob out and fetch you a sandwich,' he offered, already halfway out of the door.

'Get that key cut while you're at it,' I called after his departing form, but I wasn't sure he heard me.

It didn't take me long to check Jim's figures, and when he still hadn't reappeared with lunch, I thought I'd watch something on YouTube to distract me from my hunger while I waited. Jim was a stickler for client confidentiality and wouldn't want me to leave his office unsupervised, however trustworthy the rest of the staff were. I clicked on the internet icon and it brought up a page he must have been looking at earlier in the day. It was a document saved in an online cloud drive. I would have clicked open a different tab immediately, but the sight of my name caught my interest and I couldn't help taking a closer look. As I scanned down the page, I felt the anger start to rise. It was a list of all the employees at work and the pay increases they'd been awarded over the years. I knew that I shouldn't be looking, but as I compared their wages to my own financial situation, I felt a big sense of betrayal. How come everybody else had had pay rises yet my salary had remained stubbornly the same? None of the increases were what you'd call generous, but the point was that everybody else had been given them while I had been left out. I checked the dates and realised the change in the way I was treated compared to my colleagues had begun when Jim and I had started going out with each other.

It was a punch in the gut. I worked so hard at my job, putting in hours far longer than I was paid for, yet my own boyfriend hadn't bothered to make sure that my dedication was recognised and rewarded. I wasn't just furious, I felt hurt and cheated by him. Jim might argue that he didn't want to be seen to be favouring his girlfriend, but this was active discrimination against me, taking advantage of my status as his partner to get away with treating me differently to everyone else. It wasn't only about the money, it was about what was right and fair. He knew how much I'd put into this place, working hard because doing a good job mattered to me, but also because I knew how much the success of the business meant to him. But apparently that dedication and care was meaningless. Suddenly I was forced to view Jim in a different light and it wasn't a nice one.

One of the reasons it had taken so long for us to make the step of moving in together was because of the disparity in our financial situations. I'd grown up in a house where my dad was the main breadwinner, and made sure we knew it. I'd seen the emotional cost on my mum, having to ask him for money and justify every penny of spending to him, and I'd never wanted to put myself in that situation, not that I'd ever imagined Jim would behave in that way. But it seemed his control of my finances had been more subtle, and all the more upsetting for it. If he was this measly when it came to his own girlfriend's salary, what other areas of life had he been short-changing me in too?

I sat there stewing, a thousand thoughts swirling around my mind as I questioned everything I thought I knew about our relationship. When Jim returned, I made an excuse to get out of his office as quickly as possible. While the thought of confronting him about what I'd discovered was appealing, I didn't trust myself to do it yet. I was so hurt that I knew everything would pour out in a big emotional mess, and I'd make a hash of it. I needed to think things through, decide exactly what I was going to say to him and what I wanted the outcome of our conversation to be.

I spent the rest of the afternoon getting increasingly anxious, veering between finding excuses for Jim's behaviour and being appalled by it. Was I overreacting? Or was I not reacting enough? Part of me was desperate to message the girls and get their take on the situation, but the other part of me knew what their response would be and I didn't want other people's anger to cloud my judgement over something so important.

Just after five o'clock, an instant message popped up on my screen from Jim.

Have to stay late to finish this off. See you at home… As requested, I got a key cut at lunchtime and have left it in your pigeonhole.

For a moment, my feelings towards him softened. And then I reminded myself that his small, overdue gesture didn't change the magnitude of what I'd found out.

Back at Jim's – despite my new key, I still couldn't help thinking of it as his place – I changed out of my sober work gear into slouchy leggings, tucking my loose T-shirt up under the band of my bra and removing the bandage so that the tattoo scab could get some air. I stood in the living room, staring at my boxes of stuff, thinking about how Jim had gone through them in my absence. He'd been so casual when he'd mentioned it, but it was an invasion of privacy. I'd been looking forward to us living together for so long, but all the joy and excitement I'd been feeling had been wiped out. Now I didn't know what I wanted anymore.

Eventually, I heard Jim's car pull up on the drive. For a second, I thought about pulling down my T-shirt to conceal my 'Awesome Andreas' tattoo. And then I decided against it. It was ridiculous to think I could keep it hidden from him forever. Surely a drunken holiday tattoo paled into insignificance on the relationship sin scale when it was compared to long-term financial deception? I would be honest with him, in exchange for his honesty about the situation at work.

'Evening, what's for dinner?' Jim asked, looking at me expectantly as he came in through the door.

This was it, my moment to confront him about my discovery. But something made me stay quiet. I walked past him and stood with my back on full show, checking the contents of the fridge. It was more to give him the chance to see the tattoo than because I actually intended to magically produce food for him. If there weren't bigger issues at stake, I would have said something about his assumption that I'd moved in to become his personal chef.

'Well, I didn't have time to go shopping today as planned, so nothing by the looks of the cupboards.'

I waited for the moment when he'd ask me about the tattoo which was plainly visible on my back, the tattoo which said the name of another man.

'We'll get a takeaway,' he said, seemingly oblivious to everything except thoughts of his stomach. He scratched his chin and started riffling through the drawers for menus, selecting the type of food he wanted, and not bothering to ask me what I fancied.

It was then that I decided I wouldn't say anything yet, and would wait to see how long it would take him to notice my newly acquired inking.

It became almost a game to me as I walked around the house, leaned over at the counter as I put the takeaways on plates, and even stooped right in front of him as I pretended to drop a knife on the floor. I was practically flaunting the tattoo at him, but whatever I tried, he seemed completely unaware of the addition to my skin.

Jim took his takeaway into the living room to watch a gameshow. I went and stood in front of the television with my back towards him, but even then, he only asked me to move because he couldn't see how many points one of the contestants had got.

Eventually my frustration at my apparent invisibility and my rage at the work situation got the better of me and I muted the TV so I could confront him. Trying to keep my voice as controlled as possible, given my frustration and hurt, I asked him why everyone else in the company had got pay rises while I was still on the meagre traineeship salary I'd started out on, despite being more qualified and more experienced than most of my colleagues.

'Ah, Liddy-Lou, don't get yourself so worked up. It would have affected your tax bracket.' He said it as if it was the most reasonable argument in the world. 'And as we're together, I can handle the finances anyway. It doesn't really matter what you earn.'

I stared at him, my mouth open in astonishment. 'But it matters to me, Jim, it really matters to me. You know how that kind of thing affected my parents' relationship and eventually drove them apart. This isn't the eighteenth century, and I want to be able to stand on my own two feet. I want to be given the salary I deserve, the salary I earn from all the hard work I put in, all the experience and knowledge I bring to the business.'

He shrugged. 'Then, I'm sorry. I'll take another look at it when I can find a moment.'

It didn't sound like he'd be finding a moment any time soon and he certainly didn't sound sorry enough. I could tell his eyes were wandering back to the TV screen and that he was itching to put the sound back on so he could carry on watching the show. That tipped me over the edge. I glared at him, wondering how I could ever have allowed myself to believe that I was in love with a man who was so lacking in consideration and understanding. Even if he had thought he'd been acting in my best interests, why couldn't he take the time now to listen to my concerns and promise to act on them? As I was getting things off my chest, it seemed time to raise the other issue which had been playing on my mind, although in light of recent revelations, I felt far less guilty about it.

'And haven't you noticed something different about

me?' I couldn't keep the incredulity out of my voice at his lack of observation.

Jim struggled to tear his gaze back towards me from the silent screen where someone was now having gunge poured over them for getting an answer wrong. I could tell that my persistence was starting to irritate him.

'Something different?' he said.

'This.' I spun round and pointed at the tattoo on my back. 'How could you have not noticed this?'

I felt his gaze on it.

'Oh that. Interesting holiday souvenir,' was all he said. He might as well have been passing comment on the weather.

'Don't you want to know what it's about? Why I have the words "Awesome Andreas" on my back?'

He remained frustratingly silent. I couldn't decide whether he was doing it deliberately to wind me up still further, or whether he was genuinely unmoved by the tattoo's appearance and implied message. I threw my hands up in the air in frustration and started answering the questions he didn't seem bothered enough to ask.

'I don't know is the answer you're looking for. I don't know who Andreas is, and I don't know what inspired me to get his name on my back. I was drunk. It was stupid.'

Jim shrugged, his eyes flitting back to the TV screen.

'These things happen.' He burped. 'Excuse me.'

I think it was the burp that did it. If that explosion of sweet and sour pork-scented gas hadn't emerged from his mouth at that precise moment, I think I would have climbed down from my high horse, been grateful for his calm acceptance of my big confession and eventually got over my distress at the work situation. But something about that burp was so casually disdainful, a demonstration that he was so unbothered by issues that were really bothering me, that it tipped me over the edge. Was this what the rest of my life was to be? Tied to this man who was controlling and archaic, and apparently completely indifferent to the fact that I'd gone on holiday and got another man's name tattooed on my back? This was supposedly the beginning of our lives together, the start of something precious and wonderful. We might not be married, but we were meant to be in the honeymoon stage of our relationship, completely in love and passionately concerned about one another. When I got back from holiday, we shouldn't have been able to keep our hands off each other. He should have noticed the change in me instantly and cared about the reasons behind it. He should also have cared about my feelings over the salary situation, realised he was in the wrong and not taken advantage of our relationship to treat me badly in the professional setting in the first place. All of the hurt and the disappointment and the outrage were spinning around my mind and I couldn't grasp how the man I had thought I loved didn't understand where I was coming from. It was like a complete stranger was sitting on the sofa before me.

Jim took a sip of beer and unmuted the television, and the noise of the gameshow host filled the room once again. Was that it? Discussion held, issue dealt with?

'No.' I said the word forcefully, raising my voice over the synthetic music of the TV show.

'What's that, sweets?' Jim's question was automatic. He wasn't really interested in the answer and I didn't read any genuine regard in his affectionate manner.

'No, this is not how I want my life to be,' I said.

I thought back to the flashes of feelings I'd had from that last night of the holiday, the sense of sheer happiness and joy. When else had I ever felt like that, so completely right? And didn't I deserve to feel like that again? All my life I'd been so careful and considered in everything I'd done. Choosing a sensible nine-to-five career in a secure profession, dating a man who appeared to be steady and dependable, even if he had turned out to be an utter shit. Perhaps it was time to be spontaneous, to chase after that feeling of joy, to allow myself to live, really live, rather than just exist. Once again, I found myself thinking about the 'Awesome Andreas' of my tattoo. What if he was a real person? A mysterious individual I'd met on that night, who'd set my heart racing and inspired those feelings of happiness, who'd stirred sensible, cautious me into doing something utterly impulsive, getting a tattoo to commemorate our meeting? What if he was still out there, waiting for me?

Without allowing myself to really think about it, I got out my phone, opened up the flight app and found myself booking a one-way ticket back to Kefalonia.

Chapter Five

I t was Kat who I chose to ring from the arrivals hall of
Kefalonia airport as I paced up and down nervously
wondering what on earth I'd done. My exit from Jim's
house had been nothing if not dramatic, even though not a
single voice had been raised at any point. He'd sat open-
mouthed on the sofa as I delivered my resignation from the
company verbally, promising a follow-up email. And then,
in case he hadn't already got the message, I'd informed him
that our relationship was well and truly over too. Then I'd
picked up my suitcase, which was still packed with my
unwashed holiday clothing, grabbed a random handful of
books from one of my boxes, ordered an Uber and gone out
to sit on the kerb to wait for it to arrive as I couldn't bear
another minute stuck in the house with him. Jim had
followed me in a flap, and then stood over me, his tone
fluctuating between astonishment at my sudden departure
and embarrassment at what the neighbours must be

thinking. Sadly, the latter appeared to be more important to him.

I'd sat in a daze and let it all wash over me, almost as if this whole sequence of events was happening to somebody else. I must have been in some kind of fugue state, because I felt numb from the second I left the house, and didn't really start thinking about my situation properly until I'd touched down in Greece the next day, having spent the night at the airport to await my early morning flight.

Of course, as soon as I'd landed, my brain had gone into overdrive with the magnitude of my impetuous decision. How had I, a sensible accountant with a five-year plan, managed to toss away a long-term relationship and everything I'd worked so hard to achieve career-wise in the heat of the moment? When the man at Passport Control had asked me the reason for my trip, I'd stood there in a daze, fighting the urge to tell him the whole story, desperately seeking someone to approve of my impulsive actions, even if they happened to be a complete stranger. Eventually good sense had won over and I'd managed to croak out 'Holiday'. To tell him that I was here to search for a happiness which might not even exist would have been ridiculous. He'd nodded disinterestedly, before looking over my shoulder at the next person in the queue.

Once I'd collected my luggage, I'd had to lock myself in the toilets, fighting the urge to sob out loud as a panic attack threatened to overwhelm me. All around I could hear the excited voices of tourists looking forward to their much-needed holidays, laughing as they called out to each other between the cubicles, discussing which beaches they should visit, and what would be their first cocktail by the pool. Meanwhile, I had wanted to sink to the ground and curl up in a ball, which I probably would have done if concern about what nastiness might be lurking on the floor hadn't won out. I had never felt so totally alone and so totally out of my depth. But then again, I had never felt so alive as the fight or flight instinct surged through my veins.

In theory, there was no real reason why I couldn't have hopped on the first plane back to the UK, swallowed my pride and begged Jim for my old job back. In fact, that would probably have been the sensible thing to have done. But in reality, the thought of the sheer embarrassment I would suffer in that scenario, the utter humiliation of having to pretend that I was in the wrong, stopped me from backtracking. Yes, it had been an incredibly rash decision to come out here, but now that I was here, I needed to make the best of it, to prove to Jim, and perhaps even to myself, that I was worth far more than he had ever given me credit for. And didn't a part of me feel elated that I was finally doing something entirely for myself, rather than worrying about how my dreams would fit in with other people's? Why shouldn't I have this adventure?

The expression on Jim's face when I'd dropped the shiny new house key out of the taxi window as I'd driven off would keep me going through whatever challenges I might be about to face, I told myself firmly. Just thinking about it made me want to laugh hysterically, even though that particular dramatic gesture was going to make it much harder for Kat to go around and collect the rest of my stuff, which was exactly what I was asking her to do now.

'Sorry, you're going to have to explain it to me again,' she said. 'I think I might have taken some drugs and this must be a weird trip I'm having.' I could hear her pacing up and down anxiously.

'Jim and I are finished. I've left my job. I'm back in Kefalonia. I'm going to track down Awesome Andreas.' I spoke in short sentences to make sure I'd got the message across to Kat, but also to explain my actions to myself all over again. I knew how irrational I must sound. The whole idea was utterly ludicrous. I'd thrown away a perfectly reasonable life to chase after some romantic phantom. I had barely fifty euros in my purse, a bag full of unwashed holiday gear and random books, and absolutely zero knowledge of the Greek language beyond 'good morning' and 'thank you'. I should have been utterly terrified. I should have been queuing up to get on the first flight home. But the adrenaline from the break-up was coursing around my body along with a hefty dose of righteous indignation and I was a woman on a mission. Even the astonishment of my oldest, bravest friend at my out-of-character behaviour was not going to hold me back.

Kat cleared her throat and then started speaking very slowly and gently.

'Lydia, honey, is there someone nearby who can sit with you until I get out there? Let me check when the next flight is, and I'll scoop up Amira from work and we'll come out and be with you as soon as we can. Perhaps I should ring the consulate and see if there is someone there who could help you? I'm not sure you should be by yourself right now. I'm worried about you.'

I laughed. 'Don't be ridiculous, Kat, I'm perfectly fine.' I could picture the incredulous expression on her face and hastened to convince her. 'I promise you, everything is alright. I don't need supervision and while it's very kind of you to offer to drop everything to travel out here, I don't need collecting and taking home. I'm not having some kind of breakdown, I'm not in any danger, I'm just being spontaneous and trying to live my best life.' That was the phrase people on social media used when they posted about pursuing their dreams and living life to the fullest, wasn't it? Why shouldn't I be like them?

'If you say so.' Kat didn't sound convinced. She spoke carefully, obviously considering her every word before she said them out loud. 'Don't get me wrong, I'm delighted you've finally ditched Jim. We never knew what you saw in him, and I always had my concerns that he was controlling. After all, he constantly kicked up a fuss about you spending time with us, even when he was off with his mates all the time. And the work thing is indefensible. Classic coercive control, that, keeping a tight grip on your finances and making you dependent on him.'

Nice of my friends to keep their concerns to themselves, I thought, then told myself off. Would I really have listened to them if they had spoken out? After all, I'd been so swept up in the relationship that I'd been dreaming about marriage and babies, although hadn't holding out the prospect of those dreams been another way in which Jim had manipulated me into doing what he wanted? Perhaps it was better that I'd come to that conclusion myself, even if it meant I'd endured a different kind of heartache.

'But chucking in everything and flying off to Greece to chase after some mythical man who may or may not exist seems a bit, well, extreme,' Kat continued. 'Why can't you chop up Jim's clothes, get drunk and eat lots of pizza with your friends like normal people?'

Her words should have had a sobering effect on me, but they just made me even more determined to prove her and everybody else wrong.

'It is rather extreme, I'll admit that. And probably a tad silly. A lot silly, really. But I'm free, I'm single, I can choose what I want to do, and what I want to do is live a bit. Why shouldn't I? I've spent the last few years dutifully doing what was expected of me, and did it make me happy? I thought it did, but now I'm not so sure. I think I was existing, rather than really living. Maybe the reason I got the "Awesome Andreas" tattoo in the first place was because subconsciously I felt that, and I was trying to give myself an excuse to find my freedom. Or maybe I really did meet an amazing man named Andreas and he's somewhere here on this island waiting for me to find him again.' I felt a thrill just talking about it. I knew it was probably ridiculous, but heroines in books never got their happy ever afters by passively waiting for them to happen. It was time I channelled their bravery, and went out to discover my own dreams, rather than doing what other people wanted me to do. 'I want to find the man I deserve to be with. And who deserves to be with me. And in the meantime, I'll enjoy following my own path, experiencing something new and different and exciting.'

I was definitely talking myself further into my preposterous plan, but the more I spoke to Kat, the more I realised what I was saying was true. Why shouldn't I have some fun for a change and really live my life? And yes, I was woefully out of my depth, but what was the worst that could happen?

Kat laughed. 'Jim would definitely say you've been reading too many novels. But you're right. You deserve to be happy and not to be held back by him anymore. And I hope you have fun while you're on your Andreas hunt. What I wouldn't give to be back out there in Greece with you, feasting my eyes on all the beautiful people who live in the sunshine.' Her voice became more serious. 'Promise me you'll call if you need us. Any time, day or night. We're only a few hours away by plane. And keep us posted about how things are going. Have fun, and stay safe.'

Kat's words were echoing in my ears as I finally found the strength to exit the terminal building. I could talk the talk on the phone, but could I really follow through on my rash plans? While I was in the airport, I felt like I was still in transit and therefore not fully committed to this strange new future. Somehow walking out of that air-conditioned bubble and into the bustle and chaos and heat of the area directly outside would confirm there really was no going back now. I steeled myself, donned my sunglasses and strode out, hoping that feigned confidence would help the real thing come along.

Exiting the terminal now couldn't have been more different from when I'd walked out of it a week ago, Kat and Amira either side of me, carefree and happy, eagerly anticipating our break in the sunshine. Now I still had a sense of anticipation, but it was mixed with a hefty dose of trepidation too. Although I was surrounded by crowds of people, I felt completely separate from them. They were being shepherded by solicitous reps onto shuttle buses to holiday resorts, or jumping into taxis which would whisk them straight to their hotels. They all had someone to look out for them and they knew what to expect at the other end of their journey.

That, more than anything, made me realise how alone I was at this point. Nobody was expecting me, and I was the only person who could make things happen. Now I was an I, not a we; everything was entirely up to me, a thought that was both liberating and terrifying. After years of asking myself 'What would Jim do?', it was time to focus on 'What should Lydia do?'

First things first, I needed to consider the practicalities of my situation. With only fifty euros in cash on me, and having kissed goodbye to my regular salary along with my non-fiancé, I knew I'd have to be careful with my modest savings and make every penny, or in fact cent, count. I'd have to find somewhere to stay and a means of supporting myself before I did anything else. The backpackers I followed on Instagram made it look so effortless and fun, but now I was in their position, it felt very daunting. I'd never been abroad alone before. In fact, I'd not been abroad much full stop. My family had never been able to afford regular foreign holidays when I was a child, and Jim had always preferred UK breaks, in case a work crisis arose which only he could sort out. Was I really brave enough to follow this adventure through? And was I capable of doing it?

I told myself to woman up. If I could walk out on Jim *and* my job, then I could take this next step too. I hovered near the taxi rank, trying to summon up the courage to speak to the drivers and ask how much it would cost to get to Sami, the scene of that infamous night out. That seemed as good a place as any to base myself. The mysterious Andreas could be anywhere on the island, but it made sense to start my hunt in the place where I'd acquired the tattoo. The only trouble was, Sami was on the opposite side of the island to the airport and I wasn't sure my meagre euros would be enough to pay the taxi fare to get there, and I certainly wasn't going to take the plunge and hire a car. The thought of driving on the wrong side of the road terrified me, especially when I knew my destination wasn't exactly around the next corner. The transfer bus had taken a couple of hours to make the journey across the mountains and along the coast. But then again, we had been stopping multiple times at different resorts and I was pretty sure the driver hadn't taken the most direct route. It wouldn't do any harm to find out the facts. I decided to channel Kat's unfailing self-confidence and strode up to a group of taxi drivers who were enjoying a quick cigarette break between fares.

'*Kalimera,*' I said, using up fifty percent of my total Greek knowledge. 'How much is it to get to Sami?'

'Good morning,' replied one of the group cheerily. 'For you, fifty euros.'

My heart sank as my worst fears were proved right. Yes, I had that exact amount of money, but what was I meant to do once I arrived in Sami if I had no cash? Jim says you should always have enough cash on you to pay your journey home. While a lot of things Jim says should be taken with a pinch of salt, there was sense in that particular pearl of wisdom. What if my bank freaked out at my sudden return to Kefalonia and thought my cards had been nicked and cut them off? What if I needed to buy water and they only took cash? I remembered the guidebook saying that cash points on Greek islands aren't always regularly topped up and given that it was holiday season, they were probably in big demand. I couldn't take the risk. My dilemma must have shown on my face because the driver beckoned for me to follow him.

'*Ela,* come, you see over there? There is a bus which goes to Argostoli from that stop. You go to Argostoli, then you change there to get the bus to Sami. The journey is longer than by taxi but the two bus tickets will cost you less than ten euros, and you will see much of the island.' He smiled broadly, looking delighted that he'd been able to impart such a useful bit of knowledge.

'That sounds perfect, thank you so much.' I couldn't

believe how kind he'd been to tell me this nugget of information when he must have wanted to get the fare instead. I decided it was a sign that I'd made the right decision to come back to Kefalonia. Hopefully everyone else would be as friendly and as welcoming too.

My naïve optimism was put to the test by the journey, which turned out to be nearly as long and torturous as the holiday shuttle bus route had been. I was the odd one out, an obvious tourist among a crowd of locals who were clearly on their daily commute. They didn't do anything to suggest this was the case, in fact they smiled at me when I got on board, but I still felt rather weird. It was probably partially to do with the fact that I was still in the clothes that I'd been wearing the previous day, so I felt grimy and uncomfortable, and although I'd taken the precaution of once again covering up the tattoo with a bandage, I felt rather exposed and fearful that my fellow passengers would laugh at me if they discovered the nature of my mission.

I stared out of the window, trying to concentrate on my surroundings and live in the moment rather than worrying about my decisions and their long-term repercussions. Amira always says that's how she gets through difficult situations in the hospital, and although my circumstances weren't exactly life and death, surely the technique would still be valid.

Our route took us across the middle of the island, the smooth tarmac climbing high up through the hills and snaking its way around the steep bends. The ground on either side of the road was reddish brown, dry and dusty, but the trees were green and lush, and the gardens of the white-painted buildings were riotous with plants of all colours. Every so often there was a miniature shrine at the side of the road decorated with flowers or candles in memory of a loved one, a sobering reminder of how dangerous these mountain passes could be. But given that the other drivers seemed to make a sport of overtaking the bus on blind bends, it wasn't completely surprising. I was glad that I wasn't the one behind the wheel.

We climbed so high that my ears popped, and then eventually the bus started winding its way back down the hill. I leaned into the aisle so I could see through the windscreen, eagerly watching for a glimpse of the Ionian Sea. Despite all the drama of the last forty-eight hours, I couldn't help feeling a thrill of excitement at the thought of being back here, surrounded by that beautiful turquoise water. Living in West Yorkshire, I couldn't have been further from the sea, but I'd always loved the big skies and big views that came with coastal life. If nothing else, it would do my soul the world of good to be able to enjoy such beautiful scenery.

By the time we reached the coast on the east side of the island, there were only a handful of people left on the bus. I imagined who they were, telling myself their stories as a distraction: a mum travelling home to reunite with her family after working away, a teenager arriving to start a summer job, a yachtie about to pick up their boat and head out to sea. I wondered what they thought of me and if any of them would happen to know an Andreas.

I tried tuning into conversations to see if I could understand anything of what was being said, but I couldn't even make out where one word ended and another began. The magnitude of what was facing me seemed even bigger. I must have made my eavesdropping obvious, because someone tapped me on the shoulder and I turned around to see a woman smiling at me.

'Happy holiday,' she said, confirming my suspicion that I stood out like a sore thumb.

'*Epharisto*,' I replied, using up the other fifty percent of my Greek knowledge to thank her for her kind wishes. Her friendliness made me feel a little less alone. If I was going to stick around here for longer than a holiday, then I would have to make a stab at learning the language, a daunting prospect and yet another thing to add to my list of stuff which I probably should have considered properly before jumping in at the deep end. Numbers had always been more my thing. But I forced myself to look on the bright side, reminding myself that I was already in a good position because I knew certain letters of the Greek alphabet from studying maths. I wasn't sure realistically how helpful that would be in terms of picking up the lingo, but a bit of blind optimism was what I needed right now.

Fortunately, the road signs were written in both the Greek and English alphabets. I felt a clutch of nerves mixed with excitement as the bus turned a corner and I spotted a sign saying 'Sami'. As we descended into town, my heart started beating faster in anticipation. What was going to happen when I arrived? How would I even start my search?

I told myself firmly to take each step as it came. I was committed now. There was no point in worrying about the what-ifs. I tried to spot the hotel where I'd stayed with the girls, eager for the reassuring sight of somewhere familiar, but we'd arrived at the other end of town and I was struggling to get my bearings.

The bus screeched to a halt by the port and most of my fellow passengers quickly departed, hurrying to where a ferry was speedily coming into harbour, the water churning and chaos reigning. Moped drivers revved their engines in eager anticipation of getting on board, while foot passengers crowded along the dock, eyeing each other up to work out the best place to stand to be first on the boat. Everyone seemed to be rushing, but while there was plenty of jostling for position, people were smiling and laughing with each other.

I took my time getting off the bus. After all, with no particular plan in mind, I wasn't in a hurry to get anywhere. There was only one passenger who was moving more slowly than me, an elderly lady with a bag even more cumbersome than mine. I smiled at her and tried to appear as unthreatening as possible as I mimed helping her. She nodded and allowed me to pick up her bag. Thankfully it wasn't as heavy as it looked, although it was still a struggle to balance it with my own luggage.

Once we were off the bus, she beckoned me to follow her across the road to where a driver was waiting, engine running. I stowed the bag in the boot and gave her a final smile. And then I froze in horror as she made a sound horribly like she was going to spit at me, and muttered something under her breath.

I retreated as fast as I could. So much for doing a good deed. I hoped this wasn't an omen as to how my Andreas search in Sami was going to pan out. I dragged my bag of dirty washing to a bench on a shady side of the harbour and sat down to contemplate my lot as that crushing sense of panic overtook me once again. What on earth was I doing? The idea of tracking down Andreas had been ridiculous from the get go, but now that I'd arrived in Sami, it seemed even more implausible that I would ever be successful. Where was I even meant to start my search? And was I up to the challenges of living by myself abroad? After the odd encounter with the elderly lady I'd tried to help, I was more nervous than ever about putting myself out there.

Despite the heat of the day, the town was full of people, tourists wandering around enjoying their ice creams, and locals gossiping outside coffee shops, smiling indulgently at the visitors to their small piece of paradise. A couple walked past me, smiling and laughing together, hands entwined, completely wrapped up in their own company, their body language a perfect mirror of each other. There was a total ease in their interaction, a sense of unity, which I was beginning to acknowledge that Jim and I had never achieved. We would never have walked down a street like that, oblivious to the rest of the world, eyes only for each other. It saddened me that I had settled for less than I deserved, that I had tolerated, perhaps even indulged his behaviour, because it had been easier to go along with the status quo rather than upsetting everything by advocating for my own dreams and desires. I might be homeless and alone in a foreign country, but at least I was no longer trapped in a relationship which was never going to make me happy.

It was that thought which gave me the confidence to stop wallowing and start doing. I decided the first logical port of call would have to be the tattoo studio. Putting aside my concerns about the artist's ethics in inking me when I was tipsy, I was keen to find out if they might be able to shed some light on the inspiration behind my tattoo. Drunk Me must have made a convincing explanation as to why I wanted that particular inking on my back. Perhaps they'd even be able to point me in the direction of the mysterious Andreas? I would track down the tattooist, discover who Andreas was and then find myself somewhere to stay for the night. Sorted.

I stood up, more hopeful now that I had a plan to follow. Then I realised that I didn't have the first clue where the tattoo studio was. I pulled up the map function on my phone to help me navigate my way, but just as I was zooming in on my current location, the battery died. I was truly alone now.

Fighting the urge to panic, I told myself I could deal with this problem too. Sami was a small town, I remembered. How hard could it be to track down a tattoo parlour?

The answer was, quite hard. Despite its modest size, Sami was a thriving place with a plethora of shops and businesses tucked down streets here there and everywhere. What I really needed to do was dump my suitcase somewhere so I could explore unimpeded, but as I didn't have a base, or in fact the first clue where I was going to spend the night, that wasn't an option. I dragged it along behind me, painfully aware of the noisy clatter the wheels made on the pavements, convinced it was making everyone stare at me. I marched up and down the main streets which formed a triangle around the port, but while there were plenty of touristy shops, there was no sign of a tattoo studio anywhere. If I didn't find it in the next five minutes, then I would have to be brave and start asking people for directions, I told myself. I felt like I was sweating from every pore, while the skin of my face was growing tight, a worrying sign that I was probably causing myself some serious sun damage.

I dived down a side street in search of some shade. It was much quieter here, with more residential buildings than shops, judging by the lines of washing which were hanging up on the blue-painted balconies in between the clouds of bougainvillea. I paused in a doorway to get my breath back. I was starting to feel rather dizzy, a sick, floaty feeling which gave me unpleasant flashbacks to my hungover state the morning after I'd got the tattoo. I took a couple of deep breaths and told myself to pull it together. I couldn't fall at this first hurdle. I thought of the look of disdain on Jim's face as I told him I was leaving and forced myself to stand up straighter.

Right on cue, the wind picked up, and a shop sign over

the road started squeaking as it swung in the breeze. The sign was written in Greek, but the artwork surrounding the letters was a dead giveaway. There it was, the tattoo studio I'd been searching for, the window shaded from direct view by a couple of potted lemon trees. Finding a new surge of energy, I hurried across the street, dragging my complaining suitcase behind me, and practising what I was going to say to the artist.

But as soon as they had been raised, my hopes were dashed. The door of the shop was locked and there were no lights on, in fact no sign of life at all. I rapped my knuckles against the doorframe to see if it would bring anyone out, but no such luck. I peered through the window, my hot palms steaming up the cool glass, as I tried to spot any sign of movement. As I leaned forward, I knocked my suitcase, sending it clattering against the door.

Then I heard the sound of someone speaking in rapid Greek behind me.

Chapter Six

I turned around quickly, leaping away from the window, suddenly conscious that I must have looked like I was trying to break into the tattoo studio. There was a man standing in the doorway of the building opposite. He was tall with tousled dark hair, around my age at a guess, wearing jeans despite the heat, and he was watching me closely from behind his horn-rimmed spectacles, his expression intent. He seemed startled by my presence, but I guess I was looking rather suspicious, loitering outside the shop dressed in clothing more suitable for slobbing around in England than holidaying in Greece. There couldn't be many tourists who were so desperate to see a tattoo artist that they'd stand outside an obviously closed studio banging on the window. As my gaze locked with his, he took a step forward, knocking his elbow against the doorframe, the sudden shock of which made him drop the armful of books that he was holding. I rushed across the street, feeling unaccountably responsible for his injury.

'Are you OK? Can I help you with these?' I asked, then knelt down and started picking the books up without waiting for an answer. I couldn't read the titles, but the pictures on the covers made me wonder if they were translated copies of Jane Austen. I thought about the matching English language versions which I'd rescued on my flight from Jim's house and managed to stuff into my suitcase.

'It's OK, it's OK,' he said, kneeling down beside me, concern for his books obviously overriding his suspicion at my presence. 'It was my mistake.' We both reached for the same book simultaneously, and he snatched his hand back as if he'd been stung.

'Sorry,' we chorused.

I stood up, but the combination of high emotion and the long day without eating sent another woozy rush to my head. I reached out intending to grab the doorframe for support, but encountered the man's firm arm instead. This time it was my turn to move away quickly.

'I think you had better come in and sit down,' he said. 'You have turned a most peculiar colour. Is that your bag over there?'

He led me inside, pulled out a chair and pressed a glass of cold water into my hand, a kind gesture given that the reason he'd confronted me in the first place was that he thought I was trying to break into his neighbour's studio.

Then he fetched my suitcase and quietly pottered around, while I tried to get my act together.

Gradually the buzzing in my brain quietened down and the room came into focus. I examined my surroundings and realised I was either sitting in a bookshop, or in the front room of someone who was as big a bibliophile as me. The shelves nearly reached the ceiling and they were packed with books, mostly in Greek, but with a few English and German titles here and there. Comfortable armchairs were situated at key points around the room, perfectly placed for people to sink down into after a good browse. My host caught me looking and smiled.

'I like to keep stock for the holiday visitors,' he said, nodding towards the shelves. 'My sister says I should display them more clearly and in a more logical way, but I think people enjoying exploring bookshops and accidentally coming across a treat. Are you feeling any better? It is very hot today.'

I nodded, gingerly at first, then more confidently as I realised the movement wasn't setting off a chain reaction of nausea. I supposed what I really needed to do was have a good meal and then a long sleep, but given the situation I'd got myself into, I couldn't see either of those things happening for the time being.

'Thank you for helping me...' My voice trailed off as I waited for him to tell me what his name was.

'Alexis,' he said.

'I'm Lydia,' I introduced myself, feeling an unreasonable pang of disappointment that the guy's name wasn't

Andreas. It would be absurd to expect the first attractive man I spoke to in Sami to be the one I was looking for. Alexis nodded, then took his glasses off and started cleaning them.

'So, Lydia, what brings you to my street?'

It was such a simple question, and yet the answer was anything but.

For a moment, I considered lying and telling him I was here on holiday, ashamed to admit my impulsive behaviour and ridiculous dream. But there was something about his quiet manner, a kind of restfulness, that inspired confidence, and I decided to trust him with my story. It was all well and good making a dramatic point by running away to Greece, but time was marching on, and I was going to have to ask somebody for help if I didn't want to end up sleeping rough on a bench in the harbour. Hopefully Alexis wouldn't end up spitting at me. He seemed too kind for that kind of thing.

I took the plunge, and told him about my predicament, slightly downplaying Jim's behaviour because I didn't want to look like one of those people who go around slagging off their exes. Alexis raised an eyebrow when he heard about the tattoo, but his expression quickly returned to quiet concentration, and I found the courage to continue.

'So, I decided to return and track down the mysterious Andreas,' I said, feeling ridiculous all over again as I said the words out loud. 'And so far, it's not going well. I've failed to find the tattooist, my phone has run out of battery, I have nowhere to stay and I've been nearly spat at by an old woman whose bag I carried off the bus. Massively offending someone before I'd even properly set foot in town was definitely not part of the plan.'

'Now that I can help with,' said Alexis with a warm smile. 'You will not have offended her. Quite the opposite. I think the spitting was not because she was angry, it was because she was warding off the evil eye. It is an old Greek tradition. If someone makes a spitting sound at you, it is because they think people will be jealous of your niceness and would wish you harm, so they are protecting you from their jealousy. It was her way of showing her gratitude for your help.'

'Oh, thank goodness. I was worried that I'd inadvertently been rude or something. I really do have a lot to learn.'

Alexis laughed. 'You have come to the right place. You should be able to find all the answers you want in here.' He gestured around him at the bookshelves.

'If only I could find my dream guy in a bookshop. I don't suppose you know the Andreas I'm trying to find?' I kept my tone light, as if I was making a joke, although it was a genuine question.

Alexis seemed to think carefully about his answer, giving a final polish to his glasses and checking the lenses from several different angles before he put them back on.

'Andreas is a very common name in Greece. I was at school with many boys of that name.'

I forced a laugh, despite my pang of disappointment. 'I feared that might be the case. Still, you can't blame a girl for dreaming. I'm sure you think this must be the most melodramatic reaction to a break-up you've ever seen.'

Alexis took his time answering. Then he spread his palms and motioned to the bookcases surrounding us. 'If there is one thing I have learned from many hours of reading, it is that the heart leads us to interesting places. How can it not be right to search for happiness?'

'Thank you, Alexis. My best friend thinks I'm positively certifiable.'

Alexis crinkled his nose in confusion.

'She thinks I've gone mad,' I clarified. 'But I think she's also glad that I'm finally spreading my wings, so she's going along with it for the time being. Although, if I don't give her regular updates, she's threatened to call the consulate to track me down.' I looked across the road to the tattoo studio, half-hoping that someone might have reappeared. Sadly, no such luck. 'I must admit I'm very disappointed that place is closed. I had the idea that they would be able to point me in the right direction and make my search easier. I don't really know where else to start, and I can't wander around the street calling out for "Andreas", can I?'

I laughed again, even though I didn't find my situation funny. It just seemed pathetic.

'And you really cannot remember anything of that night?' Alexis asked, watching me closely. Perhaps he was trying to work out if I was making the whole thing up.

'Not really. Just the beginning of the night in detail, and then after that it's more like flashes of feelings more than anything. Don't ask me how, but I'm confident that it was a good night. When I try hard to think about it, all I can focus on is that feeling of rightness. I know it must sound really peculiar, but I've never felt like that before, so utterly content and happy. It has to mean something. And perhaps it's time that I listen to my gut for a change, and pursue that happiness.' If I didn't hang onto that idea, then what was the point in me being here?

'I wish you the very best in your endeavours,' said Alexis, dipping his head in a bow-like gesture. I wondered if I was being dismissed and experienced a twinge of sadness. It felt safe tucked away here in this haven of books, separate from the hustle and bustle of the main streets. Alexis had been kind, and most importantly, he hadn't laughed at me, even if he had looked at me rather strangely when I was telling my story.

I knew that this was my cue to leave. But I decided to be brave. In the last forty-eight hours or so, I had got a tattoo, chucked my boyfriend and my job, and jumped on a plane with a one-way ticket. I could be bold enough now to ask for an extra bit of help from a bookseller.

'Alexis, can I ask you a question? I don't suppose you need an assistant?' I asked tentatively. 'Sorry, this is a massive long shot, but I am currently between jobs and I'm going to have to find some kind of work if I'm going to be able to stay here for any length of time. Or, at the very least, could you recommend somewhere cheap where I could stay while I go on my Andreas-finding mission? That was another thing I didn't think about sorting before I set off. I don't think I can afford to return to the hotel I stayed in with my friends, and I don't really know where to start when it comes to searching for accommodation that's not aimed at tourists.'

I knew I sounded pathetic, like I couldn't stand on my own two feet, but Alexis had been nothing but kind to me so far, and he could always say no.

Again, a strange expression crossed Alexis's face, and I wondered if I had offended him. Then I realised that all the time I'd been in the shop, I'd been the only customer, and I wasn't really a customer at all. How tactless of me to try to get a job out of him, when he might not even get enough business at the shop to be able to employ anyone other than himself. What must he think of me?

'Sorry, I shouldn't have asked,' I quickly backtracked. Even if I had to go into every shop in town asking for a job and/or somewhere to stay, I would sort it out somehow. Anything was better than having to return home and admit defeat. 'My situation is not your problem. You've done more than enough to help me. Thank you.'

Alexis started rearranging the stack of books on the counter.

'I am not offended,' he said, reading my mind. 'I will have a think about what is best. I am not sure what I should do.'

He looked genuinely concerned. I hurried to reassure him.

'Thank you. I don't want to impose and I know I'm probably being a massive pain.'

He smiled. 'Ah, but I take the Greek spirit of hospitality very seriously. You are not a pain. Did you know that in ancient Greek the words for "stranger" and "friend" are the same? It would not be right for me not to try to assist you. However, I am not sure how I can achieve this.' He checked his watch. 'It is nearly time for the shop to close for the afternoon break. Perhaps you would like to sit in a taverna for a while, charge your phone and have some food, and I will come and find you once I have spoken to a few people about what is best?'

This was more than I could have hoped for. I helped Alexis pull down the shutters and then he led me to a quiet taverna a couple of hundred yards from the ferry port. The kitchen was on one side of the road, while the dining area was on the other. The tables and chairs were set up on two levels, some on a concrete platform with a blue and white shade above it, the rest on the beach itself. A couple of well-fed cats were winding in and out of the seats, inspecting the ground for titbits.

'It does not look like it is the most dazzling of the restaurants in town, but it is the best,' said Alexis, waving at the chef and directing me towards a table. 'In fact, it is the place where the locals choose to go. There is no menu as such, but Maria will cook whatever is fresh or whatever her husband has caught today, and it will be delicious, I promise you. Give me an hour or so, and I will return to find you.'

I sat on a rickety wooden chair at the water's edge and watched him walk down the street. After years of ignoring them, I was once again trusting my instincts and it felt good. I reached down to pick up my phone, keen to update Kat and Amira about my situation and let them know that I was still alive. When Maria came bustling over to present me with a basket of bread, I asked her if she could help. I quickly realised that my English and two Greek words were not making any sense to her, but thankfully we found some mutual ground through miming and gestures, and she carried off my phone to plug it in behind the kitchen counter. At least, I hoped that was what she was doing. I couldn't cope with a complete digital detox along with all the other challenges I was facing.

While I waited for my meal, I watched the waves lapping on the shore. There was something calming about the steady back and forth motion of the water. There was only a gentle breeze so the swell was small, just enough to make the pebbles on the beach clink against each other. The sea was clear enough for me to be able to see the tiny fish darting around in the shallows. The water looked very inviting. I was sitting so close to the edge that my feet could reach it. I glanced around me and quickly decided that this was not the kind of place where people would stand on ceremony. I kicked off my hot trainers and relished the cool sensation of the water tickling its way around my toes. I closed my eyes and enjoyed the peace of the shady spot. If I could only be certain that I'd be able to find somewhere to stay and a way of sustaining myself, then this place would be sheer heaven.

Maria bustled out of the kitchen and crossed the road to

the seating area on the beach, seemingly without concern for any passing traffic. I guessed the drivers around here must be used to running the gauntlet of waiting staff dashing between the restaurants. She placed a couple of bowls and a plate in front of me and gestured at each one in turn.

'*Tzatziki*,' she pointed at a dip in a bowl from which a delicious scent of garlic was emanating. '*Gigantes*' – this was the contents of the plate. It looked like *gigantes* were large butter beans in a tomato sauce. The final bowl was full of little pastry parcels which she called *spanakopita*. They looked rather like the spinach and feta pie that I'd had as my post-hangover breakfast in the airport, but fresher and much more appetising.

I pulled a notebook out of my handbag and employed my miming skills again to ask Maria to write down the words for each of the dishes. She happily obliged, and then I quickly wrote a phonetic version at their side so I could remember how to pronounce them. Food seemed like a good place to start with my Greek language education. I tried the words out a few times until Maria nodded in satisfaction that I'd got the correct emphasis. And then she gestured at me to start eating before the food went cold.

Last week on my holiday with the girls, Kat had taken the lead on ordering food, claiming that her backpacking days had provided her with a much more daring palate than ours, although it was funny how often our meals had involved the culturally ubiquitous side of chips. Today, I was once again letting someone else take the lead on the culinary front, but I was more than happy to follow Maria's excellent guidance. Despite the surreal nature of my personal circumstances, the beautiful surroundings and mouth-watering food made me decide pretty quickly that this was possibly the best meal I had ever eaten. The herby tomato sauce of the *gigantes* was perfectly offset by the fresh coolness of the *tzatziki*, while the salty tang of the feta made me eat the *spanakopita* so quickly, I practically inhaled it.

I tore a piece of crusty bread, and wiped it around the bowl to make sure I'd mopped up every last bit of *tzatziki*. I was sure my breath would be thoroughly garlicky by the time I finished the meal, but as Awesome Andreas was yet to arrive on the scene, it wasn't really a problem.

I decided to continue the holiday feeling by having dessert as well. This meal was going to make serious inroads into my stash of euros, but I had to eat, and hopefully Alexis would follow through with his offer of help. If I had to start wielding my emergency credit card, then it was a price I was prepared to pay for food this good.

After indulging in a delicious lemon sorbet, so sharp and sweet that it nearly brought tears to my eyes, I insisted on paying the bill, even though Maria looked cross and made it clear that she considered me a guest, another person demonstrating that Greek spirit of hospitality which Alexis had spoken about. I couldn't imagine strangers turning up back at home and finding such a warm welcome. Jim would probably tell them where to go, if he even bothered acknowledging their presence, of course. I started wondering what he was up to, and then told myself not to go there. What Jim did now was none of my business and it didn't matter to me one bit. But I couldn't help thinking that he would be astonished to see me sitting here now, comfortably enjoying a meal by myself and making my own way in the world.

'What was on the menu today?' Alexis's question interrupted my thoughts. I smiled broadly, delighted to see him again. While I had been confident that he'd return, I wasn't sure it would be with good news, but one look at the happy expression on his face and I knew that things were going to work out just fine.

'*Gigantes* and *spanakopita*,' I said, going all out on my Greek pronunciation. 'And they were excellent, the best food I've tasted in a long time. Maria is truly talented.'

He smiled. 'I said that she would look after you.' He helped himself to a leftover hunk of bread and mopped up the dregs of the *gigantes* sauce. 'And I think I have found something else which will please you. It is not in your normal line of work. You mentioned that you are an accountant, right? I am afraid that most people around here already have their own accountants or look after their books themselves. Besides, the systems here in Kefalonia might not be what you are used to. But my sister runs a hotel, and she is struggling with the housekeeping as a member of staff is having a difficult pregnancy and needs to rest. If you do not mind making beds and cleaning bathrooms, she is happy to give you a job. The pay will not be big, but enough to get by, and there is staff accommodation which you could stay in, if you like.'

I could have kissed him. 'Alexis, you must be my guardian angel. How lucky am I to have found you? You have gone above and beyond what anyone could expect. Thank you so much, you're truly kind.'

He removed his glasses again and seemed to be concentrating on cleaning them, shy in the face of my enthusiasm, but I could tell that he was pleased.

Before we left, Maria bustled out to return my phone and waylaid Alexis for a chat. Judging by the way she frequently glanced across at me, I was definitely the subject of their conversation. I wondered what they were talking about. I hoped he wasn't telling her everything about my Andreas mission. I wasn't sure I was ready to share it with everybody I met and although I hoped Alexis would tell it in a way to minimise my impulsiveness, I knew that other people would be bound to find my decision to ditch everything and head out here bizarre. But then again, if I was going to find Awesome Andreas himself, I would have to enlist the support of other people and put myself out there more than I would normally feel comfortable with. I had years of not being brave to make up for.

Maria enveloped me in a hug before we left her taverna, and although I repeated 'thank you' in Greek multiple times, it didn't feel like enough to express the extent of my gratitude. I promised myself that I would work hard to get to a place where I could have an actual conversation in Greek. I had chosen to come here, so it was up to me to learn the language, rather than expecting everyone to be able to speak to me in English, which felt rather arrogant.

'Alexis, do you have a dictionary in your shop which I could buy? I'm going to have to try to learn more than "good morning" and "thank you" if I'm going to track down the love of my life.'

He stumbled on the uneven pavement and I grabbed his elbow to stop him from falling.

'Thank you. Yes, of course I can give it to you, and a phrasebook too, if that would be helpful.' He paused and examined my face. 'Do you really think that this mysterious Andreas is the love of your life?'

I patted the bandaged tattoo gently while I thought about my answer. 'It probably sounds stupid, but whoever he is, he clearly had a big impact on me. However drunk I was, I don't think I would have got the tattoo if it didn't hold some meaning for me. And awesome is a very positive word. He obviously completely took my breath away and inspired me to do something totally out of character. I'd like to think it was because I'd met my soulmate.' I laughed. 'My ex would say I've been reading too many stories, but authors must get their inspiration from somewhere. Why shouldn't happy ever afters be possible in real life as well as in fiction? I've got to take a chance and see what happens.'

It was the first time I had referred to Jim out loud as my 'ex' and it should probably have felt weird, but actually the words tripped off my tongue without any issue. He would probably be outraged at how quickly I was finding new hope and opportunities. But I had devoted too much of my life to worrying about Jim's opinions. I consciously decided to try to leave thoughts of him behind in England, where they belonged. Time to move on. I smiled at Alexis and he nodded in understanding.

'I am a big reader. It would be foolish of me to dismiss the possibility of a happy ever after, as you put it. I promise I will do my best to help you get to know your Mr Right.'

He picked up my suitcase and led me through town. I was still hot, grimy and tired, but I felt far more settled. Everything was falling into place. It must be fate that was dictating my path. I knew I was right to take the leap and come back here. Once I'd met Alexis's sister and found out more about my new home, I would be able to turn my mind to my mission of finding Awesome Andreas.

Chapter Seven

I nearly changed my mind when we arrived at our destination. Alexis's sister Yiota was a tiny bundle of energy who seemed to have the uncanny ability to be in about fifty different places at once. She'd obviously been watching for our arrival, because as soon as we approached the driveway of the Helios Hotel, she came rushing towards us, a disapproving expression on her face; I couldn't decide if it was aimed at me or her brother. She greeted Alexis with a torrent of rapid Greek which to my untrained ears sounded distinctly like a telling-off. Despite being nearly a foot shorter than her brother, she seemed to have the ability to metaphorically tower over him, and I watched with dismay as his expression and replies turned increasingly sheepish. Although I couldn't understand a word she was saying, I could read the body language and her waving arms told me that she was far from happy.

'I'm sorry,' I said, at what I hoped was an appropriate

moment, but she flicked her hand in my direction as if she was batting a fly away and carried on berating Alexis. As was her right. Why should she take me in, a complete stranger with a bizarre background story involving a tattoo, and why would she trust me with a job? I had thought everything had fallen into place too easily and now my fears were being proved correct. Just because Alexis had gone out of his way to help, it didn't mean that everyone else would feel the same way. I certainly didn't want to repay his kindness by causing conflict between him and his sister.

I hovered uncertainly, not knowing whether to try to interrupt again, or to beat a hasty retreat. A couple of guests walked out of the hotel and sent a bemused look in our direction, wondering what drama was happening on the front step. It was their attention which spurred me into action. I couldn't allow my stupid situation to become a problem for anybody else. Fighting the urge to back off and disappear into the distance, I instead put my hand up like a child in a classroom and waited until Alexis and Yiota noticed what I had done.

'*Ela*,' said Yiota, gesturing to me to speak. I guessed that the word meant something like 'get on with it', or at least, that was the vibe I was getting.

'I want to apologise for wasting your time. You're clearly very busy and don't need a random English woman turning up expecting bed and board. I'm really sorry for intruding. And Alexis, thank you so much for your kindness, but please don't worry, I can take things from here.'

I briefly reached out to touch his arm to reassure him that I was ok, and then I turned on my heel and started dragging my suitcase back down the drive, wondering where I could go now. The afternoon was turning to evening, and as it was peak holiday season, I couldn't imagine there would be many places with beds going spare. Maybe I really would have to sleep on the beach after all.

I heard Yiota send a few more rapid-fire phrases in Alexis's direction, and then she was by my side, grabbing hold of my suitcase handle, practically forcing it out of my grasp and onto the ground.

'Wait,' she said. I couldn't help snapping to attention. Alexis took a step towards me.

'My brother is, how do you say this, not in my good books.' She shot an angry glance at Alexis as if to reinforce this. 'However, I do need help and I will not see you walk away and have nowhere to stay, absolutely not. The Helios Hotel is a place of welcome, and welcome you it will.'

'Thank you,' I stammered, still nervous and feeling like I was a massive imposition on this busy woman's time. I quickly repeated my gratitude in Greek, hoping it might warm her up to me a bit.

'Let me look at you,' said Yiota, taking my arms and scrutinising me carefully. Was she assessing whether I looked strong enough to help with the housekeeping? If so, I wasn't convinced I was going to come out of that particularly well. 'And this famous tattoo?' Her voice was studiously neutral, but I caught her sending another pointed glance at Alexis, and figured that she was not a fan of spontaneous skin artwork.

I gestured at my back, glad that the baggy T-shirt was covering the tattoo. I could almost feel her gaze boring into my skin and shivered, despite the warmth of my surroundings.

She made a tutting sound. 'Why anybody would want to get a tattoo, I do not understand. And Andreas too? Why Andreas?'

Alexis smiled apologetically at me and said a few words to his sister in Greek before he switched to English. 'Yiota likes to speak her mind.' He turned back to his sister. 'As I explained, Lydia got the tattoo because she met the love of her life. She believes his name was Andreas. And now she would like to track down that man of her dreams.'

Yiota replied in rapid Greek, her words short and sharp, then brushed Alexis to one side as she fixed me with another stern look. 'I am sorry. I forget myself. I will speak English so that you can understand until you learn my language. Now, I hear that you are happy to help with housekeeping? What experience do you have?'

I thought carefully. 'Um, I'll admit I've not done any professional cleaning. But my ex-boyfriend—' again I got a slight thrill from saying those words '—was rather old fashioned and when we were at each other's places we split the tasks between us, so I did all the household stuff – what he'd call "girl tasks" – while he did the garden. Well, I say he did the garden, but I lived in a flat, so I didn't have a garden, and he got a gardener in to mow his lawn.' So much for trying not to go on about Jim. But if it helped me get a job by demonstrating that I had at least some housekeeping experience, then it was justified.

Yiota waved her arm. 'This time, your work will be rewarded with a wage, rather than being unpaid labour.'

I decided to take it as a sign that she was slightly softening towards me.

'I think a trial is perhaps best.' Yiota nodded as she made up her mind. 'You may stay with me for a few days, I will try you on the different duties I need help with, and then, we will see what happens after that.' Decision made, she beckoned me to follow her. 'Let me show you around the Helios Hotel. It is called Helios after the god of the sun, because the sun always shines in Kefalonia.' She paused and looked around her confidentially. 'Or at least, that is what we tell the tourists. It is mostly sunny in Kefalonia, but when it rains, *po po po*, it rains a lot.'

Yiota swept into the hotel, and I scurried along in her wake, trying to keep up. Alexis reached out and took my long-suffering suitcase, carrying it as if it weighed significantly less than it did. I smiled at him gratefully. As much as I would have liked to demonstrate my independent woman credentials, I was thankful for his continuing thoughtfulness. My shoulders were aching after dragging the thing around most of the day, plus its wheels had started to make some worrying squeaking noises, and I was concerned they didn't have much life left in them. As long as the bag made it to my room intact, that was all that mattered. Hopefully I wouldn't need it for a good while after that.

The hotel was smaller than the one I'd stayed in with Kat and Amira, something which I was relieved about because it meant there would be fewer rooms for me to clean. It wasn't that I didn't want to work hard, but I needed all the help I could get to do the best job possible so I could survive my trial period and not find myself back out on the street.

The reception area was sunny and welcoming. A noticeboard by the front desk was covered in posters and leaflets advertising local excursions, and I felt a clutch of excitement about all the places there were to explore on the island. We walked through a comfortable sitting room to the wildflower-filled garden. A couple of guests were lounging by a pool, the water dazzlingly bright and inviting, while others were quietly enjoying iced drinks as they leaned on the small bar. At the far end of the garden, a vine-covered trellis arch provided shade for a bench which was carved out of the trunk of a fallen tree. It was what I'd describe as a beautiful boutique hotel, peaceful and serene, the kind of place I would have loved to stay in as a guest, perhaps with a special someone at my side.

'Are you alright?' asked Alexis quietly.

'Very alright,' I replied. If he hadn't still been holding my suitcase, I would have reached out to squeeze his hand in gratitude. I couldn't believe how lucky I was to be getting a job here.

'Sometimes my brother comes to help out at the pool bar

and make the drinks and toasted sandwiches for guests,' said Yiota. 'But often he is too busy with his own affairs to help me.'

She sent a pointed glance at Alexis.

'I'm happy to help in any way I can. I make a mean toasted cheese sandwich,' I said, hoping that it might work in my favour.

'Then already you are better than my brother. Alexis, why are you still here? Lydia and I have things to agree, and I have work to do, and you are a big distraction.'

Alexis caught my eye, and we both smothered a grin at Yiota's bluntness.

'If I am getting in the way, then I shall depart and reopen the bookshop for the evening customers,' he said.

Yiota rolled her eyes as though she wasn't convinced there would be many of them coming through the doors.

'Lydia, I hope you settle in well. Forgive my sister. She is not the tiger that she appears to be. I will take your bag to the staff quarters and be on my way.' He scribbled something on a piece of paper and offered it to me. 'This is my number, feel free to call me if you need anything. And please do come and see me at work, I am there most days, and I will make sure you get your dictionary. I am sure Yiota will help you with your language practice too.' He paused, then reached out to shake my hand formally. 'I wish you the best of luck in tracking down your mystery man.'

I felt a pang of loneliness when Alexis left. He had made me feel truly welcome in Sami and gone beyond the call of duty to help me. It was good to feel like there was at least one friendly face here. Hopefully I would win Yiota around eventually, but I got the impression that it might be a difficult task. She was clearly far too busy to spend much time holding my hand, and I would have to prove myself in my new role, and fast. I didn't want to be a burden to her after she'd done me such a big favour by giving me a trial without any credentials or proper experience.

Yiota beckoned to me to follow her back to reception where she printed off some paperwork for me to fill out. Thankfully she translated the key bits, explaining that I would be paid weekly, and that bed and board were part of the package. I happily signed on the dotted line, glad to be gaining a source of income and stability. Although I would be earning even less than I had done in my accountancy job, without the expense of rent, I was confident the modest sum would be sufficient for me to get by, as long as I was sensible. It was reassuring to know that I would be able to support myself, provided I did the job well enough to keep it.

Next stop on the tour of the hotel was my room, a small, but comfortable space on the top floor with a big window looking out towards the mountains. Yiota bustled around, tying back the curtains and checking there was a bottle of water in the tiny fridge in the corner.

'You do not have a view of the sea,' she said, 'or a balcony. We have to make sure the guests can see the Ionian, as that is a big part of the appeal of staying here.'

'Please don't be sorry. I'm grateful to have a room of my own. And the view is quite magnificent.'

I really meant it. When I was on holiday here, I'd been captivated by the stunning clarity of the sea, always sitting gazing at it and never really taking the time to turn around and look inland. The hills were every bit as stunning as the coast, wild expanses of trees and open ground, with specks of white here and there indicating where houses were nestling in the folds of the landscape.

It was the right thing to say. Yiota flashed a quick smile, then she pointed at the road winding up the mountain behind the hotel.

'If you follow that path, it is only a few miles to the Drogarati Cave. It is very spectacular. Sometimes there are even concerts performed in there among all the rocks. You should get Alexis to take you.' She paused. 'It would be a perfect place to visit with your Mr Right.' Her eyes twinkled with amusement.

'You must think me very strange, dropping everything and flying out here in search of a dream, without even considering the practicalities,' I said. 'I know how lucky I am that Alexis and you have come to my aid.'

'Yes, I think the whole thing most strange indeed.' Again she looked at me closely as if trying to read my mind. Then she sighed. 'But if Alexis wants my help in this way, then that is what I shall do, as a loving sister. Tell me, do you have siblings?'

'No, I'm an only child. It's probably one of the reasons why I love books so much and have what I'll admit is a rather vivid imagination. You're never alone when you have companions in stories. And my best friends Kat and Amira are practically my sisters. We grew up together and we know all each other's little quirks. We'd do anything for each other.' I half-wished they were here right now. Everything was easier with their support.

'Yes, I'd do anything for my brothers,' said Yiota. 'Now, are you OK to unpack? Have you had enough to eat? You must be tired after your busy adventures.'

'I am tired, but not too exhausted to get to work straight away, I promise. There is one thing I was wondering. Do you have a washing machine I could use? I left rather quickly, and I've still got my holiday clothes that need a good wash. In fact, you could probably smell them from a mile away. Not very pleasant. Sorry about that.'

Yiota laughed. 'Of course, and do not worry, I will not make you start working this evening. I think a good night's sleep will probably be the best thing for you. And then you can start tomorrow morning. The washing machines are busy right now as it was a changeover day yesterday. But when you start work, I will find some overalls for you. If you can be down in the breakfast room by eight, that would be a great help. Eleni is finding the mornings a struggle because she cannot move about as easily now and I would like to give her some time off now you are here.'

Chapter Eight

I woke with a start, my heart thudding and hot panic surging around my body. For a few moments I lay tangled in the covers, light streaming onto my eyes from a gap in the blinds, and wondered where I was and what on earth I was doing here. The scratchy sheets were unfamiliar and the dimensions of the room didn't fit either of the places I would normally wake up in. I listened carefully, trying to work out if the distant sound of running water was Jim taking a shower. But there was no atonal singing to accompany it, and it was too far away to be coming from the ensuite off his bedroom.

And then the sleepy fuzz in my brain started to clear and I remembered that I would never be waking up in a room with Jim again. I waited a few moments for the pang of separation and loss to hit me. But the only thing that happened was that my stomach grumbled and I started wondering what I might be able to find for breakfast. I quickly pulled my thoughts back from dreaming about yoghurt, fresh fruit and cake. I knew I should probably be feeling sad and guilty that irreparable differences and a misguided tattoo had driven me apart from the man I had thought I'd be spending the rest of my life with. But instead, I felt nothing, except maybe a sense of disappointment that I'd allowed myself to be taken in by him for so long.

I stretched out and tried to starfish in the bed, then quickly realised that a rickety single was not the best place to relish my solo sleeping arrangements and newfound freedom. I gingerly patted the small of my back and was reassured to find that the swelling seemed to have reduced and it had finally stopped feeling quite so tender. The fact that the tattoo was starting to heal had to be a sign that I was doing the right thing returning to Kefalonia and seeking a new life. The idea of tracking down 'Awesome Andreas' seemed no less ridiculous in the cold light of day, but then again it gave me a focus and a purpose now that I'd chucked away everything that I'd previously been working towards. Now I'd ripped my five-year plan to shreds, having a goal – any goal – was better than nothing. And why shouldn't I have some fun while pursuing this outlandish one? At the very worst, my Andreas quest would provide a good excuse for exploring different parts of a beautiful island and meeting new people along the way. And at best, I could actually meet him, that mythical Mr Right.

But how could I get started on my mission? Kat would

probably do something brave like standing in the town square holding up a sign saying 'Andreas' to see who approached her, but that felt a bit too *Love Actually* for me. I didn't want to look desperate, after all. If telephone books were still a thing, then I could have worked my way through all those people listed under Andreas. But in lieu of that old-school method, perhaps I could do a search on social media, narrowing down the location to Sami first of all, and then widening it out to the rest of Kefalonia? And that way, I'd be able to look at pictures and do a bit of due diligence/stalking first to see if any potential Andreas jogged some memories.

With the makings of a plan, I rolled over contentedly and checked my phone. Then I felt that panic all over again when I realised what time it was. Never mind daydreaming about breakfast and men (in that order!) I was due to start work for Yiota in five minutes. She was a reluctant enough host as it was, and I didn't want to give her any excuse to say the arrangement wasn't working. It would be an early end to my dreams, and it would disappoint Alexis who had been kind enough to go out on a limb for a stranger.

I rummaged through my suitcase and berated myself for not having taken the time to unpack last night. The washing machines might have been occupied, but if I'd thought about it, I could have at least rinsed some underwear in the sink so I had clean knickers this morning. Overwhelming tiredness and the strangeness of my new situation had clouded my normally practical brain and today I was going to pay the price. Alas, despite some frantic searching, a fresh pair of pants did not miraculously appear from the jumble in my suitcase, and reluctantly I pulled on a swimming costume instead. What it lacked in convenience, it at least made up for in cleanliness. I sniffed a few T-shirts and went for the one which smelled least offensive. Sadly, it was a souvenir job declaring 'I love Greece' in big letters, but then again, an open declaration of affection for their home might help me to curry favour with the locals. And although I really wanted to wear shorts – judging by the temperature of my room, it was going to be a sweltering day – I figured they might give the impression that I was here on holiday, so I pulled on the old faithful leggings again. Then I sprayed a generous amount of deodorant over my entire outfit, scraped my hair back into the neatest bun I could manage – spoiler: it wasn't very neat at all – and hurried downstairs to report for duty in the breakfast room.

Yiota took one look at me and clearly decided that my scruffy appearance would put the guests off their food. She handed me a mop, bucket and a set of overalls in lieu of a morning greeting. Then while I pulled the overalls on, she gestured at a document in Greek which I assumed was some kind of health and safety notice. Once I was dressed in my makeshift uniform, she checked me over with a critical eye, did up the top button which I'd left undone in the vain hope it might help provide some much-needed ventilation, then nodded.

'If your trial works out, I will give you a uniform like the others—' She gestured over at one of the waitresses who looked deliciously cool and stylish in a white T-shirt and beige culottes 'But that will do for now. You can start cleaning on the top floor. Every surface must be wiped, and any towels thrown in the bath must be replaced by the ones in the cupboard at the end of the corridor. Any which are not in the bath can be straightened and put back on the towel rail. It saves money. And the environment too.'

She handed me the key for the aforementioned cupboard, a great big iron thing which wouldn't have looked out of place in a Disney castle.

'Most of the guests from the top floor are booked on an excursion with an early start today, so you should not have them in your way, but do not forget to knock before you let yourself into the rooms.' I thought I saw a glimmer of something resembling amusement pass over her face. 'You may be searching for Andreas, but I would prefer that you do not search for him here by walking in on male guests. That kind of thing can give a hotel a bad reputation.'

I laughed nervously and since it was obvious that work was to be prioritised over food, I headed off to perform my cleaning duties.

Mindful of her warning, I knocked on my first door and listened carefully, before letting myself in. The room was a tip. Someone had clearly arrived back from a night out and left a half-eaten kebab on the side, along with several bottles of suspicious-looking liquid. I thought back to the hotel room we'd hastily exited on our way to the airport and hoped we hadn't left it in quite such a state. Well, if we had, then karma was repaying me for it.

I pulled up my sleeves and set to. Within minutes, I had

developed a serious antipathy for the overalls. Indestructible they might be, but breathable, they certainly weren't. Despite the best efforts of the air-conditioning unit in the corner of the room, I was soon perspiring enough to fill the cleaning bucket. There was little point in me polishing the surfaces if I then went and sweated all over them. Deciding that this was a situation where practicality won out over appearance, I stripped down to my swimming costume and continued working like that. I might look ridiculous, but at least I wasn't marinating in my own juices anymore.

After what felt like hours, but hopefully wasn't that long really, I stood back to take a look at my hard work – and get a breather – and felt proud at what I'd achieved. One bedroom down, only a dozen or so more to go. I checked my phone and was horrified to discover that I'd been in here for nearly fifty minutes. At this rate, I was going to spend all the daylight hours working, and where would that leave my Andreas hunt, not to mention my chances of seeing more of this beautiful island? I told myself not to despair. This was the first room, on my first day. I was bound to speed up, and it was more important short-term to impress Yiota and get a longer contract than it was to immediately put myself out there in the Andreas dating world.

I gave the room a final check, then lugged my cleaning implements into the corridor ready to start on the next room, only to bump headfirst into someone.

'I'm so sorry,' I said, wishing I knew how to apologise in

Greek. I had a feeling it was a phrase I was going to find very useful over the course of my employment at the Helios Hotel. I instantly clocked the man's white polo shirt and beige trousers, which was some relief as if I had to barge into anyone, it was better that it was a fellow member of staff than some hapless guest.

'*Signome*,' he said.

'I'm sorry, Signome,' I replied.

'No no no, my name is not *signome*, it is the Greek word for sorry. My wife says that it is important that you start learning our language properly as soon as possible, so I thought it was better that I apologise for crashing into you in my language rather than yours.'

The embarrassment caused my temperature to rise even further. This was just what I needed, getting caught by my boss's husband while I was dressed only in a swimming costume, and then mangling their language on top of it.

'Duly noted. *Signome*, I will make sure I use that in future. Although I'll try to avoid getting myself into situations where I need to apologise,' I added hastily.

He chuckled. 'Ah, it is a word I have to use all the time around my wife. She likes things just so and I always disappoint her. But if I got it right, she would also be disappointed, so I carry on this way.' Although he was pretending to be exasperated with Yiota, his voice was full of affection as he spoke about her. 'But that is enough about me. You must be Lydia. Welcome to the Helios Hotel. We are very pleased to have you staying with us. My name is An—'

'What is going on here?' Yiota arrived on the corridor in a whirlwind, interrupting him before he could finish his introduction, and leaving me in an instant panic. Had he been about to introduce himself as Andreas? I really hoped not, because if his name was Andreas, I could be in big trouble. I somehow knew he wasn't *the* Andreas, but given that Yiota knew about my quest, she'd probably assume I'd thrown myself at the first one I came across, especially as I was in a considerably more undressed state than I had been when she'd sent me off to work.

'I've been cleaning and got hot,' I said quickly, so quickly in fact that it probably made her believe the exact opposite. 'The room is immaculate, I promise.' I turned to open the door to show her but she stopped me in my tracks.

'The room? I hope you mean rooms? Eleni would have finished this corridor by now and she is eight months' pregnant. Angelo, have you been distracting her?'

Relief surged through me. He was Angelo, not Andreas, and rather than thinking I'd been trying anything on with her husband, she was blaming him for keeping me from my work.

'No, I promise, he hasn't. I've been attempting to be as thorough as possible and it took me longer than it should have. I think I've worked out the best way of doing things now, so hopefully the next room will take me a lot less time.'

Yiota didn't look convinced. 'The guests will be back from their excursion before you have finished. I would prefer they do not see you in your swimwear, it does not give a good impression of the hotel staff. But I understand that the overalls might be too hot, so once you have done your washing, you can wear your own clothes for the time being. If you complete your trial successfully, then we will see what can be arranged.'

Chapter Nine

By the time I'd finished work – several hours after the shift should have ended due to my painfully slow cleaning process – I wanted nothing more than to curl up in bed and sleep for a century. I knew it was bad when I was lugging the equipment back to the storage room and started eyeing up flat surfaces like the floor and the dining room tables and thinking that they looked like comfortable places for a nap. But if I went to sleep now, I would snooze straight through until the alarm went off for me to go to work again, and I wouldn't achieve anything, which would rather defeat the point of me coming out here. My lofty ambition to find the Andreas of my dreams wouldn't happen if I did nothing but work and sleep. So, after quickly texting Alexis to say I'd survived my first day and to thank him once again for finding me the job, I put my washing into the machine, pulled the 'I love Greece' T-shirt back on with a pair of shorts, and decided to start my Awesome Andreas search in earnest.

Unfortunately my bright idea to look for him on social media turned out to be not so bright after all. This was due to a combination of user error and technology, user error being my inability to work out how to narrow down my search by location, and technology being my phone's failure to translate the Greek script into something that I could understand. After several frustrating attempts to overcome the challenges by first turning the phone off and on again, and then flinging it across the room, I gave up trying and decided to channel my energy in another direction instead.

My next approach involved asking Yiota if I could use a computer.

'Do not go on any strange sites if you are searching for your Andreas,' she said, wagging her finger at me as she reluctantly led me to the office behind reception. 'A virus would be a very bad thing.' I couldn't decide whether she was referring to me or the computer getting the virus. 'If you ask me, this whole situation is very silly. And it is a mess in here,' she added, quickly swooping past me to gather up a collection of picture frames from the desk and move them out of the way.

I wondered whether I should offer to clean so I could get some brownie points, but then decided that I'd be running the risk of offending my host as the room really wasn't that messy at all. She was probably moving the pictures because she didn't want her new temporary employee seeing snaps of her during her free time. I settled down at the computer and pretended to fiddle with the mouse while I waited patiently for Yiota to give me some space. Now I was about to start it, the whole social media search thing felt a little soulless, as if picking a man out online was the same as browsing for furniture on a virtual marketplace. Doing it in front of an audience of Yiota, who was deeply sceptical about my whole Andreas quest, was even less appealing. She would probably have strong opinions about the men on screen and I didn't want to be influenced by someone else's view. Thankfully though, she was soon summoned to help direct some tourists to a nearby beach, so I could begin my exploration in private.

I'd thought it would be easier to instigate my Andreas hunt on a computer rather than on my phone so I could examine any images on a bigger screen. But I realised my mistake as soon as I looked down at the keyboard, which of course was set out in the Greek alphabet. My rudimentary knowledge of the different script from maths lessons was not going to help me get very far in typing out actual words. I stared at the jumble of shapes and tried to remember if the letter that looked like a 'v' was actually a 'v', or whether it was something else altogether. Sadly, staring at the squiggles didn't help them appear any more comprehensible, but it did give me another idea. I looked at the screen instead, and placed my hands on the keyboard as if I was going to touch type in English, and tapped what I hoped would spell the name Andreas into the search engine.

Several million results pinged up which at least let me

know that I'd managed to input an actual word. Unfortunately, it rather dashed my hope that tracking down *the* Andreas would be a simple operation. Until I worked out how to translate the results into English, or got hold of the dictionary Alexis had promised me, they were pretty meaningless, so I clicked on the image tab instead. I was confronted with page after page of potential Andreases: smiley, sad, grumpy, serious, all manners of emotions expressed by all manner of people whose only common feature was that they had the same name. Some pictures looked like they'd been taken in a professional setting, others were holiday snaps, and a few looked worryingly like mug shots. I instantly dismissed those ones. They were probably still behind bars, and if they weren't, I liked to think that even Drunk Me would have had more sense than to have used them as tattoo inspiration.

I looked carefully through the results of the first few pages in the hopes that one of the pictures would spark some recognition, but none of them leapt out at me. There were some good-looking men named Andreas out there, but I couldn't risk just going on physical appearance. I suppose one of the reasons I was beguiled by Jim for such a long time was that I'd always secretly felt that he was out of my league appearance-wise, and that I was lucky he had chosen me, which I guess was partly why it had taken so long for me to recognise and acknowledge the flaws in the way he treated me. I didn't want to fall into the same trap again.

I was on page six of the search results when my eyes started swimming and I decided enough was enough. Did I honestly think that I would be able to do a Google search and instantly find Awesome Andreas? Or was I doing this because it felt like the safe option to be tucked away in the hotel, browsing the internet, building up an imaginary picture of the man and not having to interact with anyone, rather than having to go out into the real world and speak to actual people? Because the latter option would involve me being brave, and since it had peaked with my dramatic walk out on Jim, my courage had been gradually slipping away from me.

I added the name Andreas written in the Greek alphabet to my notebook of vocabulary and decided to temporarily abandon my online search and ring my friends for a pep talk. Whatever their opinions on my recent behaviour, I knew they would cheer me up and help me find a way to move forward. Fortunately, Kat was around at Amira's place and they answered on speakerphone on the first ring. If I wasn't very much mistaken, they'd been staring at the phone willing me to call, the sixth sense of our long-established friendship making them know when I was in need of them.

'Babe, you're alive,' was Amira's opening gambit, which didn't suggest much faith in my solo survival skills. There was genuine relief in her voice. Amira was like me in having a tendency to catastrophise, so she'd probably been imagining that I was locked up in a Greek jail or something.

Kat meanwhile went for the equally subtle approach of, 'Tell us where we need to rescue you from.'

Such faith in me. My friends' reactions helped bolster my dwindling spirit.

'I don't need rescuing, thank you very much. I'm an independent woman who is more than capable of standing on her own two feet,' I said indignantly.

'And once more, with feeling,' said Kat. 'No, seriously hon, how are you getting on? We've been dead worried about you. Ouch.'

There was a slight kerfuffle at the other end of the line and I smiled as I imagined Amira nudging Kat and telling her to back off and be more subtle in her approach.

'What she meant to say is that we've been thinking about you, and hoping that you're having a good time,' said Amira. 'First things first, have you got somewhere to stay?'

'And have you shagged Andreas yet?' butted in Kat, a question which was quickly followed by a yelp as Amira undoubtedly administered another dose of pinching.

'I've barely been here twenty-four hours, and for a lot of that, I've been scrubbing toilets. If I had tracked down Andreas in that time, it would have been a miracle,' I said. 'And never mind anything as energetic as a roll in the sack, I'm so tired, I'd just want to cuddle up and go to sleep.'

'You're not going to give the poor guy much of a chance to earn his Awesome title with an attitude like that,' said Kat, throwing in a dirty laugh for good measure.

'Hold on a minute, what's this about cleaning toilets?' asked Amira.

I quickly explained how I'd managed to find both a

temporary job and accommodation thanks to my bookselling guardian angel.

'This bookshop guy sounds lovely. Shame he's not called Andreas,' said Amira. 'Is he going to help you track him down though?'

'I fear I've imposed on him enough, but it's good to feel there's someone nearby I can turn to when I need a friend. The reason I rang, apart from to hear your lovely voices of course, was to see if you have any ideas about how I can find Andreas. Things have been happening so quickly I've not really had the time or the energy to come up with a game plan, and the technology route doesn't seem to be working.'

'Oh, Lydia, you're never going to find him by sitting behind a screen,' said Kat. 'You need to put yourself out there. Put your glad rags on, head to the nearest bar and have a few drinks. After all, that's how you found him in the first place.'

'It's not the full picture of how I found him though, is it? Because it didn't happen in the bar with you guys. It must have been somewhere between the hotel and the tattoo parlour. Perhaps I should walk the streets there as a starting point. In a non-prostitute way,' I added hastily.

Once again, I racked my brains to see if any more flashes of memory came to light, but all I could picture was Alexis's bookshop and that was only because I'd visited it yesterday.

'Maybe getting drunk isn't the way forward, but I agree with Kat, you should put yourself out there,' said Amira. 'You're never going to meet anyone sitting in the hotel. And more importantly, you're not going to have much fun doing that either. You've done nothing but work and follow Jim's lead for the last couple of years. This is your chance to do what you want to do. To have a proper break and enjoy yourself. Go out there and do just that. Explore your surroundings and make the most of being in paradise. Only please remember that you shouldn't go swimming for at least two weeks, and keep a loose T-shirt on over the tattoo so it can heal properly without exposing it to the sun. Oh, and now you're not having to keep it hidden, try not to cover it up with a bandage. You want to let the air get to it.'

'Thanks, Dr. I'm now terrified of doing anything fun in case I cause myself permanent damage.'

With the girls' laughter still echoing in my ears, I decided to follow their advice and go exploring. I might as well work out the lie of the land, and if I encountered any handsome men on my travels, then so much the better. I'd pretend to trip up or something so they'd have to help me, and we'd get talking and they'd turn out to be called Andreas, and everything would be perfect. I smiled to myself. If only it could be that easy.

I lathered all exposed areas in sunscreen, pulled on my hat and sunglasses, hoping they gave me a Hollywood glam vibe while fearing they probably made me look like a vampire terrified of the light, and set off. Instead of following the main road route which Alexis had brought me along to the hotel, I decided to turn down a side lane, figuring that as long as I didn't start climbing upwards then I was probably going in the right direction towards the centre of town and the sea, rather than heading into the mountains.

It was beautifully peaceful wandering along the lane with just the occasional rumble of a distant car engine interrupting the gentle rustle of the trees in the breeze and the creak of the crickets in the grass. Every so often there was a soothing clang of a bell followed by a soft bleat from the goat who was wearing it. The air smelled of warm earth and honeysuckle, a sweet, welcoming scent so different from the pollution fug which surrounded my former place of work. I found I was walking more slowly than usual, meandering quietly between the dappled patches of shade, drinking in my surroundings and allowing them to work their magic on my soul. I felt the tension ease out of my shoulders and although I was still tired, I felt refreshed by the beauty of the landscape. I rounded a corner and was delighted to see a donkey grazing at the far end of a paddock.

'Hello,' I said, because if you don't say hello to a gorgeous donkey, what kind of a monster are you?

I'm not sure the donkey spoke English, but he certainly recognised a friendly tone of voice, and started shambling over towards me.

'I'm sorry, I don't have anything for you to eat.'

A guy on a bicycle suddenly appeared around the bend and gave me a strange look. I nearly pretended to be having a conversation on the phone, but then changed my mind. If he thought I was weird because I was talking to a donkey, then so be it.

'Andreas,' I called, feeling rather daring.

The man carried on cycling off into the distance, oblivious to my shout. I turned back to the donkey.

'Nope, it wasn't him. One ticked off, only the rest of the men of the island to go,' I sighed. The donkey blinked at me.

'Yes, you're right, I need to come up with a better plan. Watch this space. I'll see you later, my friend.'

I held my hand out so he could sniff the back of it, then he graciously allowed me to stroke his soft nose briefly before he returned to his clump of grass at the other side of the paddock.

I carried on following the lane until it widened out and the noise of traffic started to intrude. I emerged onto a street lined with colourful houses and a couple of tavernas. Was this one of the places we'd visited on that final evening of the holiday? I wasn't sure, but it looked vaguely familiar, especially the uneven pavement which I think had caused problems for Kat and me in our heels. I promised myself I'd visit each of the tavernas and see if I recognised anyone there, once I'd had my first payday, of course.

I could smell the scent of bread baking, which must have been what got me thinking about food. My stomach gave a gurgle. After skipping breakfast and working through lunch, it was high time I had something to eat. I followed my nose – literally – and discovered a bakery tucked between a jewellery shop and a clothing store.

'*Spanakopita, parakalo,*' I said, politely asking for my favourite spinach and feta pie.

I was handed a piping hot pastry parcel, carefully wrapped up in a piece of greaseproof paper by the smiling teenager behind the counter. I took my bounty across the road to sit on a shady bench where I could watch the world go by as I ate. With every mouthful, my belief in my mission started returning, along with my energy. I always teased Kat for getting hangry, but here I was discovering my mood was just as badly affected if I didn't eat. Note to self, I could definitely not survive another cleaning day without making sure I had a proper breakfast first, and any Andreas dates would have to involve some kind of food so my judgement wasn't impaired.

After I'd inspected the paper for any final crumbs, I carefully deciphered the letters in the names above the shops, comparing them to the name in my notebook, just in case any of them turned out to belong to someone called Andreas. I really needed to get that dictionary from Alexis, and soon. But before I could work out which street I needed to go down to reach his bookshop, I was distracted by the little kiosk on the edge of the square and its enticing display of ice creams for sale.

Deciding an emergency ice cream would be just the thing to fuel ideas for my Awesome Andreas hunt, I went across and selected a chocolate and salted caramel filled cone from the vast selection on offer. As I devoured the sweet deliciousness, I spotted a noticeboard on the kiosk's wall, tucked in between the stacks of crisps and boxes of chewing gum. It was peppered with index cards and bits of paper, all of which were covered in pictures of random items and messages written in Greek. I leaned in closer to examine a shot of a microwave and an inflatable unicorn float, wondering why this bizarre collection of items were on display.

'For sale,' the guy behind the counter said, gesturing at the noticeboard and answering my unasked question. 'Lost items and found items. You looking for something, you put up a notice. You find something, you put up a notice.'

'Anything at all?' I asked.

He shrugged. 'I don't see why not.'

I couldn't, could I? As the idea started to form, I wondered whether it was a stroke of genius or complete foolishness. I told myself it would be just like one of those small ads at the back of magazines, the ones full of funny abbreviations and acronyms. But what would I put?

WLTM Andreas, GSOH a bonus.

That sounded a bit too lonely hearts for my liking. Besides, we'd already met. This was about tracking him down again, rather than seeking out a new Andreas. Perhaps it would be better to mention the date we met.

Are you Andreas? We met on 7th June and I'd love to reconnect.

Reconnect? That sounded like I was approaching a business associate on LinkedIn for some blue-sky thinking.

Awesome Andreas, we met on 7th June and I long to see you again.

Nope, definitely too needy.

Searching for Andreas. We met in Sami on 7th June. Would like to reunite. L.

That would do the trick. It was short and to the point. And if I added my phone number at the bottom, instead of me chasing around trying to track down the mythical man, perhaps he would come to me. And yes, I might get a few strange calls, but maybe, just maybe, Awesome Andreas would pick up the phone and reach out to me. And maybe I'd even recognise his voice on the phone. They say that coma patients can still hear and understand people speaking to them. I'm not likening booze-induced amnesia to a coma by any means, but perhaps the same science would prevail. I imagined what kind of voice Awesome Andreas would have. Probably quiet but full of confidence, with a sexy warmth of tone which conveyed a sense of understanding and genuine care for the other person in the conversation. I smiled to myself. I was definitely letting my imagination run away with itself. But a girl could dream.

Before I lost courage, I told the guy behind the kiosk counter I wanted to add a notice to his board.

'It's two euros for the week,' he said, passing across a pen and notecard. 'If you want it longer, come visit again.'

'A bargain,' I replied, happily handing over the coins. Perhaps this would turn out to be the best two euros I'd ever spent.

Chapter Ten

For the next couple of days, I felt like my phone was an incendiary device which could go off at any moment. I was excited at the prospect of it ringing, but at the same time utterly terrified. I tried to reason with myself, reminding myself that the worst thing that could happen would be that I'd get some crank callers who I could immediately block. The notecard ad didn't give away anything too personal, such as my full name or where I was staying, and any callers certainly wouldn't get that information by just ringing me up. But I still had a niggling fear that this whole approach was completely hopeless, and that I was perhaps using it as another displacement activity, an excuse not to put myself out there in a tangible way. After all, as long as I had the dream of Awesome Andreas, I couldn't be let down by disappointing reality.

To distract myself from the terrible fear of an Andreas calling me, or perhaps worse, not calling me, I threw myself into my cleaning job with a vengeance, spending pretty much every hour of daylight working. Kat and Amira teased me on the phone, saying all the hard work was actually procrastination and accusing me of doing it because I was scared of making myself vulnerable and getting hurt in my Andreas search. They had a point, but I told myself there was no point in me trying to find him, if I then lost my means of staying on the island and couldn't get to know him properly. Alexis was the only other person to reach out to me. After receiving my initial thank you message, he sent me a picture of two Jane Austen collections in different bindings asking for my opinion on which would appeal to English customers more, and the text conversation grew from there. His messages always made me smile, even when I was up to my elbows in toilet scrubbing.

It was going to take a while before I could get up to a cleaning speed which would satisfy Yiota's demands, but at least she was starting to look almost pleased at the results of my work, or so I hoped. On day four of my stay, I was summoned into her office behind reception. She fixed me with an unblinking stare.

'How are you?' she asked, then repeated the question in Greek. Unfortunately, I was so nervous about what this meeting might be about that I couldn't take the phrase in properly. I'd have to ask her to repeat it later. If she was still talking to me at that stage, of course. I couldn't decide whether she was genuinely asking about my wellbeing, or whether this was actually a question about how I thought I was doing work-wise.

I decided to go for a neutral answer. 'I'm fine. Thank you once again for the kindness you've shown in letting me stay here.'

She nodded. 'My brother...' Her voice tailed off and she seemed to change her mind about what she'd been going to say. 'Anyway, I needed the help.'

'And I hope I am being helpful. I'm trying hard, but please do tell me if there's anything more you'd like me to do.'

'You are doing OK.' From Yiota, this felt like the height of praise. She paused for a reality-TV-worthy amount of time, then she nodded again, as if she'd made her mind up about something.

'These are for you,' she said, handing over two sets of the distinctive uniform worn by the other members of staff at the Helios Hotel.

'Does this mean I can stay?' I asked, the delight evident in my voice.

She pursed her lips. 'We'll see. I am extending the probation period.'

She didn't mention how long for, but I figured the two sets of clothing was a good sign that the new probation period was going to last longer than just a few days. If she was planning to chuck me out, then she'd have only handed over a T-shirt, or maybe not even bothered with that.

I returned to sweeping dust from the hotel's front porch

with a new feeling of satisfaction. Despite initially having the cleaning skills of an Ugly Sister rather than Cinderella, I was making a success of my new profession, and starting to carve out my own place in this world. Now, I only needed Awesome Andreas to appear on the scene, and everything would be perfect. As if on cue, my phone buzzed with a message. I'd turned the volume up to maximum so I wouldn't miss anything, and the loud ping took me by surprise, causing me to lose grip on my brush momentarily, sending the carefully piled up dust all over the porch again. No matter, I'd sort that out in a minute. But first I needed to check who had messaged me. This could be it, the moment the notice in the kiosk paid off.

With trembling fingers, I took my phone out of my pocket and pressed my thumb against the button to unlock it, but my hands were too grimy and sweaty for the fingerprint recognition to work. I wiped my palm on my overalls and tried again, telling myself to calm down and stop letting my overactive imagination run away with romantic ideas. It would most likely be a text from the girls checking in on me. Or perhaps it was Alexis with a book recommendation or a picture of a dog he thought I'd like to see. But a little voice at the back of my head wondered if it could be an Andreas, maybe even *the* Andreas. What would his first message be like? Would I read his words and hear his voice in my head, his features coming into focus at last? Could this message be something we would look back on years later and laugh about together? I told myself to stop getting carried away. It was probably a text from the phone company warning me I was about to go over my spending limit or something equally mundane. But hope still bubbled away.

When I finally succeeded in unlocking the phone, I wished it was one of those routine options. Jim's name leaped out at me, almost as intrusive in my Greek haven as if he'd walked up to the front door in person. He was still in my phone address book with a heart emoji on either side of 'Boss Jim'. He'd added those emojis in himself when our relationship had officially changed status from employer and employee to something more, but he hadn't got rid of the word 'boss', which should have rung alarm bells at the time. In those early days, my heart had started beating faster whenever I saw his name pop up on the screen. Now it was beating faster for a very different reason. A message arriving from Jim was the last thing I'd been hoping for. I'd been doing so well in not even thinking about him over the last few days, and now a text was undoing all my good work, sending me into that place of insecurity and frustration all over again. I hated that he could still have that effect on me.

Before I even read the message, I quickly deleted the hearts and the word 'boss' from my address book. I told myself I was too mature to delete his text altogether or block him, but perhaps it was really because I wasn't brave enough. My imagination would probably fill in the gaps in a worse way than the actual reality. I closed my eyes briefly and attempted a few positive yoga-esque affirmations of 'I am strong', which sounded pathetic even in my own head. Then I braced myself and looked at the message before I lost courage completely. I was disappointed that I was allowing myself to be so wound up by this.

The text was stark and to the point.

Have you had enough of being dramatic? You know you want me.

There followed a picture file, but whatever it was – and I dreaded to think what it could be – hadn't downloaded properly so the image didn't load up on the screen. My nerves turned into something very different. How dare he be so utterly dismissive of my emotions while simultaneously being arrogant enough to think I'd still be pining away for him? The man was deluded. Had he not listened to a word I'd said when I'd walked out on him? Fizzing with anger, I jabbed at the screen until I managed to delete the offensive text and the picture which would probably have proved even more offensive had it downloaded properly. A thousand potential responses swirled around my mind, many of which would have startled my friends with the number of expletives they'd contain. I even started typing out a few different politer versions of the message asking him to leave me alone. But then I decided against even doing that. In behaving the way he had done, Jim had forfeited the right to expect a response from me ever again. I could not have made it clearer to him that he had hurt me too much for our relationship to be repaired. If he was struggling to accept it, then that was his problem, but I was under no obligation to explain it to him all over again. It was time he drew a line under the whole affair and moved on, like I had.

But that annoying nagging voice at the back of my mind questioned whether I really had moved on as much as I was pretending to myself. Yes, I'd packed my bags and headed to Greece, I'd found paid work and a place to stay. But my efforts to find Awesome Andreas had been half-hearted to say the least, idling surfing the internet while knowing there was very little chance of narrowing down the options there, and leaving a tiny notecard pinned up barely in sight on a kiosk. If Jim could see me now, would he really believe that his chances of getting back with me were dead and buried?

I was so buoyed up with indignation mixed with an undercurrent of self-doubt that I decided I needed to take positive action to prove Jim's assumption wrong. The noticeboard sign was yet to elicit any Andreas callers, so I'd have one last time searching online, then I'd go out in the street and start calling 'Andreas' to passers-by if I had to.

This time I used the computer in the guest lounge which was set up for English-speaking visitors. Mindful that I didn't want to lose my place in Yiota's good books so soon after getting into them, I made sure no guests were in the vicinity, and I kept my search quick and to the point, focusing on the area where I was staying.

Within minutes, I'd found a man called Andreas who owned a grocery just outside Sami. As it was called 'Andreas's Fruit and Veg' and not 'Andreas and sons' or similar, I took a wild punt on him being single, and before I lost courage, I pinged him a quick message explaining that I was searching for a man named Andreas and asking if he wanted to meet up for a coffee. If the poor man had any sense, he'd probably ignore the message from the random English woman asking him on a date purely on the basis of his name, that is if the message didn't go straight into spam. But as Kat kept urging me, if I didn't take a chance, I was never going to achieve anything. I pressed send before I could change my mind. The less time I had to think too much about this, the better.

To my complete astonishment and slight horror, the computer pinged with a reply within minutes. Andreas the grocer was happy to have received my message and he would be delighted to meet me tomorrow. What had I got myself into?

I decided to celebrate/distract myself from worrying about my impending first date by making a trip to the bookshop. It was high time I took up Alexis on his offer of providing me with a dictionary. It would be nice to see him in person again. And it would give me another chance to check if the occupant of the tattoo studio had returned to their post yet.

I went along the quiet back street to town and waved hello to my donkey friend on the way. I cut past Maria's Taverna so I could breathe in the fresh smell of the sea, and soon arrived at Alexis's street. At least I was now able to find my way around town without any issues. Considering I'd been here for only a few days, I was feeling surprisingly at home.

My heart beating rapidly, I approached the tattoo studio, rehearsing my questions for the tattooist all over again. But once more, it was devoid of life, although it looked like someone had picked a couple of lemons from the trees which stood guard either side of the door.

'*Iassou*, Lydia, *mou*.'

I turned around and saw Alexis watching me from the doorway of his shop.

'*Iassou*?'

'It means "hello",' he said. 'Yiota tells me that she is satisfied with your work. Congratulations. My sister is what you might call a tough cookie. But once you have won her over, she will support you through everything.'

I felt a warm glow of accomplishment and beamed at him. He smiled back and welcomed me into the shop, gesturing for me to make myself at home.

'At least that's one good thing that's happened today,' I said.

Alexis's brow furrowed in concern. 'It sounds as if you have been having a difficult day.'

I explained about Jim's text, then moved the conversation on so I didn't make Alexis think I was still obsessed with my ex. If I wasted my time talking about Jim, then it would be like he still had a hold over me.

'Now that I know I'll be able to stay a while, can I purchase that Greek dictionary you said you would hold back for me?'

Alexis frowned. 'No indeed.'

I was rather taken aback. 'Oh.' Had I offended him in some way?

'What I mean is that I will not allow you to buy it. It is my gift to you.' He spread his palms in an open gesture.

'That is very generous of you. But I absolutely insist on buying it. You've been more than kind ever since I arrived. I know you say you are only being a hospitable Greek, but I need to pay my way.'

Alexis appeared to agree but reluctantly, and it was only later that I discovered he'd slipped a phrasebook into the paper bag alongside the dictionary.

I peered out of the window to see if any potential customers were heading down the street.

'Will I be in your way if I stay for a while?' I asked. 'I can help with stacking the shelves if you like?' Alexis was the closest thing to a friend I'd found in Sami and I found myself wanting to confide in him about my imminent date. There was something so calming about the bookshop, and its owner, that I would gladly settle in for the rest of the day.

'I am always happy to spend time with a fellow reader,' he said simply, handing me a pile of English language books to sort through.

'I'm meeting my first Andreas tomorrow,' I said by way of reply, the words bursting out of my mouth.

Alexis raised an eyebrow.

'And how do you feel about that?'

'Good question. Nervous. Excited. Terrified. Mostly terrified.' I paused, then admitted, 'It's been a while since

I've been on a date with anyone other than Jim. And I'm not sure I know what the etiquette is anymore.'

'What do you mean?' Alexis straightened up a pile of bookmarks which were next to the till and smiled as he asked the question.

'How do I act? What do I say? What if he thinks I'm awful? What if he's an evil axe murderer?'

Alexis chuckled. 'For a start, I think you are getting your questions in the wrong order. I would have thought the evil axe murderer issue would take higher priority over 'What if he thinks I'm awful?''

I wailed. 'You see, this is why I'm going to be rubbish at dating. I should never have started this thing. What was I thinking? I only messaged the guy because Jim's text threw me off balance. But the whole idea of searching for Awesome Andreas was ridiculous to start with. Who's to say if I do track him down that he thinks I'm awesome in return?'

My usual insecurities were bubbling to the surface and although I knew I should probably keep them to myself, I found myself baring my soul to my new friend.

Alexis took my hand and led me over to one of the armchairs.

'I think perhaps this is what you English would describe as a perfect opportunity for a cup of tea.'

He continued talking as he bustled around making the drinks, and the familiar sound of the boiling kettle and the clinking cutlery went some way to starting to settle my nerves.

'The first thing I would say is that it is very unlikely that this Andreas is an axe murderer. I know of no such men on Kefalonia.' He smiled. 'But if it would make you feel better, you can tell me when and where you are meeting him, and I can look out for you. You have my number, and if you are not happy, you can send me a message and I will provide you an excuse to leave. I am sure this is something you had already thought of arranging with your girlfriends back at home, but as I am in the same town, it might make you feel happier knowing someone is nearby. Now, do you want milk in your tea?'

The tension which had been tightening its grip on my skull eased slightly.

'I'm in your debt, Alexis. That is so kind of you.' I was touched by his thoughtfulness and sensitivity in considering the extra worries facing women in particular when they put themselves out there in the dating world.

'You are not in my debt. I will not have any feeling of obligation. Now, tell me more about this Andreas.'

I blushed, embarrassed to admit how little I knew about him. Once Alexis had heard how I'd approached a complete stranger online and proposed a date without knowing anything more than his name, he might retract his offer of support, believing me beyond help.

'He runs a grocery shop,' I said.

Was that a spark of recognition in Alexis's eyes? I waited for him to say something, but he held his counsel.

'Do you know him?' I pressed. Anything more I could find out would be a bonus.

'I cannot be sure,' was all he would say. 'I think it is better that you form your own opinions of the Andreases you meet, rather than arriving at your date with ideas already set.'

I couldn't decide whether that was ominous or not.

Chapter Eleven

The day of my first Andreas date was sunny and even hotter than the previous day. I'd like to say I woke feeling refreshed from a good night's sleep and full of excited anticipation. But the reality was that I'd spent most of the night tossing and turning as I rehearsed small talk from my new Greek phrasebook and debated whether I'd be better off fleeing the country and returning to my original life.

Thankfully the desire to run away all over again vanished with the darkness of the night, and as dawn rose, I decided to develop a positive mindset. That combined with enough makeup to cover the dark circles under my eyes should power me through.

I raced through the cleaning at my quickest rate yet, and even Yiota couldn't find fault when she did an inspection at the end of my shift.

'Perhaps dates are the way to make sure you finish on

time,' she said dryly as she confirmed that I'd completed my tasks for the day.

I raced back to my room and called the girls on FaceTime for an all-important outfit consultation and pep talk. As I hopped around in one of the hotel dressing gowns holding various clothing choices up to the camera, Kat got right to the point.

'You're not wearing those undies, are you?'

I pulled my dressing gown chord tighter so that I was no longer accidentally flashing my underwear to my friends.

'They're comfortable, they don't give me VPL, and I have no intention of them being seen by anyone but myself,' I retorted. It was the kind of underwear I wasn't really conscious of wearing, which is how it should be. The last thing I wanted in the midst of first-date nerves was to be worrying about underwires digging in or a thong riding up where it shouldn't.

Kat stuck her tongue out at me. 'Why not give yourself the option? One glimpse at those granny pants is enough to shrivel up the passion of the horniest guy, let alone what they must do to your own feeling of fabulousness. I've said it before and I'll say it again. You've got to start with the foundations. A good set of underwear does wonders for the confidence. Even if you're the only person to see it, just knowing you've got it on will make you walk taller and feel sexier. At least, that's what I always find. Why don't you wear the set you bought to distract Jim with?'

I really wished she hadn't mentioned Jim's name on today of all days. He was the last person I wanted to think about when I was already nervous enough about the prospect of going on a date.

'I've thrown them out,' I confessed. Another impetuous decision, and an expensive one. But they were tainted with unhappy and stressful memories so it was better that I was rid of them.

Kat put her head in her hands in mock despair.

'Never mind the pants, what are you planning to wear over the underwear?' asked Amira, gently pushing Kat out of the way so that she could get closer to the phone. 'And how's the tattoo healing by the way? Want me to take a look?'

'Turn away, Kat, you're not covered by the Hippocratic Oath,' I warned, as I moved the phone round and half-pulled the back of my dressing gown down so I could let Amira inspect the tattoo through the reflection in the mirror.

'Can you stand closer to the camera, babe, and lean forwards a bit?'

I heard Kat snorting in the background. 'You sound like you're directing her on some X-rated website.'

'Shut up, Kat,' Amira and I chorused.

'Can you see it now?' I asked.

'Got it fine. And it's looking really good, Lyds. That flakiness is completely normal, just an indication that it's healing up, and there's still no sign of infection. And before you say anything, I'm pretty used to doing diagnoses over video nowadays, so don't worry. Keep doing whatever it is you're doing, and all will be well.'

I pulled the dressing gown back up and nodded in relief. My feelings towards the tattoo were more mixed nowadays. The initial horror had been replaced with a kind of acceptance, and although I'd still much rather have un-inked skin, I was grateful for the catalyst the tattoo had proved to be in waking me up to my relationship situation and getting me to do something about it.

'Thank goodness for that. It would not have helped my confidence on this date to have discovered that I'd got some kind of infection. OK, and back to the other important issue. What on earth do I wear?' I sat down at the dressing table and propped the phone up on its surface while I brushed my hair. 'I want to look good, but not like I've tried too hard either. Something cool, casual and sophisticated. Oh heck, I don't think I even own any clothes which would help me create that effect.'

I put the hairbrush back down with a clatter, the nerves growing stronger.

'Can I take over now?' asked Kat. 'Only if you don't mind me boasting, this is my particular area of expertise. I'm the queen of first dates.'

'Yes, but that's because you have so many that never go beyond that,' teased Amira.

Kat laughed. 'That's because I'm extremely discerning and have no intention of lowering my very high standards. Right, take the phone over to the wardrobe and let me have a virtual rummage.'

'Um, I've not exactly got as far as unpacking my stuff into the wardrobe,' I confessed, moving my phone around so my friends could see the explosion of clothing across my bedroom floor. 'They are at least all washed and dried now. But I haven't had time to put things away properly because I've mostly been working.'

'Lydia Evans, is that the contents of the suitcase you brought on holiday with us?' asked Kat in disbelief. 'I didn't realise you'd left Jim's house so quickly you'd not even bothered to pack a proper bag.'

I cleared my throat. 'Oh, I thought you knew that. Is the rest of my stuff still OK, by the way?'

Beyond confirming that she'd collected my belongings from Jim's, Kat had remained pretty quiet on the subject, and this was the first time I'd tried pressing her for details.

Kat tutted. 'You owe me big time, hon. My new housemates are not exactly delighted that I've taken over the living room with all your oddments, sorry, many years' worth of carefully collected and collated belongings. Half of it's with me, the other half is with Dr Amira over there, who's too nice to tell you that she's worried that some of the collection is a bit of a health hazard.'

'And what did Jim have to say when you picked it up?' I don't know why I asked the question. It was like deliberately knocking against the tattoo to make it hurt.

'I thought we weren't giving Jim the airtime anymore,' said Amira gently. 'Perhaps it's time to look to the future.'

That made me even more worried than not knowing, so I said as much.

Kat's mood changed from jovial to serious. 'To be honest with you, hon, he worried both of us. The way he was talking it was like he expected you to come back any second. He got a bit teary when we took the final box out.'

'Oh,' I said, unexpectedly feeling quite guilty. I'd never known Jim to cry, and however angry I was at how he'd treated me, I still didn't feel good about him suffering.

'No, stop right there, babe. It was not in the way you're thinking,' said Amira. 'If I'm being completely honest, it was disturbing. It felt quite put on, manipulative even, as if he was doing it in order to make us ring you up and try to persuade you to return to him. I think he's enjoying imagining how he'd make you feel bad if you were to go back. It felt like a control thing. He's disappointed that his pet has disappeared, but he remains calmly confident that it will reappear and he'll be able to continue playing mind games with it.'

When Amira put it like that, Jim's behaviour did sound sinister.

'He wasn't that bad,' I protested automatically, although the words didn't quite ring true, even to myself.

'Why are you still defending him?' said Amira, her voice raised in frustration. 'I've seen men like him before and they're usually sitting next to their wives in A&E, smiling benevolently as the woman protests that she bumped into a door and that she's always clumsy like that.'

'Jim never raised a finger against me,' I said. That was one accusation I could defend him from.

'He might not have physically hurt you, but he liked twisting the knife emotionally.'

I found myself nodding. Hadn't the text from him

yesterday been yet another example of his ability to play with my feelings?

'I wish we could give you a hug, babe. Leaving him was the best thing you've ever done.'

I blinked the sudden moisture away from my eyes. However cathartic it felt to be having this conversation, it was not helping me to get in the right frame of mind before my big date. Amira seemed to realise this because she quickly moved the conversation onto a different topic.

'Anyway, we've spent enough time talking about He Who Shall Not Be Named. Your stuff is safe now, and so are you. Tell us about this Awesome Andreas that you're meeting. Are you excited?'

'I don't know if he'll deserve the Awesome title yet. In fact, it would probably be more accurate to call him Anonymous Andreas at the moment as I don't really know anything about him.'

I explained about how I'd messaged the complete stranger Andreas to arrange the date.

Kat clutched her sides as she laughed for an uncomfortably long period of time.

'I've got to hand it to you, Lyds, you certainly don't do things by halves. Most people would at least go on a dating site, but oh no, our Lydia has to message a vegetable seller out of the blue. What's the code word for when we need to rescue you?'

I pouted. 'That's all covered, thank you very much. Alexis has agreed to be my backup.'

Kat and Amira exchanged a glance.

'And before you say anything, Alexis is one of the good guys, and I know I can trust him to look out for me. If he can't help, he'll send his sister to sort it out, and believe me when I tell you that Yiota is formidable enough to put the most aggressive Andreas in his place. But I promise I'll give you a call by 9pm Greek time to let you know that I'm still alive and, if I don't, you have my full permission to call the embassy and unleash the dogs.'

'Sounds like you should be going on a date with this Alexis instead,' muttered Amira. I didn't dare say out loud that I kind of wished I was as I couldn't imagine feeling this stressed about a date with Alexis. I pushed the unhelpful thought to the back of my mind. It was another form of displacement, a way of distracting myself from nerves about my impending Andreas meeting. I needed to focus on my mission.

'Right, back to the task in hand,' continued Amira. 'What are you going to wear? How about the outfit you wore on the night out? You know, the one where you got the tattoo. You look gorgeous in it and who wouldn't feel confident and sexy in that glittery top?'

'Now there's an idea,' said Kat. 'And when you meet him, he'll go "Lydia, darling, you haven't changed a bit", and then he'll sweep you off your feet and ravish you, but carefully so he doesn't make your still-healing tattoo sore.'

'You guys are the worst.' I laughed. They were achieving their aim of making me relax before the big date if nothing else.

After much debate, we eventually decided I'd wear my

blue and white checked sundress together with a pair of straw wedge heels to give me some added height and therefore confidence.

'You'll get bonus points for the colours of the Greek flag,' said Amira. 'Cool, collected and perfect for any occasion.'

'Don't forget the shades,' added Kat. 'They'll stop you squinting in the sun, and if he's a horror, at least they'll help you disguise your reaction to seeing him.'

'I'd probably need to wear a mask to make that work,' I responded. 'You know I'm rubbish at hiding my feelings.'

'That's why we love you. And if this Andreas has any sense, he'll love you for it too. Remember my mantra, if you feel you're having to put on an act for him, then he ain't worth it, honey.'

I darted into the bathroom to pull on my chosen outfit and then applied my makeup at the mirror while the girls continued a steady stream of bolstering conversation. I knew that I'd feel lonely all over again when we ended the call, but for now, it was almost as good as having them in the room with me.

'Bit more eyeliner, hon, then you'll be done. Ready for a final handbag check. Purse? Phone? Keys? Condoms? Mace? I'm joking, I'm joking.' Kat held her hands up in mock surrender as I rolled my eyes at her suggestions.

I did a twirl as my personal cheerleaders wolf-whistled their support.

'Perfect,' said Amira. 'Let's do a final watch sync to

make sure we're in agreement about your safety check-in. We don't want the time difference to cause confusion.'

'9pm Greek time. So that's 7pm UK time.'

Amira wagged her finger at the camera. 'I mean it, babe, if you haven't called by then, I'll ring the British embassy and demand to speak to the ambassador personally. And I'll kick up such a fuss that the entire police force of Kefalonia will be out searching for you.'

'I promise I won't forget.'

'Good,' said Kat. 'Now we've done our responsible parent bit, we'll leave you with this; have fun, Lydia. You deserve to have a good time. And don't take it too seriously. I know you're hoping to meet your Awesome Andreas, and we want that for you too. But you're good enough on your own as well. You don't need a man to define you or make you whole, despite what Jim might have made you believe over the course of your relationship. You're a wonderful person in your own right.'

'I think that's the nicest thing you've ever said to me,' I said, tears starting to form again in my eyes.

'Don't get used to it,' she retorted, though I could tell she was getting a bit bleary-eyed too. 'Now off you go before you blub all over the place and ruin that makeup job we've so carefully coached you through. And remember, we want details, the hotter the better.'

She waggled her eyebrows suggestively. 'Don't do anything I wouldn't do,' was her final command.

'That gives me quite a lot of leeway,' I said.

'Exactly,' said Kat and winked at me.

Chapter Twelve

S tanding on the main street and fiddling with my phone in a bid to look busy, I thought about how much I hate first dates. In my defence, it was a while since I'd been on one, and I'm not even sure that my first date with Jim really counted given that at the time I thought I'd been accompanying him to a business dinner as a mere colleague when he'd completely surprised me by presenting me to the clients as his other half. He'd claimed he thought it would make him seem more stable and trustworthy, which seemed a rather 1950s-esque attitude, but I'd been so nonplussed by it, that I didn't know how to react. I'd barely been able to stammer out a word as we'd had pre-dinner drinks, the frustration had built as I'd choked my way through the starter, and I'd finally managed to confront him about the deception in the corridor by the restaurant's toilets between the main course and the dessert. But he'd been so surprised by my confusion and had made me think that I was the unreasonable one for not wanting to go along with his scheme; I'd ended up apologising to him, and even felt flattered that I'd been singled out for such attention. It was a perfectly executed manipulation and with the benefit of hindsight, I wished I'd been brave enough to see through it.

But what had actually happened was that before I could come to my senses, I'd got used to our names being linked together and the charade had become reality. Thinking about it now in the light of how our break-up had occurred, I really had sleepwalked my way into the relationship, settling into it out of a desire not to upset the status quo, and moulding my dreams so that they fitted into the life that Jim made me believe I wanted. I was determined that I would never allow that to happen again. At least this first date was happening at my instigation, and on my terms, but that didn't make it any less daunting.

I checked my phone for the third time in as many minutes. I was half-expecting my first Andreas to cancel on me. It was a beautiful day and he probably had much better things to be doing than meeting up with a random woman who'd messaged him out of the blue online purely because his name was Andreas and he happened to live a mile outside of Sami. I told myself to stop being negative. Just because Greece seemed to have more than its fair share of extremely attractive men, it didn't mean that they were out of my league. Perhaps this Andreas would be intrigued by the situation, and flattered that I had approached him. Perhaps he would even be The One.

I repeated this idea to myself, because the voice of

concern at the back of my head was also starting to express second thoughts about the wisdom of meeting a stranger from the internet. I knew thousands of people met their other halves online, but I suspected most of those encounters happened through dating sites, rather than after sending a message on the website of a grocery store. Beyond the fact that Andreas ran the aforementioned shop and sold the best tomatoes on Kefalonia, according to what I'd managed to painstakingly work out using my new dictionary, I didn't know much else. I'd tried to ask Yiota about him, but she'd taken offence to my inadvertent implication that living on a small island meant that everyone knew everyone else.

'It suggests we are all related to each other, and I can assure you that we are not,' she'd said indignantly.

Wary of losing my position so soon after having successfully completed my initial trial period, I'd quickly backed off. But that meant that for all I knew, Andreas could be anywhere between 18 and 108 years old, and who knew what his personality was like? Hence the decision to meet him in the most public place I could think of, the main street of Sami. At least this way there were plenty of people around and I wasn't trapped in an enclosed location if I decided I needed to make a run for it. I told myself to stop imagining worst-case scenarios. As Alexis had pointed out, the number of evil axe murderers in the world were few and far between, and that's why incidents involving them made the news. The worst-case scenario would probably be that he was a very dull man and I'd make my excuses and politely leave.

I think it was dwelling on the whole axe murderer scenario which made me jump out of my skin when someone tapped me on the shoulder. Sounding and looking like a startled guinea pig was not exactly the classy first impression I'd been planning to make.

'Lydia?' asked the man.

'That's me,' I stammered, my heart pounding as I gazed back at the impressive individual who was towering over me. I had to lean my head back to take all of him in, and if he'd been standing with his back to the sun, he probably would have blocked it out completely. Thankfully, he looked perfectly genial and hopefully harmless, not an axe in sight. In fact, he would have struggled to conceal an axe on his person as his outfit was so figure-hugging, it left little to the imagination. His white shirt was unbuttoned nearly to his waist, revealing a triangle of hairless, tanned torso. His black trousers strained across thighs which were clearly the product of many hours of squat exercises. The outfit might almost have been spray-painted on, and I was impressed at his dedication to skin-tight satin in these warm conditions. Whether he was Awesome Andreas remained to be seen, but he certainly deserved the moniker Athletic Andreas with his bulging biceps and classic bodybuilder physique. I waited for a jolt of recognition and/or attraction, but neither came.

Realising I'd been staring for a bit too long, I repeated my name, as if I was reassuring myself of my identity.

He smiled. 'I am...' He paused for dramatic effect. 'Andreas. The Andreas. The one you are looking for.'

I laughed because he said it with such an exaggerated swagger, I was convinced he must be messing around, then immediately felt bad when the smile fell from his face.

'Sorry, I'm really nervous,' I hastily covered. 'When I get nervous I tend to laugh a lot. And yawn.' Right on cue, I felt a yawn involuntarily start to stretch my jaw. I swallowed and tried to smother it. 'Sorry.'

Andreas grabbed my hand and shook it vigorously. 'Do not be nervous. I will show you a good time. And apologising is a very British thing. Be proud to yawn and laugh.'

I let out another squeak, as the bones of my hand crunched against each other thanks to the force of his strong grip.

'Absolutely. Will do,' I said. It wasn't like I was going to disagree with him while my hand was still in his. He looked at me carefully and then nodded in satisfaction. I sensed I'd passed some kind of test.

'Lovely weather,' I stammered as the silence stretched out. Again, I kicked myself. What a stupid thing to say. Of course, it was lovely weather, I was in Greece in the summer. But how else was I meant to break the silence? Say what you like about English weather, at least it gave enough variety to always provide a talking point in awkward situations. But the only reason this was awkward was because I was making it so by overthinking things. I told myself to stop, but my brain had other ideas.

'It is good training weather,' said Andreas, making his biceps twitch to make sure I knew what kind of training he was talking about. I decided he probably spent most of his free time in the gym to maintain that physique. He wouldn't be impressed with my approach to working out, which was that I didn't.

'What would you like to do?' he asked.

I nodded, grateful that he was open to discussion about it. I'd prepared my answer for this, carefully considering the options and potential outcomes as I'd lain awake last night.

'I thought maybe we could go for an ice cream,' I said, wondering if it would look rude if I took a couple of steps back. I was starting to get a crick in my neck from looking up at him. I'd worried after my initial invitation that coffee seemed too suggestive, and I'd ruled out alcohol as I was still following my vow of temperance. A full-on meal could be too much pressure, but an ice cream seemed like the perfect solution in a sunny country on a hot day, plus it had the added bonus of not committing either of us to spending a lengthy amount of time together if it turned out we didn't get on. It would also give us something to talk about. At least debating the merits of different flavours and cone options would be better than me repeatedly mentioning how sunny it was. Yes, I had thought about this a lot. But now that I was confronted by the reality of the situation, did suggesting ice cream make me seem too childish and unsophisticated? I stopped myself right there. As Kat and Amira would say, it was time I stopped worrying about what other people thought of me and did what would make me happy. I liked ice cream, so why shouldn't I enjoy it with my new acquaintance?

An expression of dismay crossed my date's face. 'Too much sugar,' he said, swiping his hand from side to side as if he was knocking away invisible ice creams. 'My body must not be tainted by such things.' As if to demonstrate this point, he flexed the muscles of his chest.

I nearly laughed, never having been confronted with this kind of peacock behaviour before, then I realised that once again, he was deadly serious.

'Of course. Sorry. Then what would you like to do?'

'I have an idea. This way.'

Athletic Andreas gestured for me to follow him, and then set off at a pace which would have been more suited to a commuter battling through the crowds on the streets of London than someone here in relaxed, sleepy Sami.

I hesitated for a moment, then decided I might as well accompany him through the centre of town. There were enough people around that I could always call for help if I needed to, and despite his intimidating physique, he wasn't setting off any alarm bells. On the negative side he wasn't setting off any tingly bells of attraction or recognition either, but I told myself to give it time. There was no point in jumping to conclusions in the first five minutes of the date.

He led me to a part of town I was yet to explore. I kept careful track of the direction we were going in, using Alexis's bookshop as the centre of my mental map. After all, he had offered me a refuge should I need it.

'Where are we going?' I asked after several minutes of

vigorous walking. How Andreas wasn't breaking into a sweat I had no idea, especially as the tightness of his outfit must have made it more challenging to achieve the large strides he was taking. I was seriously regretting the wedge heels. Pretty they might be, but the straps were beginning to rub, and I had a horrible feeling my heels were going to develop blisters. I really hoped his idea did not involve any kind of running around or exercise. The walk to get to our destination was quite enough.

'To the maritime museum. It has a temporary exhibition of Greek statues which have come from the mainland. We shall look at them.'

'That's a much better idea than ice cream,' I said, pleased to be experiencing some culture and pleasantly surprised that this was his suggestion. It seemed like a sophisticated thing to do on a date, and my estimation of this first Andreas went up. As soon as I'd seen him, I'd ruled him out as Awesome Andreas because physically he really wasn't the kind of guy I'd normally be attracted to, but I obviously needed to stop making snap judgements. This Andreas clearly had hidden depths.

We arrived at the museum and then had a brief tussle over who was going to pay for the tickets. Athletic Andreas was insistent that he should do the honours, while I was equally determined that we would split the costs fifty-fifty. It was very sweet of him to offer, but I didn't want anyone to think I was freeloading my way around Kefalonia. Besides, I'd checked my banking app before setting off and seen that my first wages from the hotel had been transferred in. I wasn't going to be buying a super yacht any time soon, but I could at least stretch to a museum ticket for myself.

'Meeting up was at my invitation, I should pay my way,' I asserted. 'Please. It's only a few euros, after all.'

'The man should always pay,' retorted Andreas. He folded his arms, determined not to give way. There was an ominous tearing sound from the seams of his shirt as the fabric did battle with his biceps.

Thankfully, the proprietor broke the impasse by announcing that as the museum was going to close in half an hour, we could go in for free. Athletic Andreas put his arm around my waist, casually resting his hand on my hip as he steered me into the room. It felt strange to be this close to a man who wasn't Jim. I wasn't sure I liked it. Not because he wasn't Jim, not at all, but because he was essentially a stranger, and I was yet to make my mind up about him. I certainly wasn't comfortable enough in his presence to be standing this close together. I neatly stepped away from his side and went across the room to pick up a leaflet giving more information about what was in the exhibition.

In spite of my uncertainty about the company, I was pleased to be getting the chance to see the artefacts on display. The exhibition consisted of the most detailed plaster casts and modern recreations of ancient Greek statues. Visitors were encouraged to get as close to them as they wanted, which gave me an amazing perspective of the craftsmanship which must have gone into creating the originals on which they were based. The figures looked lifelike and strong, if slightly exaggerated in terms of their proportions. I peered at the labels, reading about how the statues were based on the ancient ideals of the perfect form, one in which strength and grace were equally prized.

'Look at this one,' I said, calling across to Andreas as I admired the statue of a man about to throw a discus. Its stance was so lifelike, I found myself stepping out of the supposed path of the shot. There was no response from my date. I turned around and saw him at the other end of the room standing in front of a statue of a young man tying on a headband. The pose of the statue was designed to show off the strength in the guy's torso, the lines of the muscles almost hypnotic in their detail. And then I realised that Andreas was adopting a similar stance, posing in front of it so that he was mimicking the young man's action.

'What do you think?' he asked.

I wasn't sure how I was meant to reply. There was something incredibly surreal about seeing a grown man in skin-tight satin trying to impress a woman by posing like a naked statue. He dropped the stance for just long enough to gesture at his phone which was in his back pocket.

'My followers will like, don't you think? Can you take photos for them?'

And then I realised he hadn't been asking for my opinion on his appearance. He was just concerned about whether the pose would generate enough likes on his social media pages. I hoped he wasn't going to ask me to join in. I wasn't sure I'd be able to keep a straight face.

I needn't have worried as it soon became clear that my

presence was not required in any of the pictures. There followed a half-hour photography and video session, in which Athletic Andreas posed in front of every statue in the room and directed me in an increasingly bossy way as to how to take the pictures he wanted from the best angle. I had to admire his dedication to the cause as he contorted himself into various uncomfortable-looking positions in order to get the perfect pose. He even roped in the poor manager of the museum to waft a large piece of cardboard towards him so his hair could look artfully tousled while he was doing dances to add to his Instagram reels. I had never met anyone so superficial and vain in all my life, but his genuine enjoyment of what he was doing was infectious, and although the date wasn't at all what I'd hoped for, the whole situation was so surreal that I still had a good time. He was a funny guy, despite his obsession with his personal appearance.

Eventually, the museum manager had had enough and politely asked us to leave. As he closed the door behind us, I could hear him immediately turning the bolts. He was probably scared that Andreas would try to go back in for one last power pose.

'This was an amazing date,' said Andreas confidently, puffing his chest up and making his muscles ripple beneath the satin all over again.

'I can't remember the last time I laughed so much,' I answered truthfully. I had promised myself when I set out on this Andreas dating mission that I would be honest with both myself and my dates. Time to put that honesty into practice. Fortunately, I'd got a pretty good notion of what made Athletic Andreas tick, and I didn't think he'd be too devasted by what I was about to say, which made it a lot easier. I forced myself to be brave. 'Although it has been very nice to meet you and I have enjoyed learning about what makes for a good social media post, I'm afraid I can't see us going on another date. I'm not sure that we have a huge amount in common, and I'd definitely have to up my photography game. Thank you for a fun and illuminating time, though. I will never look at an Instagram picture or reel in the same way again.'

A look of surprise briefly crossed Athletic Andreas's face before he shrugged casually. 'Never mind. It was fun to have met you too, Lydia. Good luck with finding your Andreas. Don't forget to follow me.'

He named his social media handles and patiently waited for me to key them into my phone. Noticing the number of comments he'd already had in response to his statue posing post, I figured he'd soon be able to find himself another date if he wanted to. Then he kissed my cheek and strode off quickly to get another workout in at the gym.

I took the opportunity to send a text message to check in with my backup girls before they felt the need to send out a search party for me. As I was doing so, I noticed a message on my phone from Alexis that I hadn't heard arrive.

I hope you have a good evening. Here if you need me

I smiled, the words on the screen translating into the

sound of his warm voice in my head. I tapped out a brief reply thanking him, then sent another message, something compelling me to continue the conversation.

It was an interesting evening. I now feel able to take up an alternative career as a personal photographer for influencers.

His reply came quickly.

Sounds…interesting?

You could say that. I'm glad I've dipped my toe in the dating pool again, but I think my Mr Right would have spent more time admiring the ancient artefacts than himself.

Or, dare I suggest it, you?

But before I had worked out how to interpret his comment, or how to respond, another message pinged through.

Not Awesome Andreas, then? I'm sorry that it wasn't what you were hoping for.

I was touched that he seemed to genuinely care about the journey I was on.

*Alas no. Athletic Andreas definitely. Perhaps even
Arrogant Andreas at times. But sadly, not Awesome.*

The three dots appeared on the screen but it took a while
for his message to appear.

Where are you going to search for him next?

That was a very good question indeed.

Chapter Thirteen

My experience with Athletic Andreas, while not providing me with the happy ever after I'd been hoping for, at least boosted my confidence on the dating front, proving that I was brave enough to put myself out there again. The girls sent me texts filled with gifs of Beyoncé proclaiming that girls rule the world, cheering me on from afar. Alexis meanwhile followed up his check-in message, stopping by the hotel the next day, his arms full of freshly baked circular breads covered in toasted sesame seeds. He claimed Yiota had asked him to bring them, but I got the feeling he was using it as an excuse to confirm that I really was as OK as I had claimed in text messages.

'Everything alright?' he asked, watching me intently, as if wanting to reassure himself that I was still in one piece. I nodded, feeling warm under his gaze. I wasn't used to a guy looking out for my welfare like this. He was a good person, a true friend.

'You smell delicious,' I said, caught up in the intensity of his expression. 'The bread, I mean. The bread smells delicious,' I covered hastily.

I thought I detected a slight flush in his cheeks.

'*Ti kaneis? O kairos einai kalos.*' I attempted some slow and painful Greek to distract him from my awkwardness, asking how he was, and commenting on the beautiful weather.

Alexis's face lit up. '*Poli kala*, very good. You have been studying from the phrasebook?'

'I've been trying, but I'm not sure I'm doing particularly well.' I got my notebook out of my back pocket and waved it at him. 'I've been writing new vocab in here, but when it comes to piecing it together in actual sentences, I'm not having much success. I'm so worried about offending people by pronouncing something wrong, that I'm nervous to try it out on them.'

'You tried speaking to me, and I didn't get offended, quite the opposite,' said Alexis.

I gently nudged my hip against his as we walked towards the kitchen together. 'But you're too kind to take offence. I feel safe trying stuff out on you. Tell me truthfully, I can bear it. How badly did I mangle the words?'

Alexis laughed. 'No mangling at all. I knew exactly what you meant. But you were perhaps a little English-sounding. It doesn't matter. I know I speak English with a Greek accent.'

'How can I do better?'

He put the bread down on the countertop and turned to face me.

'You are doing very well.'

I pretended to frown at him.

'Fine, if you insist. I think perhaps you need to move your mouth a bit more,' he continued. 'Push your lips forward in order to get the "o" sound in the *kalos*.'

He demonstrated what he meant. I watched his lips closely, but I wasn't sure gazing at his mouth was going to help me with my linguistic skills. In fact, it proved to be rather distracting.

'Your turn,' said Alexis. 'Remember, move your mouth around the words.' He reached out and gently touched my cheek, the contact so brief that I wondered if I had imagined it.

The sound that came out of my mouth was neither Greek, nor English, but a confused jumble of the two. I pulled myself together and made a concerted effort to follow Alexis's instruction. I felt his gaze on my lips, and tried my best to imitate the movement he had suggested.

Alexis cleared his throat.

'Much better,' he said, turning aside, suddenly focused on removing a smudge from his glasses. Then he checked his watch.

'I had better go to open the shop. I can't disappoint the crowds of tourists who will no doubt be waiting on the doorstep for me.' He hurried away, but paused on the threshold and turned back to face me. 'If you would like more language practice, you only have to ask.'

And then he was gone.

The rest of the day passed in a whirlwind as I tried to concentrate on work and attempted to ignore the scene in the kitchen which kept playing on repeat in my head. I needed to focus on my Andreas mission, not get distracted by Alexis, however good a friend he was to me. When I finally clocked off, I decided to build on the experience of my first dating sortie and seek out another opportunity.

Although Kat was still urging me to go on the pull in a local bar, I knew that while my confidence was higher than it had been, it wasn't yet that high. Instead, I headed online again, and found a forum where locals and tourists posted in English as well as Greek, about everything from where to find a good beach to what was the best channel for reality shows. I couldn't care less where to catch the Greek version of *Strictly*, but what did interest me was that one of the most prolific responders was a guy named Andreas who struck me as being rather charming. Whatever people were asking about, he seemed happy to provide a helpful answer, and even better, his avatar was a picture of him with a cute dog in his arms. Admittedly the dog was blocking part of his face, but its presence definitely boded well, suggesting a sensitive, caring sort of man. Dogs were generally good judges of character.

I sent this Andreas a private message to say hi, stating that I was new to the island and asking if there was a particular place I should visit and whether he'd be up for showing it to me. After I'd hit Send, I had a brief panic that he'd think I was trying to hire him as a tour guide, but thankfully he replied with a cheery message saying that he knew just the place and if I was up for it, he'd love to buy me a drink when we were there. He added a heart emoji and a winky face, so I was pretty sure he was treating this as a date not a business transaction.

Which was how I found myself two days later jumping on the bus and travelling up to a place called Fiskardo on the northern coast of the island to meet him – and hopefully his dog too – at the harbour there. My nerves had lessened a little compared to my date with Athletic Andreas, and today I was feeling a pleasant mix of hope and excitement. This was how dating should be: joyful anticipation and the thrill of meeting someone who could become very important to me. And if he didn't, well, the sun was shining, and it was a glorious day to explore the island further.

Fiskardo was picture-perfect beautiful. Whereas Sami was very much a working port, with ferries and fishing vessels popping in and out all hours of the day and night, slightly scruffy and loveable because of it, Fiskardo seemed like its posh-and-they-know-it cousin. The buildings were a bright mix of terracotta, peach and peppermint, with sky-blue shutters expanding the colour palette. The higgledy-piggledy streets had a smarter collection of cars parked up than I'd seen in Sami, and the extra wealth was also reflected in the harbour. The boats moored here were probably worth the GDP of a small European country, and their sleek metal gangways were roped off from members of the public with stern notices stating 'Private yacht, no boarding'. Impossibly good-looking crew members maintained watch over the vessels, flexing muscles at strangers and flashing long legs at passengers as required. As I wandered between the rows of artisan bakeries and trendy bars, I overheard snatches of conversation about tennis tournaments and polo matches, while small children with names bigger than their height darted in and out of the grasp of trendy nannies. If it wasn't for the clear blue sky and glorious sunshine, I might have thought I'd taken a wrong turn and ended up on a high street in Kensington or Chelsea.

I was wearing the tried and tested sundress and sandals combination again, and although I'd set off feeling good, among the dazzling white shorts and glittering floral dresses of the yachting set here, I felt decidedly dowdy. I ran my fingers through my hair, surreptitiously trying to tame the waves which were increasingly showing a mind of their own. I half-expected a burly yachtie to block my way along the street, staring down at me, shaking their head at the pleb who'd dared to approach this playground of the rich.

Fortunately, the shop owners still seemed friendly, returning my smiles warmly, and kindly answering my request for directions to the taverna where I'd agreed to meet my next Andreas. I gave myself a stern lecture about not doing myself down. I had as much right to be here as everyone else. Designer outfits did not mean they were any better than me.

I arrived at the taverna two minutes early, but Andreas

was already there waiting for me. I instantly knew who he was because he was wearing a T-shirt with his social media profile picture on it. This did not bode well. I told myself not to be judgemental, but I couldn't help questioning what kind of person would wear a T-shirt featuring their own face to a date, or in fact any other social occasion apart from a fancy dress party. Perhaps it was a sign of a well-developed sense of humour.

I put my hand out to shake his, but he leaned forward and kissed it instead, his lips clammy against my skin.

'I am the luckiest man in Fiskardo as the most beautiful woman has agreed to be my date,' he said, looking me up and down in a very obvious fashion. No, it wasn't a well-developed sense of humour, he was just a creep. I fought the urge to pull my cardigan out of my bag and cover myself up with it as he mentally undressed me.

'I think you need your eyes testing.' I attempted a jokey tone, gesturing around at the glossy people who surrounded us. I'd never been good at taking compliments, but it was even harder to know how to react when they were delivered in such an insincere tone with an obvious agenda attached to them.

His answer was directed to my chest rather than my face. 'I have excellent eyesight.'

I had to fight to restrain my shudder. Less than thirty seconds in, and I knew without a doubt that this was *not* Awesome Andreas. But I'd travelled a fair way up the coast to meet him, and I couldn't think of a way of politely extracting myself from the date so soon after arriving, so I reluctantly allowed myself to be led to a table by the waterfront. I was angry at myself for allowing social niceties to win over my gut instinct to get away, but I felt like I had little choice.

'You haven't brought your dog with you?' I asked, figuring that a conversation about his pet was probably as good a place as any to start.

Andreas frowned. 'I don't like dogs.'

'Oh. But what about the one in your profile picture? And on your T-shirt?'

He laughed. 'I borrowed it from a shelter for the picture. Girls seem to like it.'

Kicking myself for being one of those women who'd fallen for his tactic, I perched on a chair next to the pavement, plotting a speedy exit. To my disappointment, Andreas sat down right next to me, pulling his chair up so that he was uncomfortably close. If I wasn't careful, he'd probably do the whole pretending to stretch move next so he could put his arm around my shoulders. But he didn't even bother going for subtlety. Instead, he went straight in, placing his hand on my thigh. His hand, which was bearing a ring on the fourth finger.

'You're married.' It was a statement, rather than a question.

He didn't even look ashamed.

'Yes. But when a pretty girl messages me, I hate to disappoint her by saying no.'

His fingers tapped a rhythm on my leg, straying ever

closer upwards. I grabbed his hand and removed it from my personal space.

'Well, this *woman* does not believe in messing around with someone who is already married. And in future, don't start pawing somebody without checking first that you've got their consent. Goodbye, Andreas.'

I got up so abruptly that my chair fell over backwards. I could sense heads starting to turn in our direction, but I didn't care. Now I wasn't going to let embarrassment get in the way of standing up for myself.

Andreas's air of easy charm turned dark all at once and he grabbed my wrist.

'You've been leading me on. You came all this way to see me and now you're leaving without even having a drink? I'm a nice guy. I went out of my way to book a table at this expensive taverna. You owe me. Why do girls never go for the nice guy?'

'Nice guys don't act like this,' I retorted. Somehow I managed to twist my wrist out of his grasp. The adrenaline stopped me feeling any pain, but judging by the red marks left by his fingers, I'd probably have a bruise there later.

I left the taverna in a hurry, fearful he might follow me. I was angry at him for his presumption, and angry at myself that I was feeling the guilt he'd aimed to provoke in me, even though I knew it wasn't in any way justified. How many women through the ages had ended up going along with behaviour they didn't feel comfortable with because a manipulative individual had played on their sense of politeness or obligation? I'd found the courage to call it out and reject it this time, but it had cost me. My hands were trembling and my pulse was racing, and not in a good way.

The encounter had also made me re-examine incidents involving Jim, when he'd used similar techniques to bend me to his will. He'd never resorted to physically grabbing me, but he'd certainly used my politeness and desire not to make a scene to get me to do what he wanted, our first date being a case in point. How could I have been so blind for so long? I blinked back tears, shocked at the maelstrom of emotion I was experiencing.

The meeting with Already-married Andreas had tainted my gorgeous surroundings, and I wanted nothing more than to be back in familiar territory, somewhere I felt safe. Disregarding the cost, I jumped in a taxi and headed home to Sami, the tension easing from my head every mile I put between myself and that man. But when we arrived in the town, instead of directing the driver to the Helios Hotel, I asked him to drop me off at Alexis's bookshop instead. I barely gave the tattoo studio a second glance, so intent was I on seeing Alexis's familiar features and telling him what had happened.

'You would not believe the audacity of the latest Andreas, the creepy liar,' I said as I marched in, adrenaline still surging through my veins. The shop bell clanged heavily from the vigorous way I flung the door open. By now my shock had turned into anger and I was fairly fizzing with indignation.

'*Iassou*, Lydia.' There was a note of quiet amusement in Alexis's voice at my unexpected appearance.

'Oh heck, I'm so sorry,' I said hastily as I realised that there was a bigger audience to my dramatic entrance than I'd expected. A couple of tourists had looked up from browsing the shelves and were now watching me with great interest. It was the first time I'd actually seen customers in Alexis's shop, and the last thing I wanted to do was drive them away, despite my desire to confide in the man behind the counter.

'*Persuasion*, great choice,' I said, spotting the book in one woman's hands. 'It's so beautiful. Everybody talks about loving *Pride and Prejudice* best, but *Persuasion* will always be my go-to Jane Austen book, with the gorgeous Captain Wentworth. A story of second chances, and hope. It made me cry, but in a good way.' The tourist nodded awkwardly. I realised that I was practically shouting my rambling nonsense at the poor woman. I made a concerted effort to get myself back under control. 'Sorry, I'll stop interfering and leave you to browse. Best bookshop in Kefalonia.'

Whether it was because of my recommendation, or because I'd drawn so much attention to their choices they now felt obliged to purchase, the couple went away with a heavy bag in each hand.

Alexis smiled at me. 'You should come running into my bookshop more often.'

'I'm sorry about that. I was so wound up at what's just happened that I had to tell you. Had to tell someone,' I corrected hastily, although what I had said first was more accurate. I'd wanted to be somewhere I felt safe, but the reality was I'd sought out *someone* I felt safe with, someone who I knew would put a smile back on my face. But I didn't want him to feel burdened by me. Alexis had been nothing but kind, but I was aware that I could be pushing my luck. I didn't want to be a needy friend who sucked all the attention. It was bad enough that I'd nearly driven his customers away.

Alexis nodded.

'If you do not mind me unpacking this delivery at the same time, I am very happy to listen. I am always pleased to have your company.'

I glowed at his words.

He pulled two large cardboard boxes out from behind the counter.

'We'll do one each,' I volunteered, glad to have something calming to do while I told my story.

It was an exercise in judging books by their covers. I stacked the volumes in piles according to the genres I thought they were, making the occasional stab at trying to translate their titles or authors, and then Alexis corrected as appropriate. While we worked, I told him about Already-married Andreas. Despite how upsetting I'd found the whole encounter, I played it for comedy value, enjoying making Alexis laugh at my description of the awful self-portrait T-shirt. But when I got to the bit about Andreas's fingers dancing up my thigh, Alexis looked disgusted. He instinctively reached out towards me, then picked up another book instead, clearly concerned that I might not feel comfortable with him touching me so soon after being pawed by Already-married Andreas.

'I feel like I should apologise on behalf of men. Are you sure you're OK?' He watched me closely, compassion radiating from his every pore. I self-consciously rubbed my wrist, which was now throbbing. Alexis's expression turned to one of horror as he spotted the marks on it. His voice grew even softer. 'Would you like to take it further? I will support you with whatever you choose to do. That Andreas is not worthy of being called a man.'

I shook my head quickly. I wanted nothing more than to put the entire episode in the past and forget about it.

'Thank you for your support, but he's not worth our time or energy. I can't abide people who think it's OK to say they're single when actually they're married. His total lack of honesty and his appalling attitude towards women mean he doesn't deserve any of my headspace. And you have no need to apologise. You couldn't be more different from him. He claimed to be a nice guy, whereas you really are one.'

'Do you not have a phrase in English that says nice guys finish last?' Alexis said lightly, although I later wondered if there had been a flash of disappointment in his expression first.

I reached across and squeezed his hand.

'I hate that phrase. And it's rubbish too. Being nice should be valued much more highly. It's one of the qualities I admire most about you. I feel I can trust you completely.'

Alexis held my gaze. He'd left his glasses on the counter, and without them he seemed vulnerable somehow. I found myself squeezing his hand again, wanting to convey reassurance, and how much I valued his kindness and friendship. But as I looked at him, I felt a pang of something deep within, a longing, and a question. Was friendship really the right word to describe our connection? I felt myself moving closer to him, the atmosphere between us suddenly thick with an achingly beautiful tension. I whispered his name, the huskiness of my voice saying far more than my thoughts could articulate.

'Lydia, I...' He started to respond, but the clanging of the shop bell interrupted our moment of intensity. We let go of each other's hands, and Alexis quickly jumped to his feet to welcome the new customer, apparently oblivious to what had just happened. But I still felt the sensation of his hand against mine, long after he had moved it away.

Chapter Fourteen

That night, I lay awake in bed for a long time going over and over what had happened in the bookshop. Had I imagined it, or had Alexis and I nearly shared a Moment? I felt like there had been something between us, a charge in the air. Maybe the heightened emotion after my encounter with Already-married Andreas had confused me, or perhaps there was something more to it than that. After all, Alexis was the person I'd rushed to after that disturbing date, knowing instinctively that I would find comfort and safety with him.

Daylight alas did not bring with it clarity of thought, but as I lay in bed, I realised that there was only one person I wanted to spend my day off with. Before I lost courage, I rang Alexis asking if he'd like to go to the beach with me. After yesterday's events, I felt quite shy extending the invitation. He'd been so kind since he'd rescued me outside the tattoo studio, but I couldn't work out what he really thought about me. An insecure part of me still feared that he was acting out of a sense of duty, as if I was some kind of stray animal that he felt obliged to look out for.

But I could hear the smile in his voice as he enthusiastically responded. 'I would be very happy to. I have not been to the beach much this summer. As my sister keeps telling me, I am spending too much time at work.' He dropped his voice to a confidential tone. 'But I don't think she fully understands that when I am surrounded by books, it does not feel like work.'

'If I worked in a bookshop, I'd spend the whole time reading.'

Alexis laughed. 'That is pretty much what I do, which is why it doesn't feel like work. Anyway, enough talk about my lack of business drive. Which beach would you like to go to?'

'When I visited with the girls, we went to one on the other side of the island, I think it was called Myrtos beach? It was absolutely stunning, but I'd love to go to a beach closer to home. Is there a good one in the local area?'

'I know just the place,' promised Alexis. 'It is only a short drive from town, and the water is unreal.'

Half an hour later, I was climbing into Alexis's classic Mini and trying not to laugh at the sight of his tall frame folded into the driver's seat. My attempts were not very successful.

Thankfully, Alexis's eyes were also sparkling with amusement.

'It is a shame the car does not have a sunshine roof for

me to have more headspace,' he said completely deadpan before he started chuckling at the thought. 'Perhaps I should arrange for a hole to be cut in the roof.'

'And you'd get your own air-conditioning system too,' I joked.

His car may have been more suitable for someone of a much smaller stature than Alexis, but I soon realised why he must have chosen it. No sooner had we buzzed through the centre of town and past the port, than we were on a road which narrowed as it steadily climbed upwards, with an interesting collection of hairpin bends added into the mix for an extra driving challenge. The Mini's engine may have been making complaining noises as it wheezed up the hill, but it was nipping around the tight bends like nobody's business.

'Does our destination have a name?' I had to raise my voice above the rattling.

'It is Antisamos beach.'

'And…' I pressed for more details.

'And I will not tell you anything more, but will leave you to make your own mind up about it.'

'Nobody tells me anything,' I pretended to complain but I was actually rather pleased. One of the things I liked most about Alexis was that he never felt the need to impress his opinions on me. It was liberating to be able to make my own mind up about things again.

We crested the brow of the hill, turned yet another corner and then Alexis pulled off the road into a dusty layby. I gasped as I caught my first glimpse of the beach far below us. It looked like a painting, the lush greenery of the bay giving way to a wide strip of sun-bleached white sand and pebbles. And then there was the water itself, the luminescent turquoise blending gradually into a royal blue, its surface shimmering in the light. A couple of yachts were moored in the middle of the bay, and I could see the distant splashes from people jumping off the decks and into the sea. Part of the beach had rows of colourful parasols and lines of deckchairs set out in front of a handful of tavernas, but stretching beyond the touristy bit were long swathes of untouched shore with plenty of space for people to sit quietly and enjoy the view.

'To call it breathtaking seems like such a cliché, but it really is stunning,' I said. It almost looked unreal in its pristine beauty, as if someone had cut out a picture from the glossy pages of a magazine and stuck it on the inside of Alexis's windscreen.

'Every time I come here, it looks different. The water is always changing, every day a different mood, a different shade of blue. Even in the middle of winter when it's stormy and grey, it still has a magical quality.'

We sat in companionable silence for a few minutes more, both of us wrapped up in the enchanting scenery before us. I wondered what Alexis was thinking about. He must have seen this view countless times before, but the expression on his face was as happy and wondrous as if he was experiencing it for the first time, like me. I had thought about how special it would be to see the island with

Awesome Andreas at my side, but it felt pretty good to be seeing it with Alexis.

'Thank you for bringing me here,' I said quietly.

He turned to look at me. 'It is my pleasure,' he said simply.

The sound of a car horn interrupted our quiet moment, as someone hooted to let other drivers know they were rounding the corner. Alexis started the engine up again and we zigzagged our way down the other side of the hill.

I'd half-expected the illusion of perfection to be destroyed when we got nearer, but no, on closer inspection I decided the beach was still utterly glorious. Despite its obvious appeal, thankfully it wasn't too crowded and there was plenty of space on the rough ground behind the tavernas to park up. We left the car under the shade of a tree, Alexis winding the windows down in an attempt to stop the interior cooking. He caught my questioning eyebrow.

'It won't make much difference,' he said. 'The seats will still be nearly too hot to touch when we get back, but it is worth a try. And the heat is a small price to pay.'

'Back at home, if someone left their car windows wound down, they'd probably find a half-eaten takeaway chucked in there. That is, if the car was still there by the time they got back.'

Alexis shrugged in that relaxed way of his. 'Car theft is not really a problem around here. It is harder to get away with stealing cars when you live on an island. There aren't many vintage Minis around, and the culprit would soon find themselves attracting attention. You will find if you hire a car, they will leave the keys under the wheel arch for you to collect. Everyone knows this is done, yet nobody really takes advantage of that. I am not saying that Kefalonia is perfect, no, but…'

'But it's pretty close to it,' I sighed, as we strolled along a wooden walkway straight onto the beach. I bent down to unbuckle my sandals so I could enjoy the feel of the sand and pebbles between my toes, but moments later, I was hopping around as if I'd stepped on hot coals.

'Have they got underfloor heating activated here? I think my feet are about to get cooked.'

'There is only one way to deal with that problem,' said Alexis. 'Race you.'

And before I'd properly processed what he'd said, he set off at a run down the beach, his long limbs making easy work of the distance. I attempted to follow at a quicker-than-usual pace, which was more motivated by the heat of the beach than by any real sense of competition. The warm breeze blew my hair in a tangle around my face, the pebbles forced my feet into odd contortions, and I could feel sweat dripping down my back, but I didn't care. This was a slice of heaven and I was free to enjoy it.

Alexis reached the water's edge and skidded to a halt.

'Hurry up,' he teased, beckoning for me to join him before he went into the water. He laughed as I continued my tiptoeing run towards him. As I ran, I looped my maxi skirt over my arm so I was ready for paddling. I didn't care how ridiculous I might look, nothing was going to stand between me and the Ionian. Eventually I caught Alexis up and he held out his hand. Together we stepped into the sea. It felt deliciously refreshing compared to the warmth of our surroundings, and I waggled my toes, relishing the way the gentle waves tickled my skin. Tiny fish were darting around the shallows, chasing the sparkling reflections of the light and almost dancing in formation as they decided whether or not they dared move closer to my legs. The chatter of other tourists faded into the background as I savoured the moment, leaning closer to Alexis for support as the wash from a passing boat threatened to make me wobble. He gently squeezed my hand as if to reassure me that he wasn't going to let me fall. I glanced up and caught him looking back at me. All at once, I felt very hot. I let go of his hand and waded further into the sea.

'This is torture. I'm desperate to go for a swim,' I said, fighting to dispel the sudden tension I felt rising between us again.

'Then swim,' said Alexis simply.

'If only it were that easy. My friend Amira's a doctor and she gave strict instructions to avoid full immersion for at least a couple of weeks until the tattoo has healed up properly. It's been just under a fortnight since I got it, so it might be a bit too soon. I'm still nervous about causing problems, to be honest. The tattoo has been responsible for enough trouble already.' I paused. 'Actually, it's better to say adventure, rather than trouble. After all, if I hadn't had it done, I'd probably be hunched up over a desk right now making sure columns C and F balance out in a spreadsheet, and worrying about what I was going to serve Jim for his dinner.'

I was babbling again, but since that moment in the bookshop with Alexis, I'd been looking at him in a new light. He was sending me off balance, and it was confusing.

'It has brought good along with the inconvenient.' He paused, then quietly said, 'May I see the tattoo? If that is not too personal a thing to ask?' he added hurriedly, as if he'd realised that it was a pretty intimate request.

Although I had talked about the tattoo with many now, I realised I could count on one hand the number of people who had actually seen it, and that was only in moments of necessity. Alexis had done so much for me, taking me at my word, while never having seen the proof of the thing itself. I knew he wasn't asking to see it now because he doubted me. Did he want to see it because he wished it said something else? I let the fabric of my skirt fall into the water, then slowly, carefully rolled up the back of my T-shirt. I could almost feel Alexis's eyes tracing the words written on my skin.

'Awesome...' His voice trailed away, as if he was surprised to see the reality of the words in front of him.

'... Andreas,' I finished off.

'Andreas,' he repeated. Was there a note of something like disappointment in his voice, or was I just imagining it?

Again, I experienced a moment of exquisite tension during which for some reason I imagined Alexis reaching out and tracing the letters of the tattoo with his finger.

'Lydia...' Alexis's voice was more accented than normal

and I felt my heart start to beat faster as I turned around to face him. I took a step closer, my hand moving towards his face almost without me thinking about it. Then our moment of quiet peace was interrupted by the sound of Alexis's name being bellowed across the beach by one of the waiters from the tavernas.

Alexis held my gaze for an exquisite few seconds longer, then he shrugged apologetically and hurried over to greet his acquaintance with a broad smile on his face. I waded around for a bit, telling myself to get it together. What was I thinking? I was meant to be searching for Awesome Andreas, not getting distracted from my mission by imagined moments with my friend. Alexis was kind to me because he was kind to everyone, because he was a lovely person. Thinking there was anything more to it than that was plain ridiculous.

I paddled to the shore and set up camp under the shade of a parasol. A previous visitor had left a book on a nearby table, the spine splayed open, pages baking in the sun. I reached over and automatically took note of the page number before closing it, patting the blue and white cover affectionately as I realised it was a copy of *Captain Corelli's Mandolin*.

'Very appropriate,' said Alexis, returning to my side with a couple of ice creams. Beads of condensation from the frosted glass bowls trickled down onto his hands. He set the bowls down on the table and then casually peeled his shirt over his head before settling on the lounger next to me. I blinked, glad that my eyes were hidden behind sunglasses. I was getting seriously carried away by the romance of my surroundings.

'Beautiful. The book that is,' I added hastily. 'A tale of love and conflict and misunderstandings. I'd forgotten it was set here.'

'And part of the movie was filmed on this beach. Some of the tavernas still have pictures up of the stars visiting in between scenes.'

'I'm not surprised. Film locations couldn't get more picturesque than this. The crew and cast must have counted themselves lucky to be working here. As do I. Very lucky indeed.'

'I am glad you came back.' Alexis cleared his throat. 'Anyway, we must eat this ice cream before it melts away. What flavour would you like? This bowl has peppermint and chocolate, and this one has lemon and mango sorbet. You can pick which you prefer.'

'I'm spoilt for choice. Perhaps we could share,' I suggested. An image of the pair of us playfully spooning ice cream into each other's mouths briefly flashed in front of my eyes before I firmly dismissed it. Maybe I'd got sunstroke.

The reality was more practical than my imaginings in that we set both bowls down next to each other and set to with our own spoons, but it was no less fun for it. And Alexis proved his gentlemanly status by letting me have the last spoonful.

'True lo… friendship right here,' I said, as I licked my spoon to make sure not a morsel of sweet mango goodness was left over. Heck, I'd nearly let slip the 'L' word. Where was my mind at?

I wondered if Alexis had heard the hastily swallowed word, but he quietly replied, 'I am honoured by your friendship.'

I felt a pang of something like disappointment as we settled back on the loungers. As Alexis picked up the book and started reading it, I took my vocabulary notebook out of my handbag. I had never been the kind of person who religiously kept a diary, but something about this wonderful island was making me itch to put pen to paper. It was as if I needed to remind myself that my experiences were real by writing them down. I loved reading other people's stories, but now I felt the urge to tell my own, to reassure myself that I was really here, that quiet, non-confrontational, conforming Lydia had actually done this, had stepped back from her life, reassessed and gone in pursuit of something better.

I flicked past the collection of Greek words and phrases I'd collated and found a blank page. Where to start with my story? There were still too many questions about the night of the inking, and writing about what had happened with Jim felt too much like focusing on an end rather than a beginning. And so, I started with a definite beginning: the first Andreas date with Athletic Andreas, describing how I'd found him online and detailing our eventful encounter. The words came out as more of a comedy sketch than the serious chronicling of the evening which I'd intended, but it was liberating to explore my thoughts through writing and to find a new form of expression. I realised I was proud of how daring I'd been in approaching him and putting myself out there. I found myself laughing as I wrote about Athletic Andreas's obsession with his appearance and how I'd been deputised as his personal photographer.

'You write well,' said Alexis. 'Have you ever thought about sharing your work?'

I glanced up and realised that he'd put down the book and was reading my notebook over my shoulder. I laughingly pretended to cover the page, as if I was outraged at the intrusion, but I was secretly thrilled to hear his words of praise. If it had been anyone other than Alexis, I think I would have felt exposed, but there was something about his calm acceptance of the notion that what I had to say would be worthy of sharing with others that excited me.

'I don't think I'd dare. These are just the ramblings of an accountant turned cleaner. Probably best kept to myself.'

'Don't do that,' he said softly, leaning forward and clasping my hand.

'Do what?' There was a slight time delay in me asking the question because I was flustered by his sudden closeness.

'Don't underestimate yourself. Why shouldn't your words be worth sharing with others? I for one would like to find out happens in the next chapter of your adventures.'

I found myself tracing the lines on his palm with my index finger.

'Me too.'

I'm not sure what I expected to happen next, but it

certainly wasn't what actually happened. Because Alexis stood up so suddenly that his lounger nearly tipped over and the book fell onto the beach.

'We should be going,' he said, the words tumbling out so quickly that it took me a few seconds to process them.

Without waiting for me to respond, he pulled his shirt back on, then collected the ice cream bowls, almost hopping from one foot to another in his haste to be on his way.

'Are you OK?' I asked, but he didn't seem to hear me.

I stood up slowly, reluctant to leave the haven of the beach. I took my time packing away my notebook and picking up my shoes, hoping it would give Alexis the space to answer my question. But when I looked at him, his gaze was far off into the distance. There was definitely something wrong, but I didn't have time to press him further, because Alexis hustled us off the beach urgently. I thought I heard someone calling his name, but before I could be sure, we were back at the car and he was jumping into the driver's seat.

As he'd said it would be, the interior of the vehicle was like a furnace, but Alexis seemed oblivious as he revved the engine and set the car bouncing over the rough ground back to the road.

'What's going on, Alexis?' I asked, as he checked the mirror for the fifth time.

'Sorry, I need to get back to the shop,' was all he would say.

We drove back to Sami in near silence.

Chapter Fifteen

A s I climbed the stairs to my room, weary after my day in the sun, I replayed my interaction on the beach with Alexis. We'd been having such a good time, and then suddenly, things had changed. Alexis had gone from happy, relaxed and carefree, to anxious and uptight, desperate to leave. Was it something I had said or done? I'd thought we'd been getting on well, more than well if I was being truly honest. It may have been the influence of our beautiful surroundings, but I'd once again felt that softening, a tenderness of emotion towards him, something that was hard to describe, and something that I wasn't sure I should be experiencing, given that his name was very much Alexis and I was committed to finding the Andreas of my inking. How could I come out to Greece in search of a man called Andreas and find myself hankering after one called Alexis? Was that not in some way a betrayal of the man who had inspired my inking? But then again, how could I betray someone I wasn't sure actually existed? I still hadn't managed to track down the artist who could shed light on the motivation behind the tattoo. And my own memory hadn't become any clearer. I felt conflicted and unsure about what I should do now.

When I was with Alexis, I didn't feel the need to put on an act or pretend to be someone I wasn't. I never questioned which version of Lydia I needed to be in order to enjoy spending time with him. I could just be me. He'd seen my flaws, and he didn't judge me for them. He'd heard my dreams, and he hadn't laughed at them. In fact, he'd gone out of his way to show his support.

But the very fact that he was supporting me in my quest to find Andreas argued that the tenderness I was feeling towards him must be one-sided. He'd offered to rescue me from dodgy dates, not date me himself. And when I got close to him on the beach, he'd swiftly moved away, seemingly desperate to extract himself from the situation.

By the next day, I was gritty-eyed with lack of sleep, but I'd made a decision. Alexis's friendship was too important to me to jeopardise by seeking something more, and I didn't want to put him in that difficult position of having to let me down gently. I would continue on my Andreas quest. I'd been brave enough to rip up my life plan and return to Kefalonia to seek Awesome Andreas. Now more than ever I needed to trust the instinct that had made me decide to do it and follow through on that goal.

But where could I look for him? I was done with relying on the internet to play Cupid, and given my conflicted emotions towards Alexis, it would have felt strange to go to him for advice. I pondered my next move as I cleaned rooms, zipping through them in half the time I'd taken when I'd first started work here ten days ago. If I achieved nothing else during my stay, I had at least developed serious vacuuming skills.

The answer to my dilemma about where to search for Awesome Andreas next came in the form of a stack of leaflets which were delivered to the Helios Hotel by a tour rep asking us to put them on display for the guests. They certainly attracted my attention as they advertised boat trips with a Captain Andreas. The aforementioned captain was depicted in handsome cartoon form on the deck of a beautiful boat which was gliding through cobalt-blue waves on its way to a distant island. It looked incredibly romantic, the perfect setting in which to meet the man of my dreams.

When the girls and I were on holiday, I'd been keen to go on a boat trip, but somehow between lazing by the pool and the nights out, we'd never got round to doing it. But now was my chance. I imagined sitting on the deck of an elegant yacht, drinking champagne from a chilled glass, and admiring the coastal scenery while Awesome Andreas steered the boat and told me fascinating anecdotes from his life at sea. Perhaps the arrival of these leaflets was a sign from fate pointing me in the direction of where to go.

However, Yiota was less than impressed with my idea when I showed her the leaflets and casually asked if I might be able to arrange my next day off to coincide with one of the trips being run by Captain Andreas.

As she examined the cartoon image, she tutted her disgust.

'Those trips are over-priced and more about trying to sell as much food and drink to the customers as possible than they are about taking you on a scenic tour of the island's coastline. You'd be better off not wasting your time. I will not have these leaflets on display. Put them in the recycling on your way to empty the office bins.'

I followed her direction, but kept one of the leaflets back and put it into my pocket for later. Whatever Yiota's opinion, there was something entrancing about the idea of going on a day cruise. It would be a wonderful way of seeing more of the island I was now beginning to call home.

However, thoughts of sailing through the waves with a vanguard of dolphins and an attractive Greek captain at my side flew completely out of my mind when my phone started ringing.

My initial fear was that it was Jim at the other end of the line. The *Doctor Who* theme tune was still assigned to his number, so I knew he couldn't be calling from his mobile, but that didn't mean that he hadn't picked up another phone to ring me, irritated that I hadn't risen to his bait and responded to his text message the other day. I didn't want to hear his voice, and fall into the trap of trying to explain myself to him all over again. My second, slightly more positive thought was that this could finally be a call from an Andreas who'd spotted my small ad in the kiosk, and although that option still filled me with nerves, it was for a very different reason.

'Hello,' I answered hesitantly.

The person at the other end was male, thankfully not Jim, and they talked Greek extremely quickly. Or rather, they probably spoke it at a normal pace, but it seemed incredibly fast to an untrained ear such as mine. I couldn't even recognise a simple 'hello' in among it, so for all I knew, I'd come in halfway through a speech.

I tried to find an opportunity to speak up and explain that I didn't understand, but I couldn't distinguish a moment between phrases. In the end, I put the phone on speaker and hurried in search of a colleague who could translate for me. After dashing around the office and finding no one I managed to find someone taking a rest in the staff break room.

'Eleni?' I asked, assuming that there was only one heavily pregnant member of staff.

'Lydia, hello. I've heard so much about you while I have been off work. I'm glad we are finally meeting.' Her broad grin suggested that Yiota and Angelo had probably filled her in about my Andreas quest too. I didn't mind. It made my next request much easier.

'Can you help translate? I think this might be an Andreas.'

Although I couldn't understand what he was saying, the guy had an excellent voice, deep and rather sexy for it.

Eleni raised an eyebrow, but, to give her credit, she did at least gesture for the phone to be brought over.

She spoke loudly so the speaker at the other end was forced to concede airtime to her. She asked a couple of questions while I hopped nervously from side to side. I wanted the first Andreas to call me up to be genuine rather than someone playing a prank.

Their conversation continued for a couple of minutes before she finally ended the call.

'Well?' I asked, bracing myself.

Eleni attempted to look sympathetic, but I could tell she was trying not laugh. 'I am sorry to disappoint you, Lydia, but it was not the Andreas you hoped for. He was a salesman trying to sell you some insurance. You are probably one of hundreds of people he has called at random today. I think when he realised that you didn't understand what he was saying he continued speaking so he could increase his call time minutes.'

My shoulders slumped in disappointment.

Eleni patted the seat next to her.

'Come, sit down here and tell me what you can remember of your Andreas.'

'I'm afraid that would be a short conversation,' I confessed, filling her in on the whole story.

She laughed. 'We have all done it, had too much to drink and then ended up doing something we did not intend to. Well, maybe we've not all woken up with a tattoo, but at least it will give you a funny story for you and your awesome man to tell your children one day.'

'Let's not get too carried away.'

My happy ever after dreams were a lot more theoretical

than that, especially as they kept getting interrupted with images of Alexis, something which I was trying to firmly stamp down on.

'Ah, but why not? I am looking forward to telling this not-so-little one all about how his father and I met. Unfortunately, our story is not so exciting as finding each other thanks to a tattoo. Our teacher made him sit next to me at school because he was the good kid and I was the class clown. Actually, I might leave that bit out. I don't want my son getting bad ideas.' She patted her stomach. 'I am thankful that you have arrived to help with the work. I cannot remember the last time I saw my feet, so cleaning all the guest rooms is too much for me. I hope you are enjoying it?'

If anyone had asked me a fortnight ago if I'd find cleaning a dozen hotel bedrooms enjoyable, I would probably have laughed at the idea, but now I wasn't so sure. The job couldn't be more different from my previous role, but there was something very satisfying about doing it well. As an accountant, I'd always enjoyed balancing out figures to create order from chaos. I guess that was still what I was doing, but perhaps in a more tangible way. And despite Yiota's slightly brusque nature, she'd made me feel like a valued member of the team, welcoming me into her home and making sure that I was settled and had everything I needed.

'I am, yes. I think I'm getting the hang of it, and it's good to feel like I'm making a difference. I still can't believe my luck. Every time I look out of a window, I feel like pinching myself as a reminder that I'm really here. It's such a beautiful island, and I'm so excited about exploring it further.'

'And if you can do that with a handsome man at your side, then even better.' Eleni smiled.

I grinned back.

'So, this Andreas,' she continued, a questioning note in her voice. 'Are you sure that he was…'

But I didn't get to find out what she had been going to ask because Alexis arrived. I watched him carefully, wondering if I could read in his expression the reason for his hasty departure from the beach yesterday, but he was acting as if nothing had happened.

'Yiota tells me you are visiting the hotel a lot these days, Alexis,' said Eleni. 'I wonder why that is.' She patted the seat between us, encouraging him to come and sit down. 'I was about to tell Lydia all about an Andreas I know.'

Unfortunately, before I could process her words properly, I was distracted as Alexis tripped on the tiled floor and nearly went flying. I leaped to my feet and managed to stop his fall.

'Are you OK?' he asked. His expression grew cloudy when he saw the bruise on my wrist.

'That's from my Fiskardo trip,' I said hastily, not wanting him to take the blame on himself. I quickly moved the conversation on. I had no desire to dwell on that episode. 'Anyway, the question should really be the other way round. That was quite a tumble you nearly took there. Are you sure you're OK?'

At this point Alexis seemed to suddenly realise he was still holding onto my shoulder and quickly let go. I tried to ignore the stab of sadness this caused me. He ran his fingers through his hair, looking particularly flustered.

'I am sorry. That was very clumsy of me. I have a new glasses prescription and I am still getting used to the extra sharpness of my surroundings. I hope I did not hurt you?'

'Not at all.' I gently patted his arm in reassurance. 'I'm glad you didn't end up face-planting, especially with new glasses on. They suit you by the way.'

If I wasn't much mistaken, Alexis blushed.

Eleni made a clicking sound with her teeth. 'You are turning clumsy, Alexis. And I was about to tell Lydia all about Andreas Rouvas who used to sing in a band with my brother.'

Alexis sat down in the chair with a sigh. 'Ah, Andreas Rouvas. Now that is a name I have not heard in many years. How is he?'

'Very well, or so I understand.' She clapped her hands together. 'Now I have an excellent idea. I shall host a dinner party and invite Andreas so you can meet him, Lydia.'

'That's very kind of you,' I said. It felt weird to be talking about this in front of Alexis, even though he'd been privy to discussions about my previous dates. I reminded myself that it was only in my mind that things had changed between us. I forced myself to concentrate on Eleni's invitation. A personal introduction would be a much more promising way of finding my Awesome Andreas. Eleni wouldn't be offering to set me up with someone horrible, surely? It was like a friend recommending a good plumber who wouldn't overcharge you for unblocking a drain – not that I was comparing finding the love of my life with getting pipes seen to. 'But shouldn't you be taking things easy rather than throwing a party?' I added quickly. 'You've got a lot to be preparing for, and I really don't want you to go to any trouble on my account. Perhaps you could pass on my number to Andreas Rouvas instead? If you think he's a likely candidate, that is. Sorry, person, not candidate. That makes it sound like I'm interviewing people for a job.'

Eleni's eyes sparkled. 'I am sure you will find him a very interesting individual. Whether he is your Awesome Andreas, I cannot say, but we will have an enjoyable evening regardless. Alexis, you are of course invited too.'

I cringed inwardly. Meeting another Andreas in front of Alexis had the potential to be super awkward. Even thinking about it felt like a betrayal.

Alexis cleared his throat. 'That's very kind of you, Eleni, but I would not wish to be a raspberry. Have I said the right thing?'

'It's gooseberry actually,' I said, smothering a grin. 'But if you ask me, a raspberry on a date sounds rather fun and it makes no less sense than gooseberry does.'

Eleni smiled. 'I am sure that Alexis would not be a gooseberry. You will appreciate having him there for moral support, won't you, Lydia?'

She didn't give either of us a chance to answer. She heaved herself upright. 'Now that is arranged, I will go home and start my planning. It was lovely to meet you at last, Lydia. I shall look forward to welcoming you and Alexis to my home very soon. We will have delicious food, and music and dancing, and it will be very romantic.'

'And I'll meet this Andreas Rouvas guy,' I added, because the way Eleni was talking, it sounded very much like she was trying to set up Alexis and me, and I was worried it might make him feel even more uncomfortable.

'I shall certainly call him up on the phone and invite him along.' She sent an exaggerated wink in our direction.

Now that Alexis and I were alone, the silence hung between us. It felt strange. Even when I'd first asked for his help in the bookshop, I'd been totally relaxed in his presence. Now it wasn't that I was uncomfortable, I just felt like there was a weight of something unsaid hanging in the air between us and it made me sad.

'And I should… Actually, I don't think there is anything I *should* be doing. I've finished my work, and my time is my own. It's strange not to feel like I need to be accounting for every minute, not having to justify myself to anybody. Beyond Yiota, of course, and I'm beginning to realise that she doesn't really mind how I go about it, as long as the work gets done.'

I was babbling again, but I needed to fill the silence. Fortunately, Alexis picked up the conversational baton.

He nodded. 'Yes, my sister likes to create an initial fiery impression, then softens as you get to know her. She is obviously pleased with you, otherwise she would have made it very clear to me. And to you, of course.'

'It's better to know where you are with a person. As a

boss, Jim always liked to keep people on their toes. He was a master at being non-committal, which he said allowed staff to come to their own solutions, but in reality, it made us spend half our time second-guessing what it was he really wanted.' I mimed a zipping motion across my lips, inwardly cursing that my verbal diarrhoea had led me down the Jim route. The last thing I wanted to do was to drivel on about him to Alexis, highlighting my previous bad decisions and poor judgement of character. 'Sorry, I'm at it again. I promised myself I wouldn't badmouth Jim or keep going on about him, and here I am doing just that.'

Alexis spread his palms. 'It helps to talk about these things. It is much worse to keep things to yourself and let them eat you up inside. And I don't think you are badmouthing Jim. You are working through how you feel now, which is a good thing to do. He was a big part of your life and he obviously had a big influence on the choices you have made both during and since the relationship. It is not surprising that the echoes of your time with him will still be in your thoughts.'

'I reckon if you didn't own a bookshop, you would have a very good career as a therapist, Alexis. You're being incredibly patient listening to me mithering on and on.'

'Mithering? This is a new word for me.'

'It means moaning or groaning, which is exactly what I've been doing too much of.' It was too easy to talk to Alexis. He was such a calming presence that I felt able to say whatever came into my head, something I wasn't really used to with anyone except Kat and Amira. But I needed to stop taking advantage of that. Time to change the subject. 'And speaking of new vocabulary, do you know of any Greek language classes being run in the area? I've been diligently working through the phrasebook you gave me and adding to my notebook, but I think I need more help.'

'My offer to assist still stands,' said Alexis. 'I have not much experience teaching, but I am happy to do some conversation practice. I would normally recommend the local lyceum which does evening classes, but this is not a good time of year for them. Everything stops during the main tourist season as people are very busy working.'

His expression was hard to read and I couldn't tell whether he was offering because he wanted to spend more time with me, or because he felt obliged to help. My heart hoped it was the former, but my head feared it was probably the latter.

'Then if you are sure you have the time, that would be great,' I said, deliberately not pushing to arrange when this conversation practice would happen in order to give him an opportunity to back out.

I thought Alexis might be about to say something else, but the noise of my phone ringing again interrupted us. I pulled a face. If this was the insurance salesman calling back, then he was going to get short shrift from me.

I pressed Accept, but didn't say a word.

'Hello?' The voice at the other end of the phone sounded uncertain.

'Hi, who is this, please?' I responded, although I was already confident that it wasn't my earlier caller. His voice was huskier and his accent was most definitely not Greek. If I wasn't mistaken, this caller hailed from the Antipodes.

'This is Andreas. I spotted my name in the kiosk with this number underneath it so I thought I should call.'

A fizz of nervous anticipation made me sit up straighter.

'Andreas, hi, it's lovely to hear from you.' I was so surprised that someone had actually seen the notecard that my response was possibly a bit too enthusiastic. A sentence wasn't much to go on, but so far the caller sounded friendly and warm, and even better, he wasn't trying to flog me insurance.

Alexis stood up and mimed a goodbye. He tactfully backed out of the room, and left me to my call. Any residual hope that my tenderness towards him might be reciprocated faded into nothing.

Chapter Sixteen

Disappointment at the situation with Alexis made me decide to go for honesty on the phone with this new Andreas. Well, half honesty, in that I told him about the drunken tattoo, but left out the part about my belief that the inking had been inspired by meeting the love of my life. I wasn't completely daft. The poor guy would probably run in the opposite direction if I put that weight of expectation on him right away. He seemed to find the idea of the tattoo quite funny, which was a promising sign. And he didn't launch into graphic descriptions of where on his body he had tattoos, which was even more promising.

I decided that this time, I would find out a bit more about my prospective Andreas before going straight to asking him out. My previous two Andreas dates had taught me it was better to establish some sense of initial compatibility/awareness of general humanity before I committed myself to an in-person meeting.

Thankfully this Andreas seemed up for a chat, and I soon learned that he was actually from Brisbane in Australia, but was visiting his grandparents in Kefalonia for an extended holiday.

'How lovely. When did you get here?' I asked. The notecard had specified the date I'd met Andreas, but I thought I'd better double-check this guy hadn't just got off a flight today as that would rule him out of the Awesome Andreas stakes pretty quickly.

'About a month ago? The company I work for back home has given me a sabbatical, so instead of being an accountant trapped in an office, I get to play at being an olive farmer with my *yiayia* and *pappou* all summer.'

My stomach flipped over with nervous anticipation. So, he was definitely a contender.

'What a coincidence, I'm an accountant too. Well, I'm an accountant by training, but actually I'm working as a cleaner for now. Like you, I'm trying on a different role for the summer.'

'And how are you finding it?'

I didn't take long to consider my answer.

'It's great. I enjoy that my mind is my own when I'm cleaning. And it's satisfying to know that I'm helping people to have a lovely holiday. But I'd like to see more of the island.' I made a decision. Time to commit. 'I hear the Drogarati Cave is worth a visit. Would you like to join me?'

Strong, empowered woman right here in action. Kat and Amira would be super impressed with me. Maybe this Andreas date would be third time lucky.

'Sure, sounds good to me. Shall I meet you up there in an hour?'

Ok, so that was a lot sooner than expected, but why not? It would give me less time to get myself wound up about our meeting and start doubting whether it was a good idea or not.

'Great, see you then. Oh wait, how shall we recognise each other?'

Andreas chuckled. 'Is this where we both agree to turn up holding a rose or something? I'll be honest with you, I'm not sure I'm going to source one in the next hour and get up there on time. I'll be the goofy guy standing by the ticket booth, and if we're in any doubt, we can always call each other.'

'Perfect. It's a date. See you in an hour.'

I practically flew to my room to change out of my work uniform and pulled on the first outfit I grabbed from my wardrobe. This time there was no conference call with the girls while I got ready. A pair of denim shorts and a vest top would have to do. I slapped on some makeup for added confidence, then looked up my destination on my phone. It didn't look too far away, which was a relief as I had no clue if there was a bus that went there, and I was unlikely to get a taxi at this time of day as the ferry would have just arrived in from the neighbouring island of Ithaca. Never mind, the walk would do me good.

Five minutes later, I was already regretting my decision. What the map app on my phone had failed to make clear was that although the Drogarati Cave was less than three kilometres away from the hotel, those kilometres were on a road climbing steadily upwards. It was also a road lacking in a pavement which didn't improve matters. It would not help me to achieve the objective of meeting the love of my life if I got squished en route, or melted into a river of sweat, both of which seemed plausible outcomes of this walk. I paused by a roadside stall which was selling honey and wondered whether devouring a jar of it would give me the energy to haul myself to my destination, with enough time to spare for me to find a bathroom to decontaminate myself in before Andreas arrived. If he saw me in this sweaty state, he'd definitely do a runner.

I checked my watch. If I didn't hurry up, I was going to be late. A moped whizzed past, its engine buzzing like a mosquito. I put my head down and concentrated on putting one foot in front of the other. Only half a kilometre to go, and then I'd be there. But instead of getting quieter, the buzzing of the engine grew louder once again, and then remained at a persistently irritating volume. I glanced across and saw the moped rider had circled back and was now riding parallel to me. It was rather unsettling so I tried varying my pace to see if I could lose my new companion. But whatever I did, the rider seemed to be determined to accompany me. I suddenly felt very much alone. The last-minute arrangements meant I'd not had time to tell anyone where I was heading, and the overgrown scrub at the side of the road offered far too many places for body concealment if this moped rider was up to no good. It was all well and good telling myself not to jump to worst-case scenarios but it was hardly surprising given that I was in the middle of nowhere. I put my head down and tried to pretend that I was invisible.

'Excuse me.' The man on the moped was now trying to attract my attention. His voice sounded familiar but I couldn't quite place it because of the noise of his engine.

'Hello?' I said, nervously checking the vicinity and wondering why, after nearly constant passing traffic on my walk so far, all the cars had chosen this moment to vanish off the face of the island. Why hadn't I told anyone what my plans were?

'Are you Lydia?'

'Andreas?' I asked, finally clocking the Australian twang in his voice. Well, that was a relief. Despite his lack of awareness of how a woman might feel about a moped following her on a lonely mountain road, he looked cheerful and non-threatening. He was dressed in faded, fraying cargo shorts along with a floral shirt which was flapping open to reveal an off-white top beneath it. I think in men's clothing vernacular it would be referred to as a wifebeater, but it was probably best not to start associating such words with my date.

Andreas turned the engine off and removed his helmet with a laugh. 'The very same. It's bloody hot work climbing up this hill and I've not even had to use muscle power. Do you want a lift?'

He gestured at the bike, shuffling forwards on the saddle to make room behind him. While it was flattering that he seemed to think my bum would fit in that tiny space, I really wasn't sure that it was a good idea. Already I was calculating the risks of falling off the back of the moped as we continued uphill. And what if I made it tip over while going around the corners by leaning in the wrong direction? Not to mention the dangers of not wearing a helmet, which ranged from the potentially fatal possibility of smashing my head on the tarmac to the admittedly superficial certainty of my hair turning into a massive frizz explosion in the wind. Andreas didn't wait for my answer but instead threw his helmet at me. Thankfully my reflexes kicked in fast enough for me to catch it.

'Put it on, let's get going to the cave.' His easy confidence was contagious, and somehow I found myself pushing the helmet on. It was still warm from being on his head, and to be honest, it was a little damp too, but I was committed now.

'What about you?' I asked, realising that he was handing over his only helmet. While it was a nice gesture to make, it was rather a foolish one. Amira would no doubt have plenty of disaster stories to tell from A&E involving mopeds and lack of proper safety gear.

Andreas tapped the side of his head. 'It takes a lot to crack this nut. I promise I'll only lose my head over you, not the road. And I'll make sure we go slow, just to be safe.'

He winked at me. I got the distinct impression that this was the only area in which he was agreeing to go slow. But whereas Already-married Andreas had been sleazy in his attempts at seduction, this Andreas seemed funny and straightforward.

'Hop on and hold tight.'

He didn't have to tell me twice. I gripped his waist so hard I was in danger of squeezing his last meal back up into his oesophagus. My entire body was pressed so close against him, that he must have been able to feel the underwire of my bra digging into his back.

'Woohoo,' he whooped, in a manner which did not bode well for his promise to go slow. Sure enough, he revved up the engine and we set off at a pace which felt far too fast for my liking. I'd never been on a two-wheeled vehicle with an actual engine before and initial impressions were not good. The steady incline which I'd been experiencing when I was walking now felt like a sheer cliff face, and the gently sloping verges looked like they were falling off into cavernous drops. I swallowed nervously.

'Don't worry, we'll be fine,' called Andreas over the increasing squeal of the engine as I held on even tighter. Then I worried that I might accidentally squeeze so tight I'd cause him to pass out, so I tried loosening my grip and closing my eyes instead, but that only amplified the sensation of wobbling all over the place. Just because I couldn't see the danger, it didn't mean that it wasn't there anymore. I did not want my Greek stay to end prematurely because I'd become too closely acquainted with the tarmac or fallen off a mountainside. There was nothing for it, I was going to have to wimp out and declare my terror, no matter what it made him think of me. If he didn't accept the way I was feeling, then he wasn't the one for me.

Thankfully, the moped also seemed to have had enough

because the engine started catching. It coughed once, twice, then shuddered to a halt. A couple of cars overtook us, hooting loudly, whether in support or frustration, I couldn't tell.

'That's a bugger,' said Andreas, still sounding remarkably cheerful. He leaned back and patted the side of the moped as if to comfort it. It let out a cloud of steam in response. It might even have been smoke, thinking about it. 'Guess there's nothing for it. We'll have to push.'

I staggered off the bike with distinctly wobbly legs, but grateful to still be in one piece. Andreas hopped off far more gracefully.

'My *pappou* will tell me I should stick to the accountancy in future. In fact, he'll probably do the whole 'I told you so' routine and tease me about being a feeble office worker. This old rust bucket had been knocking around their back yard probably for decades. I fancied having a go at being a mechanic and tried fixing it up to prove I'm not a complete pen-pusher.' He kicked the front tyre. 'Reckon I can still make it go again, but maybe not in time for us to be able to get to the cave. Never mind. It gives us a perfect excuse to enjoy a walk together in the sunshine.'

Despite his dubious mechanical skills, I was definitely warming to the man I had now privately nicknamed Auto Andreas. Other people might have sulked or got angry at their vehicle breaking down in front of a woman they were trying to impress, but Andreas seemed to be taking it in his stride. There was something attractive about his relaxed, easy attitude.

'Let me help,' I said, taking hold of one of the handlebars.

'Nah, don't worry about it. It's my mess, so I'll sort it out. I would offer for you to continue riding the bike while I push, but I'll be honest with you, my muscles aren't up to that.'

'Gee, thanks,' I said. I knew the comment hadn't been a swipe at me, but I couldn't resist teasing him. I smiled broadly, so he knew that I wasn't being serious.

He clapped his hand to his grinning mouth, enjoying joining in the banter. 'Ah jeez, there I go again. Speaking first, thinking second. But that's me. What you see is what you get. Right, chop chop. There's a cave to be explored and I'm reliably assured that this is one of the wonders of the world. It might not be on the official list, but it should be, or so my *yiayia* says.'

Chapter Seventeen

Thankfully after only a few more twists and turns of the road we arrived at the Drogarati Cave, or rather its car park. At the back of my mind, I'd been picturing an olde worlde cave in the side of the mountain, the kind of thing you'd imagine a hermit lurking around in, so I was rather surprised to see what looked like another standard tourist complex of shop, café and even a swimming pool attached. The car park was full of coaches and hire vehicles, and brightly dressed tourists were milling around in every direction.

'We seem to have picked a popular time for visiting,' said Andreas. He pushed the moped over to a space big enough for a car and left it propped up there. 'The old girl deserves a decent place to have a rest.'

A frustrated driver hooted at him, wheels spinning as he took off to find another place to park. Andreas laughed.

'People on holiday should learn to go with the flow and not get upset about petty things such as parking spaces.'

'And what about us? We're not really on holiday, are we?'

'We should go with the flow too. Fresh starts in a new place require a significant degree of chilling out. Audits can do one.'

I could agree with that sentiment.

'Cave time?' I asked. 'I assume it'll be obvious how we get into it when we're closer.'

'Sure,' said Andreas. 'Time to reveal my inner caveman.' He pretended to beat his chest and let out an enthusiastic roar. I laughed, unbothered by the stares we were attracting. In some ways, he reminded me of a spaniel puppy, full of boundless energy and excitement.

Andreas leaned across and tapped me on the head. 'I don't think you'll need to wear this, though, it's not that kind of cave.'

I felt myself flush with embarrassment as I realised I was still sporting the helmet he'd given me. My fingers fumbled as I tried to unclasp it, but Andreas stepped in to help. Did I imagine it, or did his hand linger on my jawline for just a little longer than was necessary?

Once the helmet was safely dangling from the handlebars of the moped, we followed the crowd through the shop and past the swimming pool towards the entrance to the cave. Andreas kept up a steady stream of chatter, asking me about my life in the UK and tactfully steering clear of too much tattoo talk. He was entertaining company and I found myself putting the pressure of finding Awesome Andreas to one side, and settling into enjoying the moment.

We wandered along the dusty path until we came to a kiosk selling water and tickets. On this date, there was no quibbling about us splitting the entrance fee fifty-fifty. Before we joined the queue to enter the cave itself, I bought a bottle of frozen water and rubbed it along my arms, half-expecting it to sizzle when it came in contact with my skin.

Andreas also waved his bottle in my direction, but mimed it going up in smoke from being so hot, setting me off laughing all over again.

'OK, quickfire round as we queue,' he said. 'Dogs or cats?'

'Dogs.'

'Madonna or Kylie?'

'Hmm, Madonna.'

'Cheese or chocolate?'

'Definitely chocolate.'

'Interesting,' said Andreas. 'I'm sorry to say but I'm not sure if we're compatible. Because I love nothing more than eating vast quantities of cheese while curled up with my cat listening to Kylie, Australian icon that she is.'

His eyes sparkled with amusement.

'Well, they do say opposites attract,' I responded lightly. 'And at least I won't have to fight you over who gets the last piece of chocolate.'

Auto Andreas pretended to flex his muscles, giving me an Athletic Andreas flashback.

'You're not an influencer, are you?' I asked quickly.

'Social media is most definitely not my thing. I prefer to live in the moment, rather than experiencing everything through a phone screen.'

I nodded. 'Good to know.'

Slowly the queue moved forward until we were at the front. We swiped our tickets and went through the modern barriers and straight onto a very old staircase. The treads were narrow and steep, and after the brightness of where we'd been queuing, it was hard to see where it was safe to step in our shadowy surroundings. I started wondering whether it might have been a good idea to keep the moped helmet on after all. As we descended into the depths, the air around us became noticeably cooler, a welcome relief in the heat of the afternoon. And then, at last, the wooden steps gave way to solid stone and we were in the mouth of the cave.

'Wow,' was all I could say, the ancient majesty of our surroundings making me lower my voice as if I was in a grand old university library. The atmosphere was clammy, and I could hear a persistent drip, drip, drip of water falling from the ceiling. Stalagmites and stalactites stood sentinel on either side of the path, and the ground-level orange lighting lent a strange glow to our surroundings, making the whole place appear other-worldly. It was like we were descending into the earth's core.

'Can you imagine how the person who first discovered this place must have felt seeing all this?' I whispered, pointing out the icicle-shaped formations which hung from the ceiling and grew up from the floor.

'I can never remember which ones are which,' said Andreas. 'Should have paid more attention in school, but I was too busy trying to impress my mates.'

'Ah, now there I can help. I was the designated homework champion in my friendship group. The stalactites hang from the ceiling – like tights hanging on a washing line.'

Auto Andreas chuckled. 'I'm not much of a tights wearer myself, but I get the analogy. Good way of remembering it. Personally, I think these things look like massive cones of sugar. I wonder what they taste like.'

He made as if to lick the nearest stalagmite, a move which resulted in one of the staff members blowing a whistle and sending a very disapproving look in our direction. She pointed at the signs which said 'No touching' in half a dozen languages.

Andreas waggled his eyebrows. 'Are they just referring to the cave or...?' He laughed and pulled an exaggeratedly leery face at me, winking so I was in no doubt that he was joking around.

I playfully pushed him onwards. 'If they get upset about people touching the cave, they're definitely not going to be happy about anything more. Right, which way?'

The walkway through the stalagmites divided ahead of us, snaking off into the darkness.

'I think we should go in this direction.'

Andreas chose the quieter path. We wound our way

further into the cave, ducking and diving as the ceiling seemed to grow ever closer. And then we rounded another corner and I gasped. The cave had opened out into a huge chamber, the light bouncing off the spiky ceiling, sending shadows dancing around the cavernous space.

'Look,' I whispered.

A cellist was sitting in the centre of the chamber, bow poised above the strings. She was dressed in a ball gown, an umbrella propped up above her to protect her instrument from the dripping water. Dotted around the walkways and ledges, an audience was steadily gathering. The low hubbub of tourist chatter quietened to nothingness, and then the cellist drew her bow across the strings, sending a note quivering into the darkness. It echoed around the chamber, achingly beautiful. I found myself being hypnotically drawn closer by the magic of the music. Listening to her play was like experiencing a moment out of time. Even Andreas grew still as we stood side by side, completely absorbed in the music.

When she finished playing, everyone was quiet, savouring the last notes until they finished reverberating around the ancient cavern. Then all at once we were applauding, the cheers and thumps of palms a sudden intrusion after the beauty of the performance. I found myself wiping away a stray tear, moved by the ethereal experience I'd just had.

'That was something else,' I said, when I finally found the strength to speak.

'We were pretty damn lucky,' agreed Andreas. 'Put it

this way, I don't think they have a concert in the cave every afternoon.'

Whatever the outcome of the date, I knew I would savour this experience for ever. It was like a spell had been cast on me by the music, and I felt dazed and moved by it.

We descended into the main chamber where the cellist had played, and slowly circled around. Although the car park had been busy and the queue long, down here in the vast cave it somehow didn't feel crowded at all, everyone giving each other space to enjoy the surroundings in their own way.

'I can't get over the way the light is reflecting off the formations.' I wasn't sure I had the vocabulary to express how magnificent it looked, so I focused instead on the practical. 'I wonder how long it took them to grow to this size.' I racked my brains, trying to remember bits from my Geography GCSE. 'It's something like a centimetre a year, so some of these must be centuries old. I mean, that one is taller than you.'

'I wonder if stalactites ever fall from the ceiling?' mused Andreas. 'It could be the start of a murder mystery plot, someone is found dead in a cave with a stalactite sticking out of them. Did it fall, or did someone arrange for it to break off?'

'Should I be worried?' I laughed. 'Here we are enjoying a romantic stroll around one of the most awe-inspiring sights of the island, and you're going on about people being impaled by geological formations.'

'If you want romance, you only have to ask.'

But before I could respond, Andreas took my hand and led me into the shadow of one of the larger stalagmites.

'I can certainly do romance,' he breathed, his mood changing from playful to serious in a heartbeat. He cupped my chin in his hand and waited for my response. Swept up in the moment, I found myself leaning towards him and then our lips met in the briefest butterfly touch, a tantalising promise of what could come. But what should have been special was ruined by the guard with the whistle once again making her presence felt. She said a firm, 'No' to us, in the same tone as I imagined she'd use on a naughty dog who'd made a mess on the carpet.

'Yes, definitely a no touching rule,' said Andreas, laughing and waving an apology.

I was glad the shadows were hiding my dazed expression. There had been no extra spark of recognition in close proximity, but there had been a fizz of something, a sense of anticipation about what could happen. Auto Andreas was definitely one step nearer to being renamed Awesome Andreas.

After exploring the pathways, we clambered back up the steep steps to the surface. It felt surreal stepping out into the dazzling sunshine again, as if we'd emerged from another land. I wouldn't have been surprised if we'd walked out to find all the tourist trappings had disappeared and we'd travelled back in time. I felt strangely reluctant to return to Sami and what passed for normality now. Fortunately, Andreas seemed similarly keen to linger.

'Drink?' he suggested. 'Something to eat?'

'That would be lovely.' My stomach grumbled as if on cue. 'As you can probably tell, all that exploring has left me with quite an appetite.'

We made our way over to the I. Andreas took two copies of the menu, one in Greek and one in English.

'I may have Greek parents, but during my rebellious teenage years, I refused to speak Greek to them. I thought my mates would call me weird. I'm regretting it now of course. I've gone from being pretty fluent as a kid to making tons of basic mistakes and struggling to put sentences together.'

'So, you're cross-checking the English and Greek versions of the menu, just to be sure? Good idea. I've been working on expanding my vocabulary, but I'll admit I've had most success in terms of memorising the names of different types of food. Clearly my stomach motivates my recall.'

'Yes, food is always a good way to kick the brain cells into gear.' He grinned broadly. 'And sometimes the English versions of the menu have some real accidental gems. Like this one. How do you fancy drunken chicken? Do you think that means the chicken was pissed, or is it actually dowsed in some kind of wine sauce?'

'I'm intrigued. But I think I might go for the safer option of moussaka.'

We browsed through the delicious food on offer and made the rest of our selections. Our table was near the pool, and every so often a spray of water flew in our direction as someone jumped in. It was actually quite refreshing.

Although we were relatively high up the mountain, the temperature was still hot, and there was little breeze to bring any relief.

'I can't wait until I can go swimming again.'

Andreas raised a quizzical eyebrow.

'The tattoo,' I reminded him.

'Oh that. I wouldn't worry too much. Sometimes you've got to break the rules.'

And with that, he took a deep gulp of his drink and fixed me with a look which made my insides flip. I swallowed, my mouth suddenly dry. Then the waiter appeared with a heavily laden tray and started laying the plates out on the table with a clatter, breaking the tension.

Andreas clapped his hands together with delight, switching from seductive to starving in a second. It took me a little longer to catch up. During the meal we chatted non-stop, and as we tucked into our dessert of achingly sweet morsels of baklava, I bravely asked a very important question.

'This has been fun. When can we do it again?'

Chapter Eighteen

Auto Andreas arranged a taxi to take me back to the hotel while he waited for his *pappou* to bring a truck up to collect him and the moped. I returned to my room feeling happier and more hopeful since the day I arrived back in Kefalonia. We'd agreed to meet in two days for lunch at a taverna in Karavomilos, where the waters from Kefalonia's famous Melissani Lake emerged to join the Ionian Sea. I didn't want to get carried away, but I had a good feeling about this Andreas.

I rang Amira and Kat to fill them in, then messaged Andreas to double-check the name of the taverna. That night I dreamt about travelling around the island by moped, the breeze blowing through my hair, a wonderful feeling of freedom in my soul.

The next morning, I checked my phone and was a little surprised and disappointed that Auto Andreas hadn't replied. There were two blue ticks next to my message, so I knew he'd read it. I shrugged it off. He'd probably checked his phone when he was tired and then forgotten to reply. If he hadn't got back to me by lunchtime, I'd send another one. I didn't want to appear demanding.

I was kept busy over the next few hours with work. It was a changeover day so it was all hands to the pump to say goodbye to one group of guests and get everything looking pristine to welcome the next lot. It didn't leave me a lot of time to think about texts or lack thereof, but every so often, I did dig my phone out of the pocket of my uniform and check the screen. By lunchtime, I was more than ready for a break, but there was still no word from Andreas. Without allowing myself too much time to overthink, I sent him a casual message hoping that his day was going well and again asking to confirm the name of the taverna. The blue ticks appeared on screen immediately, but there was no corresponding speed of response. In fact, there was no reply at all.

I told myself to chill out and go with the flow, then realised I was quoting one of Andreas's sayings. He was probably busy working on the olive farm. I had no idea what such work entailed, but I guessed they had to make the most of all the daylight they could. He'd told me himself during our trip to the Drogarati Cave that he was a laid-back kind of guy, so it tallied that he wasn't the sort to send texts instantly. He would get back to me this evening and everything would be fine. But a voice at the back of my head was already starting to doubt that he would, and with it came the insecure question of what it was about me that made him behave in this way.

The niggling, unkind voice was not helped by Andreas not replying on the actual day of what was meant to be our second date either. I'd swallowed my pride and sent him another two texts, the first one a casual question about how he was, the second openly asking whether he wanted to see me again, but although the two blue ticks appeared on the screen within seconds of me having sent the messages, no response was forthcoming. I toyed with the idea of walking to Karavomilos in case he turned up at the taverna, but fortunately good sense and personal pride intervened before I'd even stepped foot out of the grounds of the hotel.

I was slowly coming to terms with the realisation that I had been ghosted and it hurt. I knew one date didn't mean that he was under any obligation to me. But we had had a laugh together, and when we'd parted ways, he'd definitely said he would like to see me again. If he wasn't feeling it, why didn't he say, rather than cruelly stringing me along like this? We weren't in a relationship, or anywhere close to one, so I suppose I had no right to expect a response from him, but it was the height of bad manners to drop someone completely, without any communication whatsoever. And I couldn't help thinking that there must be a reason why he'd done a runner. Because that was what he had done.

Feeling foolish, I checked the local news sites, but there'd been no accidents involving mopeds, and he was young and healthy, so there was no reason to think he'd suddenly succumbed to an awful illness. Which left me questioning whether I'd offended him in some way. It made me view the whole date in a different light. When I'd thought we'd been having fun, had he been finding the encounter tedious? Or did he get his kicks out of pretending to like someone then ditching them? I kept trying to tell myself that I was relatively new to the dating scene and that this was just the way things happened now, but I couldn't help torturing myself with the fear that his disappearance was because I was fundamentally unlovable. I did at least realise it was this fear hurting me more than any pain at the thought of not seeing Andreas again.

I rang Amira, trying to make light of the situation by renaming him 'Absent Andreas', but she saw through my forced jollity immediately.

'Babe, that kind of man is not worth your time. What a rude prick. It's his loss if he doesn't want to get to know you. You are a better person and you shouldn't think of him for a second longer.'

I gave a small squeak in lieu of a response, not trusting myself to say actual words in case I let slip that I was having a little weep. I was angry at myself for being affected like this, and I knew Amira was talking sense, but personal insecurity has a lot to answer for, especially when it's ramped up by the thoughtless actions of another individual. It was stressful enough being out there in the dating world without having to navigate this kind of minefield.

Amira knew me too well to let me get away with that.

'Don't you dare shed a single tear over that waste of

space. You're a kind, lovely, gorgeous person, and you deserve only the best. The right guy won't keep you hanging like that. In fact, any decent guy wouldn't behave that way, especially when you'd obviously had a good time together. And before you deep dive into existential angst over-analysing every second of the date – yes, I'm speaking from personal experience here – in your heart of hearts, you know that you didn't do anything wrong. He's one of those silly player types, who can't see a good thing when it's staring him in the face. He should be so lucky to be with a wonderful woman like you. The girls at A&E agree, don't you?'

I heard a muffled cheer and a couple of shouts of 'Forget the bastard' in the background.

'Amira, you should have said you're at work,' I hissed, torn between being horrified I was dragging her away from saving lives, and being mortified that Amira's colleagues were now privy to the disaster that was my love life.

'Babe, in a miraculous turn of events, I'm having a break. By which I actually mean I'm hastily shovelling a stale sandwich into my mouth before going to the loo for the first time today. But honestly, I'm happy to hear from you, and everyone here is feeling invested in your adventures, so they're happy to hear from you too.'

'Thanks, guys,' I said feebly, embarrassed now I was painfully aware that I'd been on speakerphone throughout the entire conversation.

'Onto the next,' said Amira. 'That's what Kat would say, that's what the girls here think, and I am in complete agreement. Why don't you go and see your bookshop friend? He always seems to cheer you up.'

'Maybe,' I said, because Amira was in full on 'doctor knows best' mode and I knew from old that when she was like that, it was best to appear to go along with her. But in reality, going to see Alexis felt like adding an even greater complication into an already emotional situation. It didn't feel fair to burden him with yet more woes from my dating trials and tribulations. We were still texting each other, of course, but I was deliberately keeping things light. The poor guy had enough to be thinking about running his business without me constantly crying on his shoulder and needing his help. Going on the date with Absent Andreas had been my way of trying to move on from my growing tenderness towards Alexis. Running back to him now was not going to help that situation. And didn't a part of me worry that if Alexis heard too many of my dating disaster stories that he'd never change his mind and see me as more than a friend? Not that that scenario was a realistic possibility.

Amira did her best to get me fired up again before she had to dash back to her patients. It was good to talk to her, and by the end of the call, I was able to view the situation more dispassionately. But her hard work was undone when I hung up the phone and realised another text had arrived from Jim in the meantime. Why did bad things always have to come in batches? It was tough enough dealing with a Jim text when I was feeling good. To have one arrive in this slump was like kicking me when I was down. He was trying a different tactic now. Instead of the arrogant presumption that I'd be returning to him any day, he actually said he was missing me and that the house felt empty without me. I somehow doubted that was the case given that technically I'd only lived with him for less than twenty-four hours, so he couldn't possibly be missing what he'd never really had, but I couldn't help feeling bad that he still seemed unhappy. And although I knew this was an unhealthy attitude to have, in the conspicuous dearth of communication from Absent Andreas, it was gratifying that someone at least was thinking about me in a relationship context.

It was that thought which spurred me on to get myself out of what could rapidly become a negativity spiral. I volunteered to do an extra shift on Reception, hoping that processing the new arrivals would keep my mind off my phone, and stop me doing something stupid like texting Absent Andreas again, or worse, succumbing to Jim's plaintive plea to reply to him.

Yiota eyed me suspiciously when I offered my services. She may be a hard taskmaster, but, to give her credit, she was very much a believer in taking proper breaks, a new but welcome experience for me in the professional environment. Today of course I wished she was slightly less diligent about it.

'Why are you wanting to do more work?' she asked, folding her arms and giving me a searching look. 'It is not healthy. It is a beautiful day. You have done your bit, now you should go out in the sunshine and enjoy it.'

'Maybe I've had a little too much sunshine,' I said without conviction.

She pursed her lips. 'You are upset. What has my brother done?'

'Nothing, honestly,' I said quickly, amused that she had instantly leaped to the conclusion that it must be something to do with her sibling. 'Alexis has been nothing but kind to me. You are very lucky to have him as your brother.'

'That is Alexis all over, always bringing home stray animals.'

I couldn't help laughing at Yiota's bluntness, which I suspect was her purpose.

'That is better, I cannot have a sad person sitting on reception. It will give the guests a wrong impression of our lovely hotel and island. People cannot be sad on Kefalonia for long. If you insist, you can do some work in the back office. But I cannot pay you overtime, and I still think you should go and sit on the beach instead.'

Memories of the beach with Alexis confirmed my desire to keep myself occupied.

'That's OK, I just want to keep busy for a while.'

She didn't push me to find out why, but instead set me up at a computer with a pile of room tabs to go through. It felt strange to be doing something akin to my former role once again, but it was a good distraction to lose myself in the satisfaction of crunching numbers and balancing columns for a few hours. If only it was so easy to create order out of chaos in other aspects of my life. By the time I'd tallied the last bill, my neck was aching and I was ready for a break. But it was good to feel that I hadn't lost my skills. The time in front of the computer screen had clarified a few things for me, namely that Absent Andreas wasn't worth a millimetre of my headspace, and that whatever happened next, I would not be returning to life as a full-time accountant. I could stomach it for a few hours, but it was time I sought a profession that made my heart sing. And if I could find a permanent role here in Kefalonia, then that would be even better. But I was not going to achieve that unless I significantly upped the ante with my Greek skills. Without allowing myself to think about it too much, I sent Alexis a text asking if he was around tomorrow afternoon so I could take him up on his offer of language assistance. I told myself having a Greek lesson with him was very different to leaning on him for emotional support. It was time to take some positive action.

Chapter Nineteen

Alexis absolutely refused to charge for my Greek lesson. In fact, he sounded rather offended that I'd even suggested such a thing.

It will be my pleasure, he had insisted, immediately moving the text conversation on to something else completely in a manner which brooked no argument. But I'd been equally determined that his kindness towards me should not go unmarked, so before we met up, I popped along to Maria's Taverna to see if she could supply me with the makings of a thank you picnic.

'*Iassou*, Lydia, *ti kaneis*?'

She bustled out of the kitchen, greeting me with a broad smile, and I was pleased that I could reply to her question about how I was with some Greek of my own. With much assistance from my phrasebook, I stiltedly managed to explain my idea. Before long, she'd filled a basket with a loaf of freshly baked bread, a salad bursting with juicy tomatoes and slabs of feta cheese, and a tub of *dolmades*, which turned out to be a herby rice mix encased in vine leaves. Finally, she added a pot of my favourite garlicky *tzatziki*, two slices of honey-soaked *baklava*, and a bottle of homemade lemonade. I quickly scribbled down the new Greek words in my notebook and then went on my way.

As I walked towards Alexis's shop, I realised that I had butterflies in my stomach. I told myself that it was because I was nervous about the lesson. The last language classes I had attended were at school, and about the only thing I could remember from them was how to ask directions to the train station in German. As I've never visited Germany and am hopeless at following directions even in my mother tongue, it's been of limited use. At least now I had a much greater incentive to pay attention to my teacher as I was actually living in the country whose language I was trying to learn. And it didn't hurt that Alexis was much better-looking than my German teachers had ever been.

'Lydia, *mou*,' said the man himself, waving at me from across the street.

I found myself blushing, as embarrassed as if my interior monologue about his good looks had been said out loud.

'You are too hot,' he said, his voice full of concern. 'Come, let us go into the shop so you can get out of the sun. May I help?'

'Thank you,' I replied, still feeling flustered. He took the picnic basket and my bag of learning materials, and walked by my side, subtly positioning himself so that his shadow was providing me with some shade.

'This smells delicious,' he said, lifting the basket.

'It was going to be a surprise, but there's no concealing the wonderful scent of Maria's food. It's just a little thank you for the language help.'

This time it was Alexis who looked rather flushed. 'You did not have to do that. As I said, it is a pleasure to share my language with you. But I'm not going to say no to an opportunity to enjoy a meal with you, especially when it's come from Maria's Taverna.'

The shop bell tinkled as we went in. I hovered in the doorway, the nerves returning as Alexis placed the bag containing my dictionary and notebook behind the counter.

He caught the worried expression on my face and smiled reassuringly.

'I love books, you know that, and there is always wisdom to be found in their pages. But I think for language learning, perhaps it is better that instead of reading and reciting, we try speaking and listening.'

'But what about all the rules for verbs and things?' I asked, worried that even this question was betraying my ignorance.

'When it comes to languages, rules are made to be broken. Let us forget that this is a lesson, and just chat. You will be amazed at how much is learned this way.'

'I'm not sure I'm going to be up to this,' I said, leaning past him and pretending to make a grab for the books. He gently caught my hand and put it back at my side.

'I have faith in you,' he said. 'Trust me.'

'But the books…' I protested.

'*Ta biblia,*' he said, gesturing at the volumes so I could be in little doubt what he was referring to.

'Oh. Like bibliography?'

'Exactly,' he said. 'I told you this would work. Come, let us find somewhere to enjoy our picnic and talk together.'

While Alexis collected his car keys from his apartment above the shop, I took advantage of his brief absence to smuggle my notebook back into the picnic basket. Whatever he said about putting the books to one side, I was convinced that writing things down would help me to keep my mind focused on the lesson.

This time he steered the Mini away from the coast towards the centre of the island, pointing out features of the landscape and saying their names in Greek. He seemed to have endless patience as I painstakingly recited the words back to him. As we drove past the car park for the Drogarati Cave, I felt a pang of loss which I realised was nothing to do with Absent Andreas, but more to do with the fact that the trip there would have been even more magical had it been in the company of someone really special. Someone like Alexis.

'*Ola kala?*' asked the man himself. *Everything OK?*

I shook myself out of my reverie and forced myself to reply with a steady voice. Thankfully Alexis seemed to accept my slow response to his question as being language-related, rather than anything else.

I stared out of the window and hoped he'd put the renewed colour in my cheeks down to the heat in the car.

'I thought we'd visit Mount Ainos,' said Alexis, then repeated himself in Greek. 'It is the tallest mountain on the island, and the views are unparalleled.'

The road up the mountainside was narrow, and I hoped we didn't meet a car coming in the opposite direction. However much I trusted Alexis's driving ability, the thought of us having to reverse to a passing point with a sheer drop on one side was rather terrifying. The hairpin bends on the road to Antisamos beach were nothing compared to this route, and we both fell silent while Alexis gave his full attention to getting us to our destination safely. We wound our way up through mile after mile of forest, the sound of birdsong the only noise apart from the car's engine. It felt like we were the only two people in the world.

When we were just short of the summit, Alexis pulled the car off the road into an area of parched scrubland which incongruously had a car park sign on display, and turned off the engine. I remained sitting while he got the picnic out of the boot, needing a moment to myself. When he came round and opened the door for me, I realised my legs were wobbly and I found myself having to grab hold of him for support.

'Sorry, I'm not brilliant with heights,' I explained.

Alexis's face fell. 'I apologise. It is very selfish of me to have made you come here.'

I squeezed his arm. 'Don't be silly. You weren't to know. And I'll be fine once I've adjusted to my surroundings.

Besides, it's worth it for the view. We're practically above the clouds. They look like great big cotton wool chairs, soft enough for us to sink into them.'

'But perhaps they would make a rather damp picnic spot,' said Alexis, smiling at my flight of fancy. 'If you feel up to moving, there is a perfect space for eating, and our lesson, just a short walk away.'

He offered his arm to me, and I accepted, even though my legs were fine now. We clambered upwards for about ten minutes, the trees thinning out, until we came to a long ridge with a path curving along it, and there was nowhere else to climb.

'We're on top of the world,' I said, carefully turning on the spot to take in the view while making sure I didn't get too near the edge. There was no real danger of me falling off the mountain, but better safe than sorry.

Alexis beckoned me over to a concrete post.

'This marks the actual summit of Mount Ainos,' he said, patting the smooth surface.

I followed suit, my little finger grazing his. I looked up at him and caught him watching me.

He glanced away quickly and moved to one side, suddenly intent on searching for something.

'Here it is,' he said, picking up a metal container which was partially hidden in a hollow at the base of the post.

He twisted off the lid and took out a battered leatherbound notebook.

'The visitors' book,' he explained. 'Here for everyone who reaches the summit so they can record their names and if they like, leave a message for those who follow in their footsteps.'

We signed our names on a fresh page along with today's date, then flicked through the crinkled leaves of the book, our heads bent together as we looked at the signatures and comments written in dozens of different languages and hands.

I picked a paragraph in Greek at random and asked Alexis to translate it for me. He scanned through the sentences and smiled.

'It is a proposal,' he said. 'One partner secretly climbed the mountain early in the day and left this message, then the couple returned together, and the proposal was made.'

'I hope the answer was yes.'

Alexis pointed at the sentence written in a different colour ink below.

'Can you read what that says?' he asked.

I traced my index finger over the carefully written words, double checking each letter with Alexis before I finally attempted to pronounce the short phrase.

'Nai. S'agapo.'

'Very good,' said Alexis. 'It says, 'Yes. I love you.''

The words hung between us. I tried to read his expression, but couldn't tell whether the longing in his eyes was just what my imagination wanted to see there.

A sudden gust of breeze took me by surprise, making me shiver.

Alexis cleared his throat. 'Come, let us find somewhere out of the wind to sit down and enjoy our meal. It is cooler up here, especially now we've stopped climbing.'

We picked our way through the scree until we found a large, flat rock which looked like nature had placed it there for the very purpose of providing a picnic spot.

'The best restaurant seats on the island,' I said, as we settled down and unpacked the basket.

'With the best company,' said Alexis, his words echoing my thoughts.

I'd found Maria's food delicious when I first ate it at her taverna by the sea, but up here among the clouds, with a panoramic view spreading out hundreds of miles into the distance, the meal tasted fit for the Greek gods on Mount Olympus. Alexis and I relaxed into a companionable silence, all thought of language learning forgotten for the time being while we ate our feast and drank in our surroundings. It felt so right to be up here by his side, and I knew that words wouldn't do justice to the wonder of this shared experience.

But I still felt compelled to speak, to try to articulate the thoughts going through my head, to dare to voice the realisation that the happy expression on Alexis's face gave me even more pleasure than the beauty of the miraculous landscape in front of us. I took a deep breath, my heart pounding as I summoned up the courage to say the words from which there would be no going back.

'Alexis, I need to say something…'

I didn't get any further, because Alexis suddenly looked

away from me and reached his hand out, palm facing up to the sky.

'Did you feel that?' he asked.

'Sorry, what?' I wondered if he'd anticipated my speech, and this was his way of tactfully steering me away from making it so he didn't have to let me down.

'A spot of rain,' he said, palm still outstretched.

'Surely not? The sky is so blue, and most of the clouds are below us,' I protested.

But then I felt it too, a splash of lukewarm water landing on my collarbone. Before I could say anything, another spot landed on my head, and then another.

'We had better clear everything away and find some shelter,' said Alexis. 'It is not a good idea to get caught up here in a storm.' My heart soared at the reluctance in his voice. Perhaps he felt it too?

But the rapidly developing shower didn't allow me much time to focus on that. Together we quickly packed up the basket, laughing as the rain plastered our clothing to our bodies, and turned my hair at least into a tangled mess down my back. Alexis on the other hand managed to look beautifully tousled, giving me Mr Darcy in a wet shirt feels.

He took my arm once again as we hurried back to the car, a practical offer of mutual assistance as the water made the loose rubble of the ridge even more slippery and hazardous. We threw the picnic basket into the boot, then as soon as I'd done up my seatbelt, Alexis started the engine, and steered carefully out of the car park. The rain was already turning the road into a river, and I felt a clutch of nerves as I wondered whether the Mini's brakes would be up to the job of getting us down the mountain safely.

'Trust me,' said Alexis quietly, recognising my tension.

'I trust you completely,' I replied.

The rain beat a staccato rhythm on the car roof as we slowly inched our way down the mountain. I ignored my ears popping as I concentrated on the route in front of us, as if by sheer willpower alone I could make sure we both arrived back home safely. And then as the road widened out, and the slope became less steep, the noise of the rain grew softer until it was gone altogether. We drove another couple of hundred yards on a wet surface, then turned a corner onto the main road back to Sami and it was as if it had never rained at all, the car's tyres disturbing clouds of dust from the verges once again. It was surreal to be back among the traffic, suddenly surrounded by other people after all that time of it being just me and Alexis and the clouds.

'What was it you wanted to say to me?' asked Alexis suddenly.

'Sorry?' I prevaricated, although I knew full well what he was referring to. Back here in the real world, I realised I wasn't feeling as brave as I had been on the mountain.

'When we were eating our picnic. You said you wanted to tell me something. I hope you know that you can say anything to me. Anything at all.' He glanced briefly across at me before focusing his gaze back at the road.

Did I dare say something? Could I dare to risk our

friendship by voicing the idea that it was him I wanted, and not an Andreas, however awesome they might be?

I opened my mouth to speak, but the Mini bounced over a large pothole with such a jolt it somehow switched the radio on. The sound of cheesy Greek pop music suddenly blasted out of the speakers. By the time we'd stopped laughing and I'd managed to work out how to switch the thing off, the moment had passed.

'I can't remember,' I said, frustrated at myself for wimping out.

The rest of the journey was all too short, but when we arrived back at the Helios Hotel, I dredged up some of my former courage, and asked Alexis if he would like to have a drink at the pool bar with me.

'I would love to, but I am afraid I am going to have to return to the shop and reopen it for the evening customers,' he said after checking his watch. He sounded reluctant, but once again I couldn't decide whether that was wishful thinking on my part.

I waved the Mini off into the distance and headed for my room, my mind whirling.

Chapter Twenty

As I unlocked the door of my room, still thinking about the picnic with Alexis and wondering what would have happened if I had spoken out, I noticed a slip of paper lying on the floor. I bent down and picked it up. It was a ticket for a cruise on Captain Andreas's boat, taking place tomorrow. To my surprise, the handwritten note accompanying it was signed by Yiota, the trip and an extra day off a reward for my hard work. I was touched at the thoughtful gesture, that she'd gone ahead and booked this for me, despite her reservations about the touristy nature of the cruise, because she knew it was something I wanted to do.

I stared at the words 'Captain Andreas' on the ticket. Going on this trip could be the perfect opportunity to get back on track with my Andreas search, but did I really want that? The window of opportunity in which I had acquired the tattoo had only been a few hours. How well could I have got to know a person in that short space of time? Yes, I'd obviously had a powerful sense of initial connection with that Andreas, but did that really trump the deep bond that I'd built with Alexis over the course of my stay? There was more to being The One than just a name. Our friendship was admittedly counted in days rather than months or years, but it was like I'd known him forever. Yet despite my yearning for him, I was still uncertain about his feelings towards me, whether he would ever want anything more than my friendship.

I got ready for bed and tried to distract myself from the questions swirling around my brain by picking up my battered copy of *Persuasion*. But for once, the exploits of Anne Elliot and her Captain Wentworth did not provide the escapism I craved, the tale of frustrated love only exacerbating my internal debate. With a sigh, I put it to one side, and lay staring at the ceiling, forcing myself to practise counting in Greek until I finally managed to drift off to sleep.

Despite my late night, I felt more positive in the morning, determined to enjoy the unexpected opportunity to go on a trip and play tourist for the day. After all, this wasn't a proper Andreas date. It was a cruise to neighbouring islands which happened to be led by someone who had the same name as the one adorning my back.

The boat was setting off from a port called Agia Efimia a few miles up the coast from Sami. I decided to take the bus again, and hoped that the trip would turn out better than my visit to Fiskardo. It was so much nicer than getting the bus back in England. There were still teenagers squabbling on the back row and shoppers hogging extra seats for their bags, but the view from the windows was spectacular as we meandered along the coastline. The driver also recognised me and greeted me in Greek rather than English, which made me feel like I was starting to become a local.

The bus arrived in Agia Efimia an hour before the boat was due to depart so I made the most of the time exploring. The town was smaller than Sami but bustling with activity. The harbour was packed with sailing yachts, all moored up so close to each other that you could quite comfortably walk from one end of the quay to the other along their decks. A wide range of flags from different countries fluttered from the backs of the boats, and I went across to take a closer look, hoping to spot the boat I would be heading out on. The harbour master noticed my interest and wandered over for a chat in between directing yachts to their moorings.

'Stern to,' he said, gesturing at the boats.

'Pardon?' I asked, wondering if this was another important new Greek phrase that I needed to learn.

He smiled. 'The boats here are all moored stern to. With their backs against the harbour wall,' he clarified. 'It means that people can sit in the cockpit and talk to their neighbour. In some countries, they moor bow to – that is, the front of the boat faces to the land. It means they have more peace when they are sitting in the cockpit. But here in Greece we know the better way. It is always good to talk and be friendly with those around you.'

I was certainly finding that out for myself. I toyed with the idea of casually asking the harbour master about Captain Andreas, but before I could, he made his apologies and hurried away, his radio chattering, as he prepared to welcome another boat in. To my untrained eye, it didn't look like there was space left for more vessels, but clearly the harbour master knew better. There was a hubbub of shouting between the quayside and the deck of a yacht as another captain skilfully steered her vessel into a space with barely thirty centimetres' clearance either side of it. It was like having to reverse park at the supermarket, only there was an audience who seemed to get their entertainment from watching the boats. If you messed up here, everyone would know about it.

As with Sami and Fiskardo, the road along the harbour was lined with tavernas, all with big awnings hanging over the street, shading the tables from the strongest rays of the sun. I decided to take a look at the menus, but as I was about to cross the road, I spotted a familiar face. I might not have told him about my trip to Agia Efimia, but Alexis was here anyway. I felt a warm glow of happiness as I smiled across the street at him, delighted to see his lovely features looking back at me. It felt like a sign, and I experienced a thrill of excitement which far outweighed my anticipation of the boat trip I was about to go on.

'Hey, Alexis,' I called across the bustling street. But the noise of the traffic must have got in the way of him hearing me, because although he was definitely looking in my direction, he turned away and started walking along the pavement.

'Alexis,' I bellowed louder, and then waved for good measure, hopping up and down in the hope that the movement would attract his attention. But while it drew a lot of bemused gazes in my direction, to my disappointment, Alexis remained oblivious to my presence and continued striding off into the distance, wrapped up in his own world. He didn't have his glasses on, so that was probably why he'd not seen my impromptu jig on the other side of the road, I told myself, hoping that he wasn't deliberately blanking me. He wasn't the kind of person to ignore someone. But I still felt unsettled, worried that things were different between us.

I tried to dart across the street to catch up with him, but as I stepped out, a flurry of vehicles turned around the corner and accelerated along the road, the drivers determined not to hang around for a moment longer than they had to. I returned to the pavement and watched in frustration as Alexis walked purposefully off. I pulled my phone out to send him a text, then stopped myself. What would I say? That I'd seen him walking down the street? That just sounded creepy. Or that I was here about to encounter another Andreas, but I'd happily ditch my plans in a second if he gave the slightest indication that he wanted to spend time with me? No, I needed to have some dignity. I turned around and made my way back to the harbour, no longer bothered about reading menus.

Right on cue my phone bleeped, and my heart leaped in immediate response. Maybe Alexis had seen me and had sent a message to apologise for dashing off. But when I checked the screen, I was disappointed to discover it was actually a voicemail from Jim awaiting me instead. I deleted it without bothering to listen, and then I did what I should have done ages ago and blocked his number. There was nothing to tie us together anymore, no shared accommodation or workplace, no children or pets to fight over. He had no reason to keep trying to contact me, and it was about time he got the message. It was like he had some sixth sense telling him whenever I was feeling vulnerable, and was doing his best to play on that. Well, I wasn't going to let him trample on my dreams anymore.

I checked my watch. It was still too early to queue for the boat, so I settled down on one of the benches near the harbour wall and pulled my notebook out of my bag. This time, instead of focusing on my dating disasters, I decided to distract myself by writing about some of the amazing places I'd been lucky enough to visit in Kefalonia and the friendly people who had made me feel so welcome. I described the delicious food and the stunning scenery. Even the cats at Maria's Taverna got a mention. It felt good to commit my thoughts to paper, and when I read the paragraphs back, I experienced a surge of pride in what I'd achieved. Maybe Alexis's suggestion that I should pursue writing wasn't such a wild one.

'Captain Andreas boat trip customers, this way.' A man with a megaphone had started marching around the harbour summoning up guests. I carefully tucked my notebook away and joined the chattering crowd beginning to gather.

Captain Andreas's boat was sadly not one of the elegant sailing yachts moored up in front of the tavernas, but was instead a much larger, more practical-looking motor vessel tethered to the outer wall of the harbour. It was a dirty white colour, with a Greek flag hanging from the back. The flag was so big that it was trailing in the water, while the boat itself appeared to be listing to one side in a slightly drunken fashion. It wasn't exactly the romantic super yacht I'd been dreaming about, but I told myself not to jump to conclusions based on the boat's scruffy appearance, and joined the queue of tourists snaking along the jetty, excited that I was finally going to see the island from the sea.

As I was helped on board by a couple of smiling deckhands, I checked their name badges carefully. Neither of them was Captain Andreas, which was slightly disappointing as both were excellent examples of dashing Greek manhood. I found myself a seat on the top deck and settled in for the trip, looking forward to getting a different perspective on the island.

As the seats around me filled up, I realised I was the only solo traveller on the boat. Perhaps it was down to the phenomenon that when you're looking for love, all you notice is loved-up couples around you. But instead of feeling lonely, I felt proud of myself for doing this trip alone. Only a few weeks ago, the very idea of it would have made me anxious. Now I felt much more comfortable in my own skin and confident in what I could achieve.

I looked across to the wheelhouse to see if I could spot the captain, vaguely wondering whether the real-life version bore any resemblance to the cartoon form. The man behind the wheel was dressed in traditional whites, and his dark hair suggested he was a youthful sea dog, but I was at the wrong angle to see his face, so I would have to wait until he emerged onto the deck to find out more. I dismissed the thought that I was not as curious about Captain Andreas as perhaps I should have been.

The crew bustled around on the dock letting go of ropes and pulling up fenders, then the boat's speakers crackled to life with an explosion of static. They were playing a muffled recording of someone speaking, but whether they were talking in English, Greek or double Dutch, I couldn't tell. I glanced around at the other passengers, but nobody seemed to be paying any attention to the announcement. One of the crew members gave a cursory wave in the direction of the lifeboats, so I figured that this was the safety briefing, but it was over pretty much as soon as it had started. The horn sounded, making everybody jump, and then with a cloud of exhaust fumes, we set sail.

The first part of the trip was everything I'd imagined it would be. We cruised slowly up the coast of Kefalonia, the boat cutting effortlessly through the glistening azure waters while people posed for pictures and tucked into the generous hospitality on offer. We sailed past Fiskardo which looked even prettier from the sea, waved at the haughty occupants of a super yacht which was moored offshore, and then the boat headed out into the open ocean. I'd been worried in case I felt seasick. After all, I'd never been on a boat trip like this so didn't know if it was something I was afflicted with, but thankfully I seemed to have pretty good sea legs. At one point a school of dolphins appeared, leaping happily in and out of the waves as if they were racing the boat. I couldn't quite believe that this was really happening. I must have taken hundreds of photos of the sights we sailed past, and I regularly sent updates to the group chat with Amira and Kat until they joked they'd had enough of being tortured by stunning scenery. I also considered sending a picture or two to Alexis, but my uncertainty about the incident in Agia Efimia held me back.

We cruised up towards the nearby island of Lefkada, stopping on the way at a cave where Captain Andreas showed off his seafaring abilities by inching the boat practically inside it. His crackly commentary informed us the cave had been used during the Second World War to hide a submarine in. I watched the waves crashing against the rocky roof and experienced a moment of misgiving. If the engines failed right now, we'd be in trouble. Fortunately, Captain Andreas's navigational skills were better than his sound equipment, and soon we were safely away from the rocks and heading to our next destination, the island of Skorpios, which I managed to glean between bursts of static once used to belong to the Onassis family. I tucked away the nuggets of information, vowing to write about the trip once I returned to dry land. An idea was half-forming in the back of my mind that maybe I could pitch a blog post about the boat trip to holiday companies as part of their marketing. It might be an unrealistic ambition, but as I'd been telling myself throughout my stay here, if I didn't try, I would never find out.

The crew moored the boat in a quiet bay so that people could sunbathe on the deck or go for a swim as they desired. Some guests lined up outside the wheelhouse, taking advantage of the break to enjoy a meet and greet with the captain. I hovered in the queue feeling unaccountably worn out. My fellow passengers were happily posing for pictures with Captain Andreas and having a chat with him. It would be very easy for me to do the same: casually introduce myself and quickly establish whether or not he was the Andreas I was looking for. But as I stood there, bracing myself against the rocking motion of the boat, I started to wonder how I would react if I did recognise him as the Awesome Andreas who'd inspired my tattoo. Would I be thrilled? Or would I feel sad that he wasn't Alexis?

Chapter Twenty-One

C aptain Andreas noticed me loitering at the back of the queue and came over to introduce himself. He was conventionally attractive, like his crew, and his air of complete confidence spoke of a man who knew he was in charge. But his features weren't familiar, and when he spoke, his voice didn't spark any recognition.

'Welcome, welcome aboard. I hope you are enjoying the trip?' he asked politely.

'I feel like a proper tourist,' I said. 'I've learned so much today, and I can't get over how wonderful our surroundings are. The Ionian is beautiful.'

'I am biased, but I cannot think of another sea that is so perfect.' He wrinkled his brow. 'And what is your name? If you don't mind me saying, you appear familiar. Have we met before?'

I felt a jolt of nerves. In all the time I'd been considering how I would recognise Awesome Andreas, it had never really crossed my mind that he might recognise me first. The idea threw me. Did the man standing in front of me hold the key to those missing few hours? The idea was unsettling. But then again, he didn't seem to even know my name. If he was Awesome Andreas, maybe he'd been similarly tipsy. Or maybe I was overthinking again and this was a standard line that he used on all the tourists.

'I'm Lydia. I work at the Helios Hotel in Sami, and my boss bought me a ticket for the trip.'

Captain Andreas nodded thoughtfully. 'I live in Sami and I am excellent with faces, but I do not think it is there that I have seen you.'

I actually felt relieved. He seemed like a perfectly decent guy, but I didn't want him to be my Awesome Andreas. It was a quick judgement to make, but I felt instinctively it was the right one. Once again that know-it-all voice at the back of my head piped up, urging me to accept that I didn't want to search for an Andreas any longer, and that I should focus on working out how to lay bare my feelings for Alexis instead.

'Let me think, it will come to me,' said Andreas. 'And in the meantime, may I offer you a drink? I do not like to see my guests empty-handed. We like to have fun on this boat.'

Before I could answer, a sudden gust of wind sent a rogue wave crashing against the side of the boat. I could feel the salty spray even high up by the wheelhouse. The swimmers in the bay whooped with delight as they body-surfed the swell, while those who remained on board grabbed hold of the railings to steady themselves. Captain Andreas glanced at the sky, and rubbed the back of his head.

'I think perhaps we have some interesting weather coming in. It was not forecast, but the weather at sea does not always conform to what is expected of it. If you will forgive me, I will go and check the radar. I will be back in a moment.'

I looked up at the sky, but it seemed as flawlessly blue as it had when we set off. The swell was maybe slightly bigger than before, but aside from the burst of choppiness caused by the rogue wave, the rocking motion of the boat was still relaxing. The water looked inviting and deliciously refreshing in contrast to the heat of the day. Maybe it was even time to take the plunge and go for my first swim of my stay. I leaned on the railings and watched the people in the water. Some were wearing snorkels, kicking slowly up and down as they peered at whatever was living below the surface. Others were racing around the boat, competing to do as many laps as possible. I thought those who were floating on their backs probably had the best idea, soaking up the sunshine while being rocked gently by the waves. But I wasn't sure that I would be able to achieve their levels of relaxation given the conflicting thoughts spinning around inside my head.

A member of crew made his way up the stairs from a lower deck holding a tray of fresh juice. He gestured at one particular glass, which was decorated with a large slice of orange which had a tiny paper Greek flag sticking out of it.

'The captain asked us to make it especially for you,' said the sailor with a smile. 'A special treat for a special passenger.'

It was a generous gesture, but rather showy, and it got me wondering once again where Captain Andreas thought he recognised me from.

My thanks were interrupted by another crackly announcement over the speaker from the captain himself.

'Ladies and gentlemen, please make your way to the swim ladder and get back on board. We will shortly be setting off on our return to Kefalonia. We're expecting some breezy weather this evening, so it is better to travel before the worst of it comes in.'

I felt a pang of disappointment. No swim stop this time and even worse, a premature end to the trip.

As we set off, Captain Andreas poked his head around the wheelhouse door again. I hoped he had left the boat in some kind of automatic steering function because it was rather worrying that he wasn't holding the wheel, especially given the reason for our early departure.

'Is your drink good?'

He waved the twin of it at me, and said, '*Yamas* – or cheers, as you say in English.'

I took a sip of the juice and nearly choked as I realised it was actually alcoholic punch, and a very strong one at that. I forced a smile and waved my thanks while wondering how I could subtly pour it over the side. Although I wasn't wholly opposed to the idea of drinking again, on my own terms, it would definitely be in moderation. Judging by the tiny sip I'd had so far, I'd probably end up with an entire tattoo sleeve if I drank a full glass of this. I seriously hoped Captain Andreas's version was virgin as I didn't fancy our chances of a safe return otherwise.

He was clearly a bit of a mind reader, because he answered my unspoken question by gesturing at the juice carton on the windowsill of the wheelhouse.

'Do not worry. You are safe while I am in charge. As captain, I never drink any alcohol, even when I am not at sea.' His eyes sparkled. 'And I now remember where I saw you. It was in Fiskardo. You seemed in a hurry to leave. Nobody should be in a hurry to leave Fiskardo.' He smiled broadly. 'I run a boat trip which stops off there, if you would like to see it on another occasion. Or if you would not like to visit it on a boat trip, perhaps you would like to join me for dinner there instead?'

In all my time in Kefalonia, I had been the one asking Andreases out, so I was rather startled to be on the receiving end of an offer of a date. It was flattering and I'll admit I felt an instant confidence boost. Why shouldn't I accept the invitation? After all, despite his casual approach to steering his vessel, he was pleasant, polite, and rather pleasing on the eye. What wasn't to like? This could be the start of a wonderful relationship. But something held me back. Or rather *someone*. Because in that moment I knew with absolute certainty that I couldn't say yes to this perfectly decent man, because it would feel like I was stringing him along. Because the guy I really wanted to spend time with was on shore and his name was very much not Andreas. And although I wasn't confident that Alexis reciprocated my feelings, I would never know for certain until I actually spoke to him about what was in my heart.

I did what I had to do. 'That's a really lovely invitation, and I'm very flattered, but no thank you. I've got a boyfriend. No, that's not true. He's not my boyfriend yet, but I very much hope he will be one day.'

Captain Andreas shrugged his shoulders good-naturedly. 'No problem. I hope that this man recognises his luck. If he does not want to be your boyfriend, then he is a fool. I will look forward to seeing you on another boat trip instead. Perhaps you could bring your man.'

He passed me a leaflet, then returned to the wheelhouse humming happily. I was relieved he'd taken my rejection in good spirits.

I settled in for the journey home, willing the boat to speed up so I could see Alexis again. It was time to be honest with him and tell him how I felt. It came with a risk that I could get hurt, but I now knew that I would rather take that chance and it pay off, than spend the rest of my life wondering 'what if'.

But the weather had other ideas. As we left the shelter of the bay, a gust of wind caught the boat, sending several sunhats flying. The swell was growing bigger, and once we headed into the open water of the wide stretch between the islands, the gentle rolling motion of the sea turned into an urgent chop, jolting the boat around uncomfortably.

I tried not to worry, but it was difficult when the horizon was pitching around at odd angles. It would be just my luck that after deciding to take the leap and speak to Alexis, I drowned in the meantime. I told myself not to panic, that I was once again jumping to the worst-case scenario, but it was difficult to stay calm when the boat was lurching up and down so much. As the waves buffeted the sides of the vessel, I gripped onto the railing and wondered what to do if we started sinking. Should I wait to follow the directions of the crew, or take matters into my own hands? The land was still visible, but it was difficult to get a proper perspective of how far away it actually was, and with the waves being so high, I didn't fancy my chances if I had to swim for it, not to mention the added hazards of other boats in the vicinity.

I sidled along the deck towards the sign for the lifejackets. If it came to it, I wanted to be in a good position to get hold of one. Judging by the relaxed approach to the safety briefing which we'd had on first boarding the ship, I didn't trust that they'd actually have a sufficient amount of lifesaving equipment for everybody on board, especially as the decks were so crowded.

From the deck below, I could hear the sounds of dinnerware crashing to the floor. I highly doubted they'd chosen this moment for a traditional Greek plate-smashing session. Conditions must be worse than expected. There were a few muffled cheers, but most people seemed to have turned quiet as the weather grew louder. It all felt eerily *Titanic*-esque, although hopefully the water wouldn't be quite so lethally cold if we all ended up in it.

I gasped as I saw Captain Andreas walking casually

down the steps from the wheelhouse again, waving and smiling at my fellow passengers as if he was on a royal visit. Why had he left his post? Surely, he should be doing everything in his power to keep the boat under control and prevent us from disappearing into a watery grave? Or maybe he was doing the same as me and getting in prime position near the lifeboat? Traditionally a captain is meant to stay with the ship until the bitter end, but he seemed to prefer a relaxed approach to his duties. He smiled broadly at me as he walked past.

'Relax. It is all good,' he said confidently. I only hoped he was right. He might think he was keeping his passengers calm by walking around and chatting with them, but I for one would prefer to know that his full attention was on steering us out of this situation.

Having been proud about my lack of seasickness symptoms on the outward journey, I was now worried that my smugness had been premature. The last time I had felt this queasy I was struggling down the aisle of the shuttle bus on the way back to the airport with Kat and Amira. I forced my mind away from that image. It was not going to help me feel any better.

I tried to fix my gaze on the horizon as I did battle with my growing wobbliness. I wasn't the only one. There were quite a few grey faces around me, and the carnival atmosphere from earlier in the trip had been replaced by a quiet undercurrent of alarm. The boat's strange list to one side which I had spotted at the dock seemed even more pronounced, and I noticed a few of the other passengers had also started shuffling towards the lifejackets.

I took my phone out, melodramatically wondering if now should be the moment I sent a message to Alexis, declaring my feelings before it was all too late, but a wave of nausea sent me cross-eyed and I nearly dropped it over the side. With trembling fingers, I managed to stuff it back in my bag and curled up at the railing, praying that we would reach land soon. My earlier warm feelings towards Captain Andreas had been replaced by outright dislike. He was still striding among the guests, offering words of comfort, squeezing shoulders and laughing about the conditions, but I couldn't see much to laugh about. I should have listened to Yiota when she warned me about this trip in the first place.

What felt like several days later, but was probably less than an hour, we finally reached the sheltered channel between Ithaca and Kefalonia, and the wind instantly dropped while the boat settled back into its earlier gentle rhythm. Captain Andreas's voice came over the speakers, much clearer than it had all trip.

'Ladies and gentlemen, it will not be long until we are back at Agia Efimia. Do not worry, it is all smooth sailing from here. You will not be coming face to face with Poseidon today. We hope you have enjoyed your adventure with us, and please do join us again soon.'

There was a smattering of faint applause around the boat from those who still felt strong enough to put their hands together. I took a deep gulp of fresh air and hoped Captain Andreas was right.

It was a subdued crowd who eventually staggered down the gangplank at Agia Efimia and back onto Kefalonian soil. I was so relieved to reach dry land, I felt like kneeling down and trying to hug it. I returned to the bench I'd sat on before the trip, and took a few deep breaths, grateful to still be in one piece. Captain Andreas gave me a cheery wave as he strolled past with his crew, all of them looking sickeningly healthy and unmoved by the events of the trip. To be fair, it was probably all in a day's work for them. I put the leaflet about the Fiskardo sailing trip in the nearby recycling bin. It might be safer to stick to land-based activities in future.

I checked my watch and realised if I hurried, I could catch the bus which was due to return to Sami in the next five minutes. I wanted to get back there as soon as possible, to seek out Alexis and tell him how I felt. I had missed so many opportunities to be open with him, and it was time that fear stopped me avoiding the conversation I knew I needed to have. I was still terrified about the outcome, of course, but taking the safe option wasn't always the best course.

I hauled myself up from the bench, legs still shaky from my hours on the boat, and managed to wobble my way down the street to secure the last seat on the bus. This time I was indifferent to the views unfolding outside my window as the bus travelled along the coast. Once I'd stopped feeling queasy, I spent the rest of the journey rehearsing the conversation I would have with Alexis, lips moving silently as I tried out different phrases. But it was hard to rehearse something where I only knew my own lines. How would Alexis react? Would he welcome my declaration or shrink away from it? Whatever happened, I knew he would be compassionate in his response, but could I cope with a gently delivered rejection?

Chapter Twenty-Two

Despite having built myself up to have the conversation with Alexis, I decided it would probably be a good idea to stop by the Helios Hotel first and freshen up. My skin was salty and tight after the boat trip, and I knew my confidence levels would be higher once I'd had a wash and got changed. Just to make sure I didn't chicken out once I'd reached the sanctuary of my room, I sent Alexis a text asking if he could meet me in the harbour in an hour, not allowing myself much time for the nerves to build up further. And then I had the quickest shower of my life, threw on a clean sundress and a bit of makeup – Alexis had seen me bedraggled and soaked on a mountainside, so I didn't think leaving off the eyeliner was going to make any crucial difference at this stage – and then set off for the harbour.

I made it down there with fifteen minutes to spare having half run along the main road rather than taking my usual quieter route through the back streets. Sami was starting to come alive with the Friday night crowd, a mix of tourists and locals heading out for an evening of food, conversation and dancing. The smell of barbequing meat drifted ashore from a yacht moored up in the harbour, the clinking of its rigging against the mast providing a tuneful contrast to the chugging engine of a fishing boat bringing in the day's catch.

I wandered along the jetty and found a bench which was slightly set back from the others to sit on, and settled down to watch the sunset while I waited for Alexis. Streaks of copper pink were appearing across the horizon, bathing everything in a glorious golden glow. As the darkness slowly descended, the nearby restaurants grew livelier with the clatter of cutlery and the chatter of diners. For a moment, I felt a pang of loneliness, sitting there on the outside, observing from a distance all the happy friends and families having fun together. But then someone quietly sat down on the bench beside me and I didn't feel alone any longer.

'*Iassou*, Alexis,' I said, without even turning round. I would recognise his footsteps anywhere.

'*Iassou*, Lydia *mou*, how was your boat trip?'

I felt a thrill of happiness. He frequently addressed me as 'Lydia *mou*', but it was only now that I considered the meaning and potential significance of the phrase. 'My Lydia.' Did he mean it in the way I hoped he did, or was it a common manner of address between friends in Greece? I had to find out.

'It was an…experience. I'm not sure I will be venturing out to sea again any time soon, and certainly not when it's windy. But I'm glad I did it. It was good to see things in a new light.'

'And what did you think of Captain Andreas?'

This was it, my moment to be honest and say what was on my mind.

'He was *Alright* Andreas.'

'Ouch,' said Alexis.

'That sounds harsh. He was a perfectly decent guy, but just not the guy for me.' I turned to face Alexis, my stomach contracting with nerves. This was it. 'In fact, I think I might be done with the whole Awesome Andreas search. The boat trip got a bit dicey, and it made me realise that life's too short to waste time following the wrong path, or keeping quiet when I should speak out. You see, the thing is, I have met someone awesome in Kefalonia, and I care for him a great deal, but his name isn't Andreas.'

It was hard to read Alexis's expression in the gloaming, but I thought I heard a sharp intake of breath. What would his reaction be when I came out and said it? Did I dare I carry on? I thought about all I'd been through in the past few weeks, all the brave steps I'd taken since I'd walked out on Jim and chosen a new direction in life. Having achieved so much, I couldn't fall at this hurdle. And it might not turn out to be a hurdle at all. I took hold of Alexis's hand, finding courage in the warmth of his palm against mine.

'Alexis, you're the guy I can't stop thinking about. You're kind, caring, gorgeous inside and out, you love books, you go out of your way to help random strangers like me, and basically I think you're awesome.' No going back now. 'And I was wondering if you would like to go to Eleni's dinner tomorrow night with me? Not as friends – although I hope we'll always be friends whatever happens – but as someone even more special, my date.'

My heart was pounding so much when I asked the question, I worried that passers-by would hear it too. I'd put everything on the line. Now it was up to him. The silence seemed to stretch out forever as I waited for Alexis's answer. I was torn between dread and optimism. I knew that however he answered, he'd be kind. But I really didn't want to be on the receiving end of the sort of kindness which involved, 'Thank you, but…' If Alexis said no to my invitation, I didn't know what I would do. It would be a wound I wasn't sure I would recover from.

I peered through the dusk, trying to make out his reaction. Did he feel the same way? Was he happy? Or was he trying to think of a way of letting me down gently, overwhelmed by my praise, and embarrassed that he wasn't able to reciprocate?

'Are you sure?' he asked eventually, his words soft and hesitant.

My insides twisted with half fear, half hope.

'I'm very sure. I've never been so sure of anything. In fact, I don't know why it took me so long to see what was staring me right in the face from the moment I met you in the bookshop. I like you. I like you a lot.' If truth be known,

I almost wanted to use another L word, but I didn't want to overwhelm him, or make him feel pressured.

Still, he hesitated, and the fear started to outweigh the hope. This was a moment which would define our whole future. Although I felt like I'd known him forever, I couldn't anticipate what his response would be. What would I do if he said no? It would change everything between us. Even if we both pretended that we could carry on as friends, this conversation would always be hovering in the atmosphere, tainting every interaction with awkwardness on his side, and unbearable loss on mine. The green shoots of everything that I'd been building here in Kefalonia would wither and die, and I would have to start over somewhere new, because the thought of being here and not having Alexis as part of my life was too painful to contemplate. Maybe I should have waited, held back until I was sure of his answer, kept to the safe option. But I had taken a chance on Greece, and I had to take this chance too. I swallowed, my mouth dry with nerves.

Then Alexis reached for my other hand with his and the noise from our surroundings shifted into nothingness as I focused on what he was about to say.

'Yes. Yes, that would make me very happy. I like you too. A lot,' he echoed my words. 'Since the moment we first met, in fact. I would love to be your partner for Eleni's dinner.'

His first 'yes' was hesitant, but the second was more confident, and by the end of his speech, his voice was certain. It was still hard to see his features properly in the shadows, but I could tell that he was smiling.

I found myself laughing with sheer relief. In all the date invitations I'd issued since I returned to Greece, I'd never been so nervous. But I realised now that none of them had mattered so much to me.

Alexis shuffled up so we were side by side and put his arm around me. I rested my head against his shoulder and it felt like the most natural thing in the world. I could hear the thudding of his heart in his chest as we snuggled together watching the lights from the boats in the harbour dancing on the dark water.

'I never imagined this would be the outcome when I set out on my Awesome Andreas quest,' I said. 'I feel like the whole thing was leading me to this moment, that everyone I've met along the way helped play a part in me coming to this realisation. Does that make sense?'

It was probably not very tactful of me to bring up the dates I'd been on over the last couple of weeks, but when I was with Alexis, I felt safe to speak my mind, to be completely myself and not worry about the reaction.

'It's all part of life's journey,' he replied simply. 'I am glad that we are together here now.'

Then my quiet sense of contentment was spoilt by a sudden realisation. 'Oh no, we can't go to Eleni's dinner together.'

Alexis's arm stiffened. 'What's the matter?' he asked.

'What about Andreas? Andreas Rouvas – you know, the guy that Eleni was going to invite for me to meet. I still want to go with you, of course, but how are we going to solve that? It would be the height of bad manners to uninvite him, and I don't want him to think he's got a chance with me, when I've only got eyes for you. I mean he probably wouldn't be interested in me anyway, but what if he is? Oh, this is really awkward.' I was gabbling again.

Alexis chuckled. 'I think it will be alright. He won't mind.' He sounded supremely relaxed about the whole idea.

'You say that, but it's still really bad to get him to turn up expecting a blind date with me, only to find out that I'm there with someone else.'

'Andreas Rouvas is ninety-two and has remained happily single throughout his life. While of course I think he would be a fool not to fall for you, perhaps we should accept in this situation that I have a biased viewpoint because I like you, and that actually it's safe to assume that he will not change the habit of a lifetime and fall for you.'

I could tell Alexis was trying not to laugh, but I was confused.

'He's ninety-two? Then why was Eleni trying to set me up with him?'

Alexis cleared his throat. 'Ah, well I think that could have something to do with the fact that Eleni is what you might call a hopeless romantic.'

'There's hopeless romantic, and then there's just hopeless. If Andreas Rouvas has not been interested in a relationship at any point in his ninety-two years, why would she think he'd change now? And I'm sure he's lovely and everything, and while older gentlemen have their attractions, he's perhaps a little *too* old for me. I mean, he could be my great-grandfather at that age.'

'I haven't explained properly. Eleni is a hopeless romantic and I think she was trying to set you and me up. Do you remember that she teased me about how often I was visiting the hotel? It is not my usual habit, and she knew that. She could see straight through what I was doing. I'll admit that I was finding excuses to stop by so I could see you. Eleni and I have been friends for many years, and she's always enjoyed playing matchmaker. This way she looked like she was supporting your Andreas search, but actually she was arranging it so that we would spend the evening together.'

Now I joined in with his laughter. 'And didn't you mind? You must have realised what she was up to at the time.'

Alexis kissed the top of my head. 'I was rather pleased. I am a bit of a hopeless romantic myself.'

'You should have said something sooner. Then that would have spared me the drama of some of those Andreas meetings.'

'You were very certain that Awesome Andreas was the one for you. I did not want to stand in your way when you were so determined that this was the right thing to do. After all, I have read many books in which the anti-heroes come to bad ends. I hoped that one day you would notice me. But I'll admit that it was hard to see you going on dates with other men, when I so wanted to be in their shoes.'

'You're your own worst enemy,' I teased him. Then my voice grew serious. 'And of course, you're not the anti-hero. You should always be the hero of your own story.' It felt like the conversation had got very deep, very quickly. 'But I'm glad that we found our way to each other in the end. Goodness, what a day of drama. From near drowning to asking you out. I feel quite exhausted.'

Alexis laughed again. 'You were safe with Captain Andreas. It is an old boat with its own character but it is definitely sea-worthy and goes through all the proper checks. My br... relative works in the yachting industry and knows all the inside gossip. Captain Andreas is one of the best. He may look like he's running a party boat, but he is very careful to make sure that his guests are properly looked after, and that health and safety rules are followed.'

'There you go again, making other people the heroes in your story.' I squeezed his waist.

'I will try harder to be the hero in the future.'

He traced his finger down the side of my neck and along my collarbone, sending a delicious fluttering sensation across my skin. I pulled myself even closer to him so there wasn't a millimetre of space between us as we sat side by side. I could feel his breath tickling the top of my head and every receptor in my skin tingled at his proximity.

'What time is Eleni's dinner tomorrow?' he asked softly. It took a while for me to process his question.

'Eight-thirty-ish, I think?'

'I should warn you that a dinner party with Eleni and her husband Stephano always involves dancing and goes on late. Much as I am enjoying sitting here with you, perhaps we should get an early night as we'll need plenty of energy tomorrow evening.' He hesitated, suddenly realising what he had said. 'When I say we should get an early night, I mean in our separate accommodation, of course. I am a gentleman.'

'You would be no less a gentleman by spending the night with me,' I said, reaching up and cupping the side of his face. There was nothing I wanted more than for Alexis and I to get to know each other at a deeper level, preferably in a more private setting.

'Lydia, first there is something I should…' Alexis started to respond, but he was interrupted by a group of loud tourists who chose that precise moment to stumble past the bench and start wolf-whistling at us.

Alexis stood up, automatically putting himself between them and me. By the time they had staggered on their way, the moment of intimacy had passed.

'Let me walk you home,' he said. 'It is getting late.'

And although we took our time returning to the Helios Hotel, our hands linked with each other's the whole way, when we arrived at reception, he gave me a chaste kiss on the cheek and took his leave.

'Until tomorrow,' he promised, then strode off into the darkness.

Chapter Twenty-Three

I spent the next day in a daze, still not quite believing what had happened. Part of me was desperate to sing the news about the development in my relationship with Alexis from the rooftops, or at the very least tell Amira and Kat. While they'd probably be surprised at this twist in my journey, I knew they'd be thrilled for me. But the other superstitious part made me decide to hug the knowledge to myself for a little while at least. I didn't want to jinx something so new and so precious. The insecure voice at the back of my head still questioned whether I was good enough for such a lovely man. So, I kept my head down, worked hard through my shift, and thanked my lucky stars that Yiota and Angelo had taken a rare day off to visit friends in Argostoli on the other side of the island. Yiota with her perceptive powers would have been bound to spot the change in me straight away, and I wasn't sure I wanted

Alexis's sister to know about our date before we'd even had it.

Although I had promised myself when I travelled back to Kefalonia that I would savour every single moment of my stay, I couldn't help wishing the day away, so eager was I for it to be evening so that Alexis and I could be together. I finished stowing the cleaning materials back in the cupboard, and was just getting my phone out to text Alexis and check I hadn't dreamed the whole thing, when he messaged me first, arranging to come and pick me up at the hotel so we could walk to Eleni's apartment together. It was a thoughtful thing for him to do, and I felt reassured once again that everything was going to be wonderful. Alexis would never be the type to ghost me.

This time, I didn't spend ages riffling through my wardrobe and agonising over what outfit to choose for the date. It wasn't because I didn't care – quite the opposite – but because I knew that Alexis would make me feel beautiful in whatever I was wearing. I twisted my hair up in a simple bun, and then picked out a loose-flowing sundress. The pre-date nerves were nowhere to be seen, and I was full of excited anticipation, confident that tonight was only the start of something wonderful.

As I was getting ready, I caught a glimpse of the fateful tattoo in the mirror. The swirly writing still looked strange on my skin, but I was finally growing used to it being there, and had even developed a certain affection for it. I could appreciate the beauty in the design – Amira was right when she said the artist knew what they were doing – and I was grateful for the adventure it had led me on. Perhaps I would never remember why I had chosen those particular words to be inked, but I was glad I had chosen them, as they had brought me to Alexis, albeit in a roundabout way. Maybe at some point in the future I would get it covered up, but there was no rush.

Just before eight o'clock, I headed downstairs to meet Alexis, early in my eagerness to see him again. But it turned out he must've felt the same way because he was already there waiting for me, intelligent eyes sparkling behind his glasses, a heart-melting smile on his lips. I'd half-feared it might feel strange, knowing that we were embarking on this evening as something more than friends, but the second I saw him, I knew that everything would be fine.

My pulse started racing as he leaned towards me, his hand resting on my waist. I reached up and held his shoulders, every sense in my body eager for his kiss. And then his lips landed on my cheek, lingering there for just a second longer than would be customary between mere friends.

'Lydia, *matia mou*, I am so glad to see you,' he said softly. I didn't have to know the exact translation to work out that it was a term of endearment, and the tenderness in his voice nearly compensated for the disappointment that our first proper kiss was still yet to happen.

We walked hand in hand along the quiet back street to town, the air thick with the sweet scent of jasmine. We'd walked this way together before, but it felt so much better to be doing it *together* together, palms clasped, hips brushing against each other as we strolled along, savouring every step of the walk, and spinning the journey out into twice its normal length. Although I was looking forward to joining in the festivities at Eleni's home, I wished that for this first date we were able to enjoy it alone. But there would be time for that later.

Sami was getting ready for another busy evening. Waiters were putting extra chairs out at the tables in the tavernas along the sea front, and bar staff were polishing glasses, preparing for the influx of guests refreshed from lazy afternoons by the pool, ready for a fun evening of conversation and laughter. We stopped at the florist's to buy Eleni a bunch of flowers to thank her for her hospitality. Alexis picked out a large white daisy from the bunch and tenderly tucked it into my hair.

'A sunny flower for a sunny person,' he said, tipping my face up towards his, and setting me off blushing.

We turned away from the main shopping precinct into a quiet residential street with a low apartment block at one end. The front of the building was a faded honey colour, though it was difficult to see it behind the riot of bougainvillea. On the top floor, a blue chair balanced on a rickety balcony, clearly a favourite spot for someone to sit and watch the world go by. High above our heads, washing lines zigzagged across the street.

We buzzed the intercom and after a brief pause, Eleni leaned out of a window three floors up.

'*Ela*, come straight up,' she called down into the street. 'I will not climb down the stairs to greet you, if you don't mind. I am not sure I will make it back up again.'

'I don't blame you, you should put your feet up,' I replied, leaning back against Alexis as I shouted up to her. He responded by bending his head and placing a kiss on the nape of my neck, which made me want to abandon the party all over again. I forced myself back into sociable mode.

'Maybe we should have offered to bring food, instead of just bringing flowers. The last thing Eleni probably feels like doing in her condition is cooking for everyone.'

'She would be most offended if we had brought food,' said Alexis, holding the door open for me, and slowing his pace to match mine as we climbed the stairs. 'She was very clear in the invitation that she would be host and I know how much she enjoys looking after everybody. But I agree, I hope she is putting her feet up.'

Of course, when we arrived at Eleni's apartment, we realised she was doing anything but. She instantly clocked the fact that Alexis and I were holding hands, and pounced on him kissing both his cheeks and talking enthusiastically in Greek. I understood about one word in twenty, but my comprehension was still better than it had been when I first came to the island. And I was confident that it would improve still further, now I was going to be spending much more time with my personal tutor.

Eleni's husband smiled indulgently at his wife as she chattered. When she finally paused for breath, he made his own greetings.

'You must be Lydia,' he said, leaning forward to kiss my cheeks. 'I am Stephano. It is a pleasure to meet you. I have heard so much about you.'

'Good things, I hope.' I smiled.

'You are helping by doing my wife's job now she is too pregnant to do it. Of course, I have heard many good things about you.'

Eleni turned to me and gave me an enthusiastic hug. I only just managed to stop the flowers being crushed.

'These are for you,' I said, handing them over before they suffered any further damage.

Eleni went into paroxysms of delight and spoke very quickly again. I managed to keep up as far as the first 'thank you' but after that I lost the thread.

'I'm sorry, my Greek still isn't quite up to scratch,' I apologised.

'It is I who should be sorry,' replied Eleni. 'I am so excited to see you both together that I am getting carried away. I will repeat what I said before. Thank you so very much for the beautiful flowers. You are a generous and kind person, and I hope you and Alexis will be very happy together. I am only disappointed that he did not come to his senses sooner.' She winked up at Alexis and I swear I saw him blush. 'I hope you are very hungry because I have prepared a feast for us.'

She hustled us into the tiny flat and down a dark corridor. 'I thought as a treat we could eat outside. We have been working on something very special which I am dying to share with everyone. That is why I told Stephano we needed to have a dinner party, but of course the real reason was to make romance happen. Come, follow us. It is probably best that you go first. If I go and get stuck, that will cause problems for everyone.'

Stephano reached up and undid the latch on a hatch in the ceiling which I hadn't spotted before. He pulled it down and a set of wooden steps slid into the room.

'You don't...' said Alexis.

Eleni clapped her hands together. 'We do, we have created a roof garden. Our own little piece of paradise. Come, come, you must look.'

She gestured up the steep steps.

'After you,' said Alexis.

I hesitated. The steps were closer to a ladder than actual stairs. But if Eleni could manage it while heavily pregnant, then there was no excuse for me not to have a go.

'I'm right behind you. I won't let you fall,' said Alexis.

I took courage from his reassurance and started climbing.

We emerged into an explosion of colour. Dozens of pots overflowing with lavender scented the air, and lush green undergrowth trailed onto the chalk-white roof. The waist-high parapet was barely visible behind the dancing foliage.

'I am speechless,' said Alexis. He turned and helped Eleni up the final step. 'You are a miracle worker. How did you keep this quiet?'

'Ah well, I am very good at keeping secrets, as you know.'

'Don't forget to enjoy the view,' said Stephano, emerging

behind his wife holding a tray of drinks.

I was glad he had pointed it out. I had been so absorbed in admiring the beautiful garden that I had completely failed to notice what was beyond the rooftop. The whole of Sami was laid out before us, bathed in the beams of the setting sun, fairy lights twinkling from balconies.

Eleni smiled. 'It is very special, is it not?' she said. 'Every day I get up and I think how lucky I am to live in this place.'

'I feel the same,' I replied. 'Sometimes I wake up in the middle of the night terrified that coming out to Kefalonia was all a dream, and that I'm really back in the UK and will have to face another day wrestling with spreadsheets. But then I hear the distant sound of the sea and I know that it's all ok. This is another "pinch me" moment right here.'

Eleni paused at a faint sound from the apartment below. 'Ah, that will be the neighbours. As I mentioned, I have invited a couple of people to make sure that this evening is a proper celebration.'

Eleni's definition of a 'couple of people' turned out to be every resident in the street. They poured up from the ladder in a seemingly never-ending stream, chattering loudly, voices progressively raising in the battle to be heard. I started to worry about whether the roof was up to bearing everybody's weight.

I was quickly separated from Alexis and passed around the gathering to be introduced. Everybody wanted to hear my life story. I kept quiet about the Andreas quest and didn't make a big deal of the fact that I was here this evening with Alexis, but they found my sudden move to

Greece novelty enough, and I was quizzed on my views of Kefalonia by many people. My answers must have been satisfactory because I soon found myself with a whole bunch of new friends determined to make sure I stayed.

'You will have heard of the spirit of Greek hospitality,' said Eleni, laughing. I looked across the crowd and caught Alexis's eye.

'Yes, I learned about it very early on in my stay. Everyone is making me feel so welcome, saying that I am now part of the community. It's more than I could have ever wished for. I only hope I can find my niche and make sure I can support myself properly, if I'm to stay here longer term.'

She nudged me with her hip. 'I will want my job back some time, but don't worry. We will find plenty to occupy you when that does happen. The community in Sami is very caring and likes to look after its own, both those who are born in the town, and those who find their way here. Let me introduce you to someone.'

She led me through the chattering crowd to a quieter corner of the rooftop where an elderly man was sitting smoking a cigarette. He was watching the proceedings with a benevolent expression, while he clacked a loop of worry beads between his fingers.

'This is Andreas Rouvas,' said Eleni with a smile.

He leapt to his feet and kissed me on both cheeks, his movements quick and easy. If Alexis hadn't told me he was ninety-two, I would have assumed he was at least three decades younger.

'I'm honoured to meet you,' I said.

He nodded, as if this was to be expected, then fixed me with a perceptive gaze.

'Tell me about yourself,' he commanded.

Figuring that Eleni would have said something about my Andreas quest, I started there, but he held his hand up to interrupt me.

'No, tell me about your qualifications. What your talents are. What you want out of that side of life.'

Surprised, I opened my mouth, automatically about to recite the five-year plan that I'd always aimed for career-wise, then I stopped. I didn't need to pretend anymore.

'I'm a qualified accountant, but the more I think about it, the more I want to combine working with words as well as numbers,' I admitted. 'Since I've been here, I've found such pleasure in writing about my experiences, and the amazing people I've met. I don't know if I could make a success of it, but I'd like to try. I'm doing shifts at the Helios Hotel for now, but perhaps longer term I could develop other work, maybe helping businesses write English versions of their websites and information leaflets, doing blog posts for them, that kind of thing.'

I was rather surprised that I was confessing to a complete stranger the plans that I'd been secretly contemplating, but there was something about Andreas Rouvas's shrewd expression which invited confidences.

'It would take a lot of drive to build up a business like that. But it is very possible.'

He gave me another assessing look, then nodded, as if he'd made up his mind about something. Then to my complete astonishment, he fished a very plush-looking business card out of his shirt pocket.

'Give me a call. I may be able to introduce you to a few people,' he said.

Then he stubbed out his cigarette, lit another one and settled back down to watching the guests milling around.

Eleni looked very pleased with herself as she led me away.

'Did you know that he would do that?' I couldn't help asking. It felt like I'd passed some kind of test I didn't know I'd been sitting.

She smiled. 'Andreas Rouvas has, how do you say it, a lot of fingers in a lot of pies. Now you are friends, you will soon find yourself in a position where you have to turn away work, trust me, I know this well. Now if you will excuse me, I had better return to preparing the food.'

She hurried off, leaving me feeling rather startled by the whole exchange. I looked down at the card with its gold swirly writing. There was a line of Greek script which I would have to look up when I got back home, but then beneath that there was a list in English of at least a dozen hotels and businesses based all around Kefalonia and the neighbouring island of Ithaca. And at the very top, just below Andreas Rouvas's name it said, 'Owner and proprietor'. If I wasn't very much mistaken, I'd just been introduced to one of the Ionian islands' most successful – and senior – businessmen, and he'd offered to help me achieve my embryonic ambitions. This evening was turning out to be truly special, in more ways than one.

Chapter Twenty-Four

Alexis was called into service helping Stephano set up an outdoor oven on the corner of the roof. Soon the delicious smell of roasting meat and sizzling vegetables had my mouth watering. Eleni bustled around, picking fresh herbs from the pots by the oven and squeezing lemon juice from her own small lemon tree. She didn't measure any ingredients but seemed to know instinctively exactly how much she needed to add in.

The guests started a human chain to bring all the crockery and cutlery to the roof, and then after an unspoken signal, they all surged forward to help themselves to the food.

Eleni clapped her hands. 'Lydia first,' she decreed. The crowd parted to let me through. I would normally have been embarrassed about being singled out for such attention, but the gesture was done with such warmth that I felt touched by her kindness. Eleni piled my plate high with enough food to keep me going for several weeks. She watched as I took my first bite.

'Delicious,' I said, relishing the fresh flavours of the food. 'I think this is one of the best meals I have ever tasted.' It was certainly up there with the picnic we'd had on Mount Ainos, but perhaps it was the company for both meals which helped to give them that extra edge for me.

Eleni beamed, then turned to Alexis. 'All food in Greece should taste like this. Why have you not been taking her to proper places to eat, Alexis?' She told him off. 'You need to sort that out. I am sorry Lydia. Alexis is clearly not looking after you properly.'

Alexis held up his arms in mock surrender as Eleni playfully slapped his chest on her way past to put some more souvlaki on the barbeque to roast.

'I can only apologise, Lydia *mou*. I promise to try harder from now on,' he said earnestly.

'You don't need to try at all with me. I like you just the way you are,' I said quietly.

'I am very lucky. And I feel the same way about you. But there is something…' He hesitated, concern clouding his features.

I felt a pang of nerves, worried about what he might be about to say. I didn't want anything to spoil this wonderful evening. I reached up and kissed him on the cheek.

'Whatever it is can wait. Eleni has given us strict instructions to enjoy ourselves, and so enjoy ourselves we shall.'

Alexis looked like he wanted to speak more, but Stephano swung by to inspect our plates.

'Do you have enough to eat? Eleni will never forgive herself if our honoured guests are hungry.'

'I shall be the size of a house if I eat all this,' I protested, as he added an extra scoop of *tzatziki* onto my plate.

'You need to keep your energy up,' said Alexis, the sparkle back in his eyes. 'After the eating, there will be dancing. Do you remember how I warned you?'

As the sky fell darker, the drinks flowed and the hubbub of chatter grew louder. I turned hoarse from having to shout to make myself heard. People kept on pressing glasses of chilled *retsina* into my hand and adding extra delicacies to my plate. I'd long since accepted that my vow of temperance was not going to be possible at this party, but I was trying my best to go steady, still traumatised by the horrible hangover I'd experienced post-tattoo night.

Just when I thought the party couldn't get any livelier, Stephano emerged from the apartment holding a musical instrument with a long neck and bulbous body.

'And now the party really starts,' said Alexis, clapping his hands in joy. 'Stephano is going to play his *bouzouki* for us.'

The first two notes sent a shiver through my body. The tune started slowly, then gradually accelerated until Stephano's fingers were dancing hypnotically over the strings at lightning speed.

'What do you think?' asked Alexis.

I struggled for the right words to express how wonderful I was finding the evening.

'It's so very Greek.' I laughed.

Alexis joined in, delighting in my enjoyment of proceedings.

'This is how life should be,' he said. 'And now, we dance. Come on.'

He took my hand and led me to the line which had already started to form.

'I've no idea what to do. I've got two left feet at the best of times,' I protested.

'Follow my lead. It is very simple. It is not about looking good. It is about feeling the music and letting the rhythm guide you,' he said. He looked so alive and happy that I couldn't resist following his lead.

He stretched his long arms and gestured for me to do the same. His left hand rested on my right shoulder. I reached up to rest my right arm on his left shoulder and then we joined the long line of people all facing Stephano.

Stephano played a chord, and started a slow tune. We took a step to one side and then the other. Just when I had got used to that little sequence we stepped forward. Everyone around me tapped their right foot behind their left and then stepped forward again, raising their knees. I stumbled slightly, but Alexis held me up, softly squeezing my shoulder to make sure that I was alright. All of a sudden, everyone lunged down and back up again, and the whole sequence was repeated. The men at either end of the line clicked their free hands in time to the music. Slowly I became accustomed to the pattern and relaxed into the rhythm, just as Alexis said I would.

Then Stephano's fingers started flying across the frets and the movement of the line grew more chaotic as we skipped forwards and backwards.

The music reached its climax and everyone broke apart. Alexis seized my hands and spun me, both of us laughing like children. We whirled round and then came to a gasping stop, still holding onto each other. Caught up in the moment, I found myself reaching up to touch the side of his face. He leaned down towards me, then our lips were only a breath apart. I could smell the subtle scent of his aftershave on his neck, warm and spicy. It sparked a memory of something, but before I could retrieve it, I was distracted by Alexis gently pulling me even closer, his hand resting on the small of my back. I smiled as I imagined his fingers tracing the words of my tattoo. His lips curved against mine, and I closed my eyes, savouring the magical moment of our first kiss.

And then I heard someone shout. In a daze, we broke apart. The music had stopped, and there was a crowd gathered around Eleni. Although I couldn't understand what people were saying, I thought I could guess what had caused the commotion.

'She's not...' I started.

Alexis turned to me with a broad smile on his face.

'She is. Eleni is having the baby.'

I couldn't think of a more joyous reason for our first kiss to be interrupted, although I wondered if Alexis was also secretly wishing the baby could have held on for thirty seconds longer before making his presence felt.

How we got Eleni down from the roof garden and into Stephano's car, I do not know, but somehow, the chaotic crowd of slightly drunk guests managed to pull together to make it happen. Stephano fortunately had stayed away from the booze in solidarity with his wife, so he was able to drive them safely to the hospital, as everyone cheered them off in the street. It would certainly be a party which would go down in Sami folklore.

'What an amazing evening,' I said to Alexis as we walked back to the Helios Hotel. My whole body was fizzing with excitement, both from the drama with Eleni, and with anticipation at what was about to happen between us.

Our fingers were entwined as we walked and every so often, he stroked his thumb across the palm of my hand, sending delightful shivers through my skin. When we reached the back streets, I took advantage of the lack of passers-by to pull Alexis into the shadow of a tree, pressing him up against its trunk while I whispered a husky invitation in his ear to continue the kiss we'd begun on Eleni's rooftop. He responded with a trail of them, starting on my collarbone and moving slowly up my neck with tender torture until his lips were tantalisingly close to mine. Then the jarring bray of a donkey made us jump, interrupting our cocoon of intimacy and bringing us crashing back to awareness of our surroundings.

'Our friend would like us to move on,' said Alexis, as we both laughed.

He looped his arm around my waist, his hand resting on my hip, as we walked the last stretch back to the Helios Hotel, and made our way through the quiet gardens. In the meadow beyond the swimming pool, fireflies were darting around busily, sending sparks of light through the darkness. We paused on the dimly lit terrace.

'You are home safely,' said Alexis.

'Would you like to come up?' I asked, nerves and anticipation and happiness whizzing around my veins in a heady mix. I wanted nothing more than for him to agree, and I was confident that he would. Once again, I wondered how it had taken me so long to realise what was right in front of me. Without giving him a chance to answer, I reached up and kissed him, relishing the feel of his mouth on mine.

'Please say yes,' I breathed against his lips. I could feel his heart thudding against my chest.

'Yes.' The word was husky and faint, but it was there. But before my soul could sing, suddenly, he took a step back and ran his hand through his hair, his face clouded with confusion. 'I mean, no. I shouldn't. I can't.'

'Alexis, what's the matter?' I said, taking a step forward, trying to close the distance between us again. But that gulf remained, even though we were physically close.

'There's something you need to know,' he said, the words stilted and uncertain. 'And when you find out, you won't want this at all.'

He gestured between us.

'Alexis, that's—'

But before I could finish my sentence, he took the words right out of my mouth with what he said next.

'I know who Awesome Andreas is. I've always known.'

Chapter Twenty-Five

I t felt as if the world had shifted, throwing everything I thought I'd known up in the air.

'What do you mean, you know who Awesome Andreas is?'

It was a daft question to ask, because there had been no room for ambiguity in what Alexis had said, but I still couldn't process the meaning behind his shocking statement.

'I think I know who Awesome Andreas is.'

He'd stepped back from the ledge slightly with those words.

'You *think*, or you *know*?' I pressed.

He took his glasses off, as if he couldn't bear looking at me in proper focus. 'I know,' he admitted reluctantly.

'So, you mean to say you've watched me run around chasing random guys purely because they're called Andreas, you've watched me go through the emotional turbulence of putting myself out there and getting hurt, yet you've known all along who I should have been approaching?' I fought to keep my voice steady, but the sense of betrayal was sending a physical ache throughout my body. Suddenly I felt very tired.

'It sounds worse when you put it like that,' he said, a tremor in his voice. 'I know it was wrong of me. I've always known it was wrong.'

He started cleaning his glasses on his shirt.

'On no you don't. Put them back on. You don't get to buy yourself time to think while you hide behind polishing your glasses. Speak to me. Why didn't you tell me? You know how important honesty is to me. I made that very clear when I came running to you after the incident with Already-married Andreas. And you know how much I've invested in my Andreas search, how much it mattered to me.'

I still wasn't shouting, but I think he found my quiet persistence even more unnerving. I looked at the man in front of me and for a short, terrifying moment, it was like a stranger was standing there. How could things go from so perfect to this painful shock?

'It's not a good enough excuse, but it's because I fell for you when we *first* met and…'

But I didn't get a chance to hear the rest of his explanation or query his strange emphasis on the word 'first' because somebody was saying my name. And it was the last person whose voice I would expect to hear in Greece.

'Lydia.'

I turned around and felt my body turn heavy with dread as my eyes confirmed what my ears had already told me.

'Jim. What on earth are you doing here?' Now there was a note of slight hysteria in my voice. There was only so much drama I could cope with in one evening.

'I've come to bring you home,' he said simply, as if it was the most obvious thing in the world. It sounded like I'd just popped out to the shops, and he'd decided to give me a lift back because it had begun raining.

'What on earth do you mean? It's the middle of the night for goodness' sake. How did you even know where to find me?'

Jim looked rather pleased with himself. 'I went to the hotel where you stayed with the girls, but they said you weren't there, so I showed your picture to a few people around town and they pointed me in this direction. I've been here for hours, waiting for you.' Then he frowned, his voice taking on the condescending tones I was so horribly familiar with. 'It is very late, Liddy-Lou. Where have you been? Anything could happen when you're out after dark.'

I started laughing in overwhelmed reaction to everything that was happening. Better that than opening my mouth and screaming until I had no voice left, which was what I really felt like doing. This evening had had more ups and downs than a rollercoaster, and I had had enough. Jim waltzing in and trying to pretend that I was here on some kind of minibreak and that he still had the right to question me about my comings and goings was the final straw. I threw my hands up in the air.

'This is too much.'

So many thoughts were spinning around my head that I couldn't properly process what was going on and how I should be reacting.

Alexis stepped back into my line of sight, although to give him credit, he did at least keep a respectful distance away from me, giving me the space I so desperately needed.

'Lydia, I know this is a lot to ask, and I don't deserve a second of your time after what I have done, but please let me explain,' said Alexis. Despite everything, the break in his voice sent a shard of pain through me, and I had to fight the urge to reach out and comfort him.

'Is this man bothering you?' asked Jim, standing up straighter, inserting himself between us as if he was preparing to square up to Alexis.

I grabbed his shoulder, ready to pull him out of the way if I had to. Despite everything, I was not prepared to stand by and see Alexis get hurt.

'Jim, please will you back off? I don't understand why you're here or what you're hoping to achieve, but this situation is absolutely nothing to do with you, and I would really appreciate it if you stopped interfering. I am perfectly capable of fighting my own battles.'

I looked between the two men, Alexis defeated and sad, Jim still posturing with his innate sense of self-righteousness, and I knew I had to get away. I needed time to think. I turned my back on both of them and walked into the hotel. I started climbing the stairs to my room, but thoughts of how I'd wanted to end the evening climbing these steps hand in hand with Alexis intruded. I swerved towards the staff room instead, not able to bear the contrast of reality with the ache of what might have been.

I recognised Jim's footsteps starting to follow me, but to give Alexis credit, I heard him quietly telling my ex to wait until the morning.

I curled up on the couch, wrapping my arms around my knees as if by making myself as small as possible, I'd be able to squeeze all the hurt and pain away. Even though it was a warm night, I found myself shivering. Dealing with Alexis's revelation would have been enough of a bombshell by itself, but having Jim on the scene made things so much more complicated. I knew that I wouldn't be able to concentrate on the situation with Alexis until I'd dealt with Jim, and I'm ashamed to admit that I was scared about how I was going to go about that. Logically, I knew that he could only have a hold over me if I allowed it to happen, but I felt so vulnerable right now that I was afraid that Jim would turn on his forceful charm and manipulate me into doing something I would regret – like taking the coward's option of walking away from the island and putting this whole interlude behind me.

I thought I'd never be able to rest again given the turmoil of thoughts doing battle in my head, but somehow, eventually, I drifted off into a dreamless sleep. I woke several hours later as shards of light from the dawn came through the open windows of the staff room. My neck was stiff, but I suspected the ache in my body was as much from the emotional strain as the physical discomfort of having spent the night on the ancient sofa. I stretched as best I could, then tiptoed to the door and checked the corridor. I wouldn't put it past Jim to be out there waiting for me. At the moment, I didn't feel ready to face anybody, let alone him.

Thankfully the corridor was deserted. I padded quietly to my room and shut the door behind me with a sigh of relief. I stripped off the dress I'd put on with such hope last night and dived in the shower, finally letting the tears flow freely as the lukewarm water pummelled my back. I felt like such a fool. I thought of all the times I'd confided in Alexis, all the opportunities he'd had to tell me the truth about Awesome Andreas, and yet he had remained silent. I couldn't understand it. He'd always seemed like an open book. How could I have misjudged him so badly?

As the water grew even more punishingly cold, I steered my thoughts away from Alexis and reluctantly focused on the Jim situation. I had believed myself free from him, but now he'd intruded on my safe haven, I was left with little choice but to confront him and make it absolutely clear where we stood. If this had happened before Alexis's revelation, I would have gone straight to his bookshop, seeking his support and advice on how to handle the situation – so much for trying not to think about him – but now I was unable to do that. As my skin turned almost translucent with cold, I came to a decision. I would ring Amira, and see what she had to say. She was always good in a crisis, and unlike Kat, she was more likely to focus on the practical side of what to do. In a situation like this, it was important to have a friend by my side, if only through the power of technology rather than in person.

I stumbled out of the shower and tried to get my circulation going again properly by rubbing my limbs vigorously with the towel, but I feared the reason I felt cold wasn't really to do with the temperature of my surroundings. I quickly pulled on some shorts and a T-shirt, thanking my lucky stars that today was my rostered day off from hotel duties, and then dialled Amira's number, hoping that she was already up and about.

'Kalimera, my friend,' she answered cheerily, thankfully sounding very much awake. 'You've caught me heading home from work with a dirty takeaway burger on the passenger seat. I was just thinking about you. My colleagues on the night shift are dying for an update on your love life. Speculating about your adventures kept us going through a particularly torturous few hours in A&E last night, and I need more tales from you so I have a reason to carry on talking to the cute new registrar.'

'I'm sure you can talk to him anyway without having to use me as an excuse,' I said half-heartedly.

'Where would be the fun in that?'

I attempted to laugh, but it came out more as a pathetic gurgle.

'Hold on, I'm pulling over,' said Amira. 'This sounds like a conversation which requires my full attention.'

I heard the sound of the indicator, and then the engine

stopped. Amira's voice returned, and this time it was less echoey, as if she'd taken me off hands-free and was now clutching the phone to her ear.

'Babe, I'm here. Tell me.'

The kindness in her voice was almost unbearable, and I wished desperately that I was in the car with her, the comforting smell of greasy fast food hanging between us, instead of sitting here alone in my austere staff bedroom, so far from everything familiar.

Although I'd promised myself that I wouldn't say anything about Alexis and only tell her about Jim, I found myself pouring it all out, from the joy of us getting together, to the hurt of his confession, and the sense of betrayal and heart-breaking loss which remained.

'And now Jim's turned up too,' I finished, with a sob.

'Stuff doesn't happen by halves to you, does it? Oh, Lyds, I wish I could give you a hug. I'm on back-to-back nights and we're already down on staff, otherwise I'd be hopping on that plane to get out to you right now. Do you want me to send Kat over? She's got a gig next week, but I think she's resting until then, or working on material, whatever it is creative types claim they're doing when they're not in front of a crowd.'

'It's OK, just speaking to you is making me feel a bit better.'

Much as I missed my friends, this was my mess to sort out. I lay back on my bed and stared up at the shadows on the ceiling. From this angle they looked like people looming over me, the shades of those who'd hurt me bearing down with malicious intent. I turned onto my side and fixed my gaze on the blank wall instead, my phone tucked between the pillow and my ear.

'Why do you think Jim's here?' I asked. I couldn't stop thinking about the look on his face when he'd stepped towards me. Had it been one of lonely longing, or was it something more sinister?

'Well, if he's trying to present it as some big romantic gesture, then we both know that's nonsense, right?' said Amira, her voice full of kindness. 'It sounds like another classic power play to me, straight out of the coercive control textbook.'

'I hate that he can still provoke a reaction in me,' I admitted shakily.

'It's not a sign of weakness in you, I promise, Lyds. He's manipulative and he knows exactly which buttons to press. But you are better than him. Surely he must realise that he's going to get nowhere with this dramatic gesture. Tell me you're somewhere safe at the moment?'

'I'm doing a classic Lydia and hiding in my room, hoping my problems will go away. I could really do without all this. I want Jim to leave, but I'm scared he'll hang around getting in the way and making things worse. I'm feeling a little fragile right now.'

'Understandably so,' said Amira. 'But you're not going to let that influence your behaviour, are you, babe?'

I closed my eyes and once again replayed the scene on the hotel veranda with Alexis's revelation and Jim's sudden appearance. What would I have done if Jim hadn't shown up? Would I have given Alexis the chance to explain, or would it all have been over between us before it had even really started?

'I think I need to talk to him.'

'Alexis, or Jim?'

'Well, both really. But perhaps Jim first. Get it over with.'

'You won't…' Amira hesitated.

'Won't what?'

'You won't let him persuade you to come back to Yorkshire? I know you're stronger than that, but I also know how convincing he can be when he puts his mind to it. Don't get me wrong, we'd love to see you, but you being in Greece seems so right somehow. This conversation aside, you've been happier and more alive in the last few weeks than you have been in years.'

I sighed. 'You make it sound so simple. But how realistic is it to stay here, and what would I achieve by doing so? I have no proper home, my language skills are minimal…'

My voice trailed off. Perhaps I was catastrophising, or perhaps I was finally coming to my senses. Could I really bear staying here with things as they were with Alexis?

'But nothing has really changed,' insisted Amira. 'These things were issues before you returned to Kefalonia, but you still went ahead and did it anyway, because you're a brave person. Because you believe in yourself. I can't tell you how proud I am of you.'

While I was touched by my friend's kindness, it felt like she was describing somebody else. What if what she saw as bravery and confidence was really just a wild overreaction to an emotional situation? I thought I knew what I was doing, but everything that had happened since I got to Kefalonia could be taken as evidence that my judgement was way off. The situation with Alexis could even be interpreted as the ultimate proof of that.

I wrapped my arms around me, my hand on top of the fateful tattoo. Now it had healed, I could no longer feel the difference in my skin, but I still knew exactly where it was. I had met an Andreas after all that night. But since then, I'd fallen hard for an Alexis instead, and look where that had got me. I'd run away from England to avoid a messy situation, and here I was in an even messier one.

'Are you still there, Lyds?'

'Yep.'

'What are you going to do?'

I sighed. 'That is a very difficult question. And I'm not sure I know what the answer is yet.'

Chapter Twenty-Six

I stayed in my room for a good few hours, examining my thoughts, creating a mental spreadsheet of pros and cons, battling with what I should do next. But as I gazed out of the window at the majestic wildness of the mountain, I kept returning to the same answer. It was time to stop running away. Despite all the hurdles, and the complete mess that was my personal life, there was the potential for me to create something here in Kefalonia, to carve out a worthwhile future for myself, regardless of the Alexis situation. Everything I'd been through over the past few weeks proved that I was more than capable of standing on my own two feet and facing whatever challenges were thrown at me. Now I just had to decide to back myself once again, and take control of my destiny.

I padded over to the dress which I'd worn last night and fished Andreas Rouvas's business card out the pocket. The Lydia of old would have been hesitant to follow this lead, shrinking from proactively creating an opportunity for herself out of fear of the unknown or concern about what other people would think. The Lydia of today knew her worth, and was no longer afraid to take a chance. If local business tycoon Andreas Rouvas said he might be able to send work my way, then I was certainly going to take him up on that offer of assistance.

After an illuminating phone call, I went downstairs in search of something to eat, my appetite apparently having not got the memo about the emotional trauma I was going through. I turned onto the final flight of stairs and stopped when I spotted a familiar figure loitering in the reception area.

'Hello, Jim,' I said, not entirely surprised to see him there waiting for me. I made a mental note to speak to Yiota about tightening the hotel's security.

'We need to talk,' he said.

I braced myself for dread to pool in the pit of my stomach, but was pleased to find only a complete sense of indifference instead. I paused one step from the bottom, so that I could be at the same eye level as Jim. And then I looked at him, really looked and double-checked with myself that I was happy with what I'd decided to do. The answer came easily.

'I am happy to talk,' I said. I held up my hand to stop the expression of smug satisfaction which appeared on Jim's face. 'But I will only do so if you promise to listen, really listen, to what I have to say.'

'That's fine. As long as you listen to me too,' he couldn't resist adding as an afterthought.

'Jim, I always listened to you. And I think that was a big part of the problem.'

'You needed my guidance.'

'But that's the thing, I didn't. When I started out as your trainee, of course I looked up to you as my boss and mentor, the person who could help me to develop into a competent, successful accountant. But that inequality continued into our relationship, to the point where you were reluctant to give me a key when we moved in together or let me keep all my stuff, because you hated letting go of any vestige of control.' I could tell from his expression that he still didn't get what I was saying. 'I was always capable of standing on my own two feet. It was you who was keen to create this illusion that I was so dependent on you. You never wanted a partnership of equals, and I would never now settle for anything less than that. It was inevitable it would end badly for us.'

'Like this has ended well for you?' Jim gestured around at the hotel. 'I hear you make a living nowadays scrubbing skid marks off toilets and cleaning up other people's rubbish. Classy.'

I shrugged, unmoved by his attempt to make me feel small.

'It's an honest living, and it makes a positive difference to other people. If you look down on it, then that's your problem,' I said. 'I have the respect of my boss and colleagues, and my mind is my own. It's given me space to

EMILY KERR

think about what I really want to achieve in life. And I am determined that I will pursue those ambitions. The best thing about my life now is that I don't need anyone's permission to live it the way I want to.'

Jim slowly deflated in front of me. The more I stood up to him and asserted myself, the less he seemed to know what to do with himself. Whatever he'd been expecting when he'd flown out to Kefalonia to track me down, it definitely hadn't been this: a confident, assured woman who knew what she wanted, and who was no longer afraid to go after it.

'What about that Alexis chap? I overheard your conversation. You say you prize honesty, but it doesn't sound like he's been very honest with you,' he said, puffing up his chest again.

I waited for the instant stab of pain to subside before I answered him. 'That is a matter for me and Alexis, and quite frankly, it is none of your business. Goodbye, Jim. I hope you enjoy the rest of your stay, and have a safe journey back home. I wish you the best for the future, but in case you are in any doubt, I will *not* be featuring in it.'

I turned my back on him, and strode purposefully towards the cloakroom before he could see my carefully constructed armour melting away. My heart was racing, my appetite had disappeared, but I was proud that I'd once again stood up to him. This time, Jim could be in no doubt about my feelings and about my intention to choose my own path in life, a life which would not involve him. Whether he went straight home or not, it didn't matter. I

312

had stood up to him for one final time, and shown him that he could no longer cow me into doing what he wanted.

But that had been the straightforward bit. The next challenge facing me was the Alexis situation, and I didn't have a clue where to start with that. I perched on the closed toilet lid and looked at my phone. According to WhatsApp, Alexis hadn't been online since we'd exchanged messages before our fateful first date last night. So, he couldn't even bear to show his face in the virtual world either? Sounded about right. Then I stopped myself. This was Alexis I was badmouthing. Alexis who had been nothing but kind to me, who set my brain buzzing as well as making my heart sing – but who also seemed to have been nursing a great big secret throughout our acquaintance.

I thought carefully back through our every interaction, examining his behaviour in a new light and remembering what he had said to me. He had never actually out and out lied about not knowing Awesome Andreas, but he had certainly steered clear of revealing the truth. And now that I came to think about it, hadn't there been warning signs that he'd been keeping something from me? The way his Greek conversations had always seemed to last longer than his supposed direct English translations when he introduced me to Maria and Yiota back at the very beginning, his tendency towards clumsiness when our chat steered too close to the identity of Awesome Andreas. Could it in fact be that he wasn't the only one who knew who Awesome Andreas was? Had he enlisted the help of Yiota, Eleni and others to keep his secret?

But, I reminded myself, Alexis was no Jim. He'd never coerced me into doing something against my will, and he'd never pushed to have a relationship with me. Quite the opposite in fact. It was only when I asked him out that he confessed that he had been harbouring tender feelings towards me from when we first met. When we *first* met. I wondered. Could it be that I'd encountered Alexis before my return to Greece? Was he there on that night when I got the tattoo? Maybe that was how he knew who Awesome Andreas was.

I felt my heart start beating faster as Alexis's status changed from 'last seen yesterday' to 'online.' My fingers hovered over the screen, but before I could formulate a message, Alexis got in there first.

I considered writing you an apology and a declaration of love worthy of Captain Wentworth, but I owe you more than that. This is probably too much to ask of you, but would you consider meeting me so I can explain and apologise in person?

He remembered that *Persuasion* was my favourite Jane Austen book and the character Captain Wentworth my ultimate hero. Not that I should let that influence my decision, but I was touched that he'd recalled a throwaway comment I'd once made. *Persuasion* was a book about second chances. In the past I might have thought I owed Alexis a second chance. Now I knew I didn't owe him anything. My actions were my own, and should be freely undertaken out of choice, not out of any sense of obligation. I stared at the message on the screen and considered my options. To reply, or not? To give him that chance or not? Actually, it was an easy decision. I was going to give him the opportunity to explain things to me, not because I had to, but because I wanted to. What would happen after that, I had no idea, but I needed to understand.

I started tapping out a quick message, telling him to meet me at Maria's taverna. And then I changed my mind and said I'd go to his bookshop. It felt right that we have the conversation in the place where this had all started.

I unlocked the cloakroom door and emerged to find Yiota hovering outside, waving a feather duster around in an unconvincing way.

'*Kalimera*, Yiota.'

'Is it a good morning, though?' she replied. She pretended to examine a picture frame for cobwebs, then let out a sigh. 'Look, it is none of my business, and I told myself when my idiot brother first asked me to give you a job that I should not get involved, but involved I am, so I will say something. When Angelo and I arrived back from Argostoli last night, we saw Alexis walking down the street and he told me he had finally confessed to you.' She made a tutting noise. 'I will not tell you how he was, because it would not be right to put pressure on you that way, and if I am honest, he has brought this situation on himself. I knew from the very first moment that this would be the outcome.' She reached out and clasped my arm, fixing me in her perceptive gaze. 'But I will say this. At the end of the day,

Alexis is a good man. He made a foolish decision, and then he got deeper into trouble than he realised he could get, and in the course of doing so, he has caused you and himself great pain. I will respect whatever you decide, but I love my brother, and he loves you, so I hope that you will be able to work things out between you. I will say no more.'

'So, you did know from the very beginning,' I said, feeling even more foolish. She didn't deny it, but mimed zipping her lips and after a brief moment of hesitation, strode off to carry on pretending that she was preoccupied entirely by cleaning. At least I knew now that her initial reluctance to employ me hadn't been a personal thing, but was instead more to do with her frustration at the position Alexis was putting her in. I knew I'd proved my worth since then.

I took my time walking down the back street to town. Even though every step reminded me of the passion-fuelled slow progress we'd made along here in the opposite direction last night, I still preferred the quiet, needing the peace to examine my thoughts further. Until I heard Alexis out, I couldn't decide what I wanted for our future, whether we would even remain as friends, let alone become lovers. But I could determine what the rest of my future held. As I leaned on the gate waiting for my donkey friend to shamble over to me, the sun sparkling and the breeze softly tickling my skin, I was even more determined that whatever happened, I wasn't ready to say goodbye to all of this. My conversation this morning with Andreas Rouvas had confirmed that there were good opportunities for me here, that with hard work and determination, I could make something of myself. And that's what I was going to do, regardless of the outcome of my conversation with Alexis.

'Besides, you'd miss me, wouldn't you, you disruptive beast?' I addressed the donkey. 'Probably best that you interrupted us when you did last night. A lot has happened since then.' He blinked. 'Yes, you're right. I should stop putting off the dreaded moment. I'm going. Wish me luck.'

The donkey hee-hawed in response which I chose to interpret as an expression of goodwill, rather than disappointment that the treats he'd been hoping for hadn't transpired. Then I picked up my pace and made my way to Alexis's bookshop.

Chapter Twenty-Seven

When I arrived in the street, I instantly realised there was something different about it. Whereas before the window of the tattoo studio had been permanently shaded and dark, now a light was shining inside. The artist was back in residence. For a second, the skin on my back itched, as if memories of the night I'd got the tattoo were finally stirring. I hesitated, wondering whether I should go and speak to the tattooist about that evening, and find out about Awesome Andreas that way. I quickly dismissed the idea. It wouldn't give me the full picture, and there were many questions that the artist wouldn't be able to answer. I needed to hear from Alexis himself.

There was a 'Closed' sign on the bookshop door, but I paid no attention to it and went in anyway, the bell jangling in a far too cheery manner for my current state of nerves. For the first time, I crossed the threshold and didn't feel immediately at ease, which was probably something to do with the nervous energy coming from the man standing in the doorway to the back room. Alexis didn't look much better than I felt. There were dark circles under his eyes, and the buttons of his shirt were done up in the wrong order so one side was longer than the other. I'd never seen him looking less than perfectly turned out and I had to fight to ignore the tenderness it provoked in me. If he'd had a bad night's sleep, it was because he had brought it upon himself.

He made as if to rush towards me, then stopped himself, holding onto the counter as if in need of its support.

'Lydia, thank you for coming,' he said quietly. 'It is far more than I deserve.'

I tipped my head, acknowledging the truth in his statement. Now that I was here, I found myself uncertain what to say. I had so many questions that I didn't know where to start with them. And so, I stayed quiet and waited, ignoring Alexis's gesture for me to sit in one of the squishy armchairs. Nothing was going to make this situation more comfortable. I had done my bit in returning to the bookshop and giving him the opportunity to speak. It was time for him to explain himself.

Alexis quickly looked me over, as if checking that I hadn't come to any physical harm from Jim, then nodded, seemingly unsurprised by my silence. Without further prompting he launched into his confession.

'I have spent all night trying to think about how to say this to you, where I would start were you to be kind enough to grant me the opportunity to talk to you again. But now you are here, it is clear to me. And I promise my complete honesty to you, whatever it might cause the outcome to be.'

I folded my arms, waiting for him to continue. If he was looking for reassurance from me, he hadn't earned it yet. It was easy to promise future honesty, but much harder to make up for a lack of it in the past.

Alexis nodded as if he could read the thoughts going through my mind. 'The explanation you are looking for is as follows. When you stepped in here two and a half weeks ago, fresh off the plane from England, and asked for my help in finding somewhere to stay, that was not the first time we had met. We also met when you were here before then on holiday. The night you got the Awesome Andreas tattoo.'

I closed my eyes and attempted for the millionth time to remember that evening, but try as I might, I still couldn't picture when and where Alexis and I had encountered each other. Had he been just another face in the crowded bar, a stranger who bumped into me on the dancefloor? I took a deep breath, frustrated that the memories were still elusive. But then a faint recollection of something stirred.

'Your aftershave. That slight spicy scent, I remember it now. You must have been wearing it that night. And you had it on yesterday evening when we went to Eleni and Stephano's apartment. I knew it smelled familiar; I just couldn't place it.'

He nodded. 'Yes, I was, that's right.' He paused, waiting to see if anything else came back to me.

'And was it here that we met?' I asked hesitantly. When

I'd first returned to Sami and settled into the Helios Hotel, I'd tried to remember the fateful night again, but all I could picture was the bookshop. I'd assumed at the time it was because I'd just been there, but maybe that had actually been a memory from my original visit, although how I'd ended up in a bookshop after leaving my friends on the dancefloor to return to the hotel, I didn't know.

'Actually, it was in the lobby of your hotel. I'd stopped by there to say hello to a friend as I'd been away for a while. You walked in through the front door and it sounds like a cliché, but you lit up the room with your smile. You came over to the reception desk where my friend was working, and we got talking because you recognised the cover of a book I was holding and asked me if I knew of any others like it. My friend soon left us to it. I'm ashamed to admit that I didn't know you were drunk – we had such an interesting conversation.'

'My friends tell me that Drunk Me still manages to act remarkably sober,' I said. 'The curse of normally being the sensible one of the friendship group. But having done the liquid maths with Kat and Amira, you're right, I really hadn't drunk all that much that night. I think it just had a greater effect on me because I rarely drank. Jim was always against the idea.'

A shadow crossed Alexis's face at the mention of my ex. Once more, his eyes darted over me, as he reassured himself that I was unharmed after my earlier encounter with Jim. I nearly told him that I'd sent Jim packing once and for all, but quickly crushed the impulse. He hadn't yet given me a reason why I should ever trust him with that kind of personal information again. While I was glad that he was finally filling in the blanks of that night, my frustration and anger were growing that he'd not done it before.

'We talked non-stop, then you persuaded me to let you have a look at the bookshop, even though it was long past closing time. I was so happy to meet someone who shared my passion, who understood me. I was proud to show it to you, and your delight when you saw it got me here.' He patted his chest.

My arms remained stubbornly folded.

Alexis continued his explanation. 'When you returned to Kefalonia, you told me that you were searching for your soulmate who you believed you had met on that night. It sounds absurd, but it felt that way to me too. During that first conversation, we didn't even get close enough to touch, yet I had never connected with another person as I connected with you. When I saw you, it was like I recognised you, like I knew you already, and had been waiting for you to arrive.'

I forced myself to stay quiet, even as he articulated the very thoughts that I'd had about that evening. Although my memories of it were so limited, hadn't I too recalled that strong sense of contentment and utter joy, that feeling of rightness? But it didn't change the current situation.

'Then, when we were in the shop, I went into the back room to look for a volume we had been talking about, and when I came out, you had disappeared. I walked up and down the street looking for you, but it was like you had never been there, like you were a phantom I had created in my imagination. I feared I would never see you again. I knew you were a tourist and you had told me it was your final night on the island. I didn't know how to find you again, we hadn't even exchanged names. The only hope I could cling onto was that you knew where my bookshop was, but it was too much to dream that you would visit Sami again. And then, when you returned here a few days later, I was so surprised and overjoyed. Until you told me about your tattoo, and straight away I knew what must have happened, who you must have met after you left my bookshop.'

Alexis picked up a photo frame from underneath the counter and stared at the picture. Then with great effort he turned it around and passed it to me.

'Awesome Andreas is the one on the left,' he said simply.

I found myself staring at a picture of two very familiar-looking men. They had their arms around each other's shoulders, and were mirror images of each other, except one was wearing glasses and one wasn't.

'I don't understand,' I said stupidly, although the explanation was plain to see, right there in front of me.

'Awesome Andreas is my twin brother. He's the one you've been looking for all this time.'

Chapter Twenty-Eight

'You think after sharing what you've described as a magical time with you, I then went on to meet your twin brother Andreas and found him even more to my liking?' I said. 'Just how much adventure do you think I got up to in one night? If you don't mind me saying, it seems rather far-fetched to me.'

Although I had no way of knowing that what Alexis said wasn't true, I instinctively felt that scenario must be wrong.

Alexis refused to be swayed. 'Andreas works on boats normally, but he was in town that night because he had been looking after my shop while I was away. My brother is everything I am not: outgoing, charismatic, sporty. I am not surprised you fell for him. He is a good man. Even when we were at school together, he always had a lot more attention. When he is around, nobody notices me. That is not me complaining,' he added hastily, 'it is just the way it is. I am normally ok with that.'

Frustration joined my growing sense of incredulity. 'Well, obviously I did notice you on that night, Alexis. Just because I'm attracted to you, it doesn't mean I'd be attracted to your brother too. I'm sure he's a perfectly decent guy, but I couldn't care less how sporty and outgoing he is. I fell for you over these past few weeks because of your kindness, your intelligence, your quiet thoughtfulness. Do you honestly believe that when we first met we had this amazing once-in-a-lifetime type connection, then I walked out of the bookshop, bumped into your brother and immediately fell so head over heels for him instead that I had his name tattooed on my back? The idea is utterly absurd.'

He shrugged sadly. 'Why is that any less absurd than you falling instantly for me? And the fact of the matter is that it is *his* name that you have tattooed on your back, not mine. You always said it must have taken something extraordinary for you to have got a tattoo, however drunk you were. Andreas is that extraordinary person. The awesome man who inspired you to do something so out of character. I realised what must have happened the moment you told me about the tattoo.' He paused, struggling to find the right words to continue his confession. 'I should have said something right then, as soon as you'd returned and told me of your quest, but I was a coward and I was selfish. I felt such happiness when I saw you again, and then that happiness was crushed by your story and by the fact that you didn't seem to recognise me. I foolishly decided I would keep quiet, hoping that by spending time with you, you would fall for me again, or at least start to remember what had really happened. It was very wrong of me. I have not been fully honest with you, and I will never be able to forgive myself for ruining what might have been.'

'And you enlisted Yiota into your deception?' I needed to know the full facts. I noticed him flinch when I used the word 'deception'.

Alexis removed his glasses and rubbed his eyes. 'Yes. I am even more ashamed about that. I took advantage of the fact that you did not speak Greek to explain the full situation to Yiota and Maria right in front of you. They both told me I was a fool, that it was the wrong thing to do, and that I should be honest. And I knew that myself. But from the second you walked into the bookshop and I didn't tell you what I knew right away, it then felt too late to turn back from that path, and before I knew it, I was getting myself into more and more trouble. The longer I left it, the more impossible it seemed to be able to tell you the truth. I told myself that I was only buying some time, so you might remember on your own terms what we had, but it was wrong of me, very wrong. When you asked me out, I knew that I had to confess. I tried, but the moment was never right. I should have tried harder. I will never forgive myself for the stupid choices I have made. I can offer no excuse for my behaviour. It was not what you deserved from me.'

He sat down behind the counter and put his head in his hands briefly, exhausted by his outpouring. His entire body language spoke of the shame he felt and his disappointment in himself. Then he looked up again, and sent me another apology-filled glance before writing something down on a piece of paper.

'Here, this is my brother Andreas's phone number. I should have given it to you long ago. You can finally speak to your Awesome Andreas again.'

He pushed it into my hands. I stared at the number until it went blurry, my mind churning with confusion. I closed my fingers over it, and put it in my pocket. Suddenly I needed to be outside in the fresh air. The bookshop was stuffy with emotion and I couldn't work out what to do next.

'I need to think.'

To give him credit, Alexis didn't say a word to try to stop me, but quietly stood to one side and watched me leave with a look of utter resignation on his face.

I walked down the street in a daze, my trainers scuffing through the dust. It felt strange that life was carrying on as normal out here when I had been having such a momentous conversation. I blocked out the happy chatter of holidaymakers as I tried to interrogate my feelings. I thought back to Jim's deception and how hurtful that had been, and how manipulated and abused I'd felt because of it. Even now, I felt sick thinking about it. But how did I feel thinking about what Alexis had done? Hurt? Yes. Disappointed? Certainly. But was it a fatal blow? Were Alexis and I over before we'd ever really started?

Jim's deception had taken place over the course of years,

and had been a calculated choice from the start, motivated by the desire to control. Keeping me on low pay had been another way of keeping me on a tight leash, just like withholding the key to his house for as long as possible had been, and he'd made the most of the position of power it had put him in. The only reason he had confessed to what he had done had been because I had confronted him about it, and he had had no choice. Even then, he had showed little to no remorse, and seemingly didn't understand why I was so upset about it. He had continued to harass me, even going so far as to turn up in the place I had escaped to.

This situation with Alexis was painful too, but if I really examined it, I realised that the deception he had got embroiled in felt like it was of a very different nature. What Alexis had done was wrong, and he shouldn't have done it. He was very aware of that, and I was certainly not going to make excuses for him. But I did acknowledge that it stemmed from a spur-of-the-moment decision to be sparing with the truth. And I could understand how, once he'd made that decision, things had spiralled out of control until he was out of his depth and unable to go back. He'd kept quiet about his Andreas suspicions when I'd first sought his help, and then he'd asked his sister not to mention their brother, and relied on the discretion of his friends to keep the secret. He had hoped that time would allow me to rediscover our connection and fall for him once again, but he had never gone beyond that hope. He hadn't used the situation to his advantage to make a play for me, but instead he'd offered his friendship and support, always being there for me, and giving me the space I needed to come to my own conclusions about what and who I wanted. He'd never forced his opinions on me, and he'd stood by and watched me go off on Andreas dates, offering to look out for my safety, even though it must have caused him great pain. He had only showed his true feelings when I had declared mine first.

I thought back to the rooftop party at Eleni's last night and remembered how he had kept trying to tell me something, but I had hushed him. And when we had returned to the Helios Hotel and I'd kissed him and invited him up to my room, he had refused because he wanted to be honest with me first. He would have confessed everything then and there if Jim hadn't arrived on the scene with his usual bad timing. Alexis was no cruel manipulator like Jim. Ultimately, I knew he was a good man. He'd allowed his heart to rule his head, and now he was paying the price. I had hopped on a plane back to Kefalonia because I had taken a chance. That decision had served me pretty well, all things considered. Perhaps it was time to take another chance, although this one felt like much less of a gamble.

I stopped in the middle of the street, and looked around me, trying to get my bearings. My distracted wanderings had brought me to the Athena Hotel, the very place where Kat, Amira and I had stayed. Feeling nostalgic, I waved at the proprietor who was busy checking in a coachload of guests who'd obviously just arrived off the midday flight. He gave a distracted wave back, clearly not having a clue who I was or why I was waving at him. I looked across the street to the bar the girls and I had been drinking in. This was where it had all begun. Now it was time for me to return to the bookshop to see where my next chapter led me.

I retraced my steps to Alexis's shop, going at a much quicker pace than before, despite the fuggy heat of the day. The closed sign was still up, but this time the door was locked. I tapped on the frame and peered through the window, my breath steaming up the cool glass. There was no reply from within.

'Alexis,' I called through the letterbox.

I heard the sound of hurrying footsteps, then the key quickly turned in the lock.

'You came back,' said Alexis, looking past me into the street as if he expected to see somebody else with me.

I pulled the piece of paper out of my pocket which had his brother Andreas's number on it. I showed it to Alexis so he could be in no doubt what it was, then I ripped it up and stepped past him to put the pieces in the recycling bin next to the till.

Alexis looked shocked. I could tell that he wasn't even allowing himself to hope anymore.

'Alexis, you may have acted foolishly, but I accept there was nothing malicious in what you did. You got in over your head, and then were trapped in an impossible situation of your own making. I know that fundamentally you are a good man, and if we are to remain...' I hesitated, not sure what word to use. '... In contact with each other, then I trust that you will always be honest with me.'

'If you give me the chance to redeem myself, I promise that I will always be completely open and truthful with you,' he said fervently. 'I cannot tell you how very ashamed I am of myself.'

'Enough of the self-flagellation. I forgive you.' They were just three small words, but they were from the heart.

Alexis wiped his eyes. 'Thank you. I do not deserve your forgiveness, but I am honoured that you are giving it to me.'

I went over and hugged him, my heart breaking at how sad he looked. As I held him close, I inhaled the faint trace of his spicy aftershave once again.

I stepped back and fixed him with a stern look.

'My forgiveness is freely given. But you have got to get it out of your head that I fell for Andreas. However convinced you are that this whole meeting your twin scenario happened, I am sure that you're completely wrong. Whatever insecurities have led you to believe that Andreas is the more attractive twin, and that you're second best, you should stop listening to them. In my opinion, it's very much the other way round.' Alexis actually blushed, which I found sweet. 'And I'm absolutely certain that I've never met your brother Andreas in my life. No, wait...' I paused, a memory stirring to the surface. 'I tell a lie. I think I may have seen him from a distance, when I went on the boat trip from Agia Efimia. I was convinced the man across the street was you, and that you hadn't noticed me. It felt strange at the time, because you appeared to look straight at me, and I was jumping up and down waving like a right muppet, but you seemed completely oblivious, as if I was a total stranger. I'd assumed it was because you hadn't got your glasses on, but it must have been your twin that I spotted.'

I saw a spark of hope in Alexis's eyes. 'He is often at Agia Efimia working on the boats. But if he didn't respond to you… We nearly bumped into him at Antisamos beach as well. That was why I was so rude and hurried you away, even though we were having such a good time. I knew I should have stayed to let you see each other, but I lost my nerve, fearful that you would hate me for not having told you straight away.'

'Well, if Andreas didn't recognise me in the street in Agia Efimia, then it would suggest that he didn't have a clue who I was. But I know one way in which we can settle this.'

'We can call Andreas,' said Alexis. I could hear the reluctance in his voice and I knew he was still convinced that when his brother walked into the room I would go running to him. But I didn't have time to delve into the long-seated family dynamics which were clearly at play here. I had already decided there was a much simpler method to get the answer we needed.

'I don't think we need to involve Andreas in this. Come on, let's go and visit my old friend the tattoo artist. I've got a bone to pick with him about why he tattooed me when I was drunk. And more to the point, he should be able to answer the important question of why I asked him to tattoo the words "Awesome Andreas" on my back.'

Chapter Twenty-Nine

The smell of antiseptic hit my nostrils as soon as we stepped over the threshold. The interior of the studio felt familiar, with its walls covered in artwork, and I was pretty sure I knew which of the two black couches I'd lain down on to get the tattoo, even though the exact memories of the occasion didn't come flooding back. If I closed my eyes, I thought I could remember hearing the buzz of the needle, and the scratching sensation of it running over my skin.

'*Iassou*,' said the guy emerging from behind the black curtain which divided front of house from the rest of the shop. His face lit up as soon as he saw me.

'Ah it's Awesome Andreas girl.'

Then he glanced across at my companion and his expression changed into one of total horror.

'*Malakas*.'

I didn't need to have my Greek dictionary with me to recognise that that was some kind of expletive.

'I cannot believe what I am seeing in front of me. I think I might know what this is about,' the tattoo artist continued. 'I may have made a very terrible mistake.'

I glanced at Alexis. Did he feel the same leap of hope that I did?

The tattoo artist switched into rapid Greek, but Alexis interrupted and asked him to return to English.

'Lydia needs to be able to understand what you're saying, Niko. After all, she is the one with the tattoo.'

But I noticed the tension in his shoulders had eased somewhat. Had something already been said to confirm my suspicions? Niko's speech had been too quick for me to understand.

Niko nodded. 'You have come about your Awesome Andreas tattoo, am I not right?'

'Yes. I was hoping you could explain exactly how I ended up with a tattoo about a man whom I've never met.'

Niko looked mortified as I confirmed his suspicions.

'I am so ashamed. I have a spotless reputation, spotless, but this mistake, this is the worst thing that I have ever done in my whole career.'

He sat down behind the counter and started sketching out a design, clearly needing to keep his hands busy while he explained what had happened.

'It went as follows. It was a quiet night, and I was beginning to think that I should close when you rush in. You are talking fast, you look very happy, very determined.

You tell me that you have just met the love of your life, the awesome man from the bookshop and that you have to get a tattoo to mark it.' He smiled as he remembered the scene. 'You were very sure of yourself. You say it is time that you are brave and make a change for yourself. I mean, of course I try to talk you out of it, even though it was a quiet night and the money would be good. The flash of love like a lightning bolt is very rare. To get a tattoo in honour of someone is a big thing. Even I have not done that.' He indicated the full sleeves of tattoos on his arms, and gestured at the rest of his body so we knew that there were many more beneath his clothes as well. 'It is there for ever, and if you wake up the next day and say, "No, I do not love him after all", then it is a big mistake. But you insist. You tell me all about talking with him in the bookshop, and how it was like you had always known each other. I look out of the window, and I see a man walking down the street from the bookshop. And I know that Alexis is away and that Andreas is looking after the shop for him, so I go fine, you are very, very sure of your decision to have a tattoo to mark this special love, you say Andreas is awesome, so let us tattoo that. I know he is a good man, and I am happy that he has met this woman who is so in love with him.'

He smiled again. I got the impression that beneath the tough guy exterior there lurked another hopeless romantic. Then he frowned. 'But you must remember all this yourself?'

'I was pretty drunk. I actually remember very little of it at all,' I confessed.

Niko's sketching became more rapid. 'Then I am in even more trouble. I am so careful all the time. I do not understand how I could make such a mistake. You did not smell strongly of alcohol. You speak very clearly, you listen to me and hold my expression. I ask if you are sure, and you say yes. I have seen many drunk people and not given them tattoos. With you, I had no idea.'

He looked so disconsolate that I felt sorry for him.

'It's OK. It wasn't your fault, I've accepted that now. Well, doing the tattoo bit anyway. The actual name on the tattoo, we'll discuss in a minute. My friends say Drunk Me is only a slightly more outgoing and daring version of Sober Me, so I can understand why you wouldn't have realised I was rather tipsy. But there is one thing I'm still confused about. Didn't you check with me what the guy's name was or question why I didn't seem to know it?'

Niko put his pencil down. 'I did check,' he insisted. 'When I refer to the bookshop man as Andreas you do not say I am wrong, and when I point out of the window at the man walking down the street away from us, who I am sure is Andreas, and say you are lucky to have met him, the love of your life, you agree.'

He actually stood up and re-enacted the scene to emphasise his point. Did I have a vague recollection of seeing the outline of a tall man striding along the darkened street, or was my memory playing tricks on me?

'Only it was me that you both saw walking down the street,' said Alexis. 'I was searching for Lydia. If I'd been walking in the opposite direction, you'd have recognised it was me, and not Andreas.' He pointed up at his glasses. 'There are other slight differences between us, but this is the most noticeable one that people use to distinguish us by.'

'That makes sense,' I said. 'But I'm surprised I didn't let slip during the appointment that you were the one who'd told me the name Andreas, and that up to that point I'd had no idea what my bookshop guy was called. Judging by what you've both told me of that evening, I was in a pretty talkative mood.'

Niko pulled a face. 'I ask you to be quiet while I tattoo. Of course, if you are in pain, or want to stop, you can speak, but I prefer to be able to concentrate. You may even have gone to sleep for a bit. It is most unusual for people to do that when it is their first tattoo.'

'Maybe that was another sign that I wasn't as with it as you thought I was,' I said wryly.

He nodded his head in acknowledgement. He hadn't been as diligent as he should have been, but from the sounds of it, I'd been pretty determined about getting the tattoo, and the poor guy had obviously been pleased at having the business on a quiet night. I couldn't really blame him for what had happened. And as it turned out, it had all worked out for the best anyway.

Niko pushed across the sketch he had been doing. It was of an island scene, the sea lapping against a beach on which there was a lounger and parasol. In the background a mountain faded into the distance. It was recognisably the Sami coastline, with a couple of artistic liberties.

'I can do a cover-up for free. See here, the name will be

hidden in the lounger and the shading of the beach. It would not be much bigger than the artwork you already have, although it would take a while longer to do it because there is more detail to put in.'

I examined the picture carefully. It was very beautiful. He was clearly a talented artist to have produced such a sketch so quickly, and Amira had said that his work had been careful, and cleanly done. I hesitated. Now I was stone-cold sober, I wasn't sure I was brave enough to put myself under the needle. I couldn't really recall the pain during the tattoo, but I could certainly remember the stinging afterwards, then the swelling and the days of disgusting flaky skin. Did I really want to put myself through all that again?

'Or I can create a design that will cover the word Andreas, and I can put Alexis on instead,' Niko offered.

I laughed. 'No thank you,' I said quickly. I turned to Alexis. 'That is no slight against you. But I realise now that I don't need words on my skin to declare what is in my heart.'

His expression of joy said it all. I wanted to kiss him until we melted.

Niko cleared his throat.

'Cover-up?'

'Maybe later,' I replied. 'I will consider my options. But there's somewhere very important we have to be first.'

Chapter Thirty

'What gave me a small kernel of hope – which I told myself I didn't even deserve to feel – was that you didn't immediately ask who Awesome Andreas was when I said I knew. You just wanted to know why I hadn't told you about him,' said Alexis, some time later as we lay sprawled between the tangled covers of his bed in his apartment above the shop. It was growing dark outside, and through the half-open shutters I could hear the sounds of the street coming to life again after the afternoon break in business.

'It never occurred to me to ask. I was so focused on you, and what we could have together, that the thought of actually encountering an Andreas was awful. Of course, I'm very much looking forward to meeting your awesome twin Andreas...' I paused, raising my eyebrows so he could be in little doubt that I was teasing him. 'But only because he is your family and very important to you, and therefore very important to me.'

Alexis leaned over me to pick up his glasses, then propped himself up on his elbow so he could look at me properly. He reached out with his other hand and started tracing patterns on my back, sending a delicious shiver throughout my body. I snuggled in closer.

'I will be delighted to introduce you to him,' he said.

'No fear that I will run off with him?'

'I trust you. Besides, I seem to remember you referring to me as the "hot twin" a short while ago.'

'Can I borrow your glasses? I need to check.' I laughed and gently pushed him back onto the covers, pinning him beneath me while I pretended to carry out a thorough examination of his features. He did his best to distract me by clasping my waist and turning the tables so that I was now the one lying among the pillows. I reached up and cupped his head in my hands. 'Seriously, you'll always be the hot twin to me. Even though it's only been a few weeks, I feel like you know me better than anyone ever has. I fell for you the second moment we met – that is, when I walked in your bookshop and asked for your help. It was the second moment, but it's the first one where I was stone cold sober and which I can remember fully, so it's the one that really matters.'

'Perhaps it is my bookshop that you really love me for,' suggested Alexis with a smile.

'Naturally,' I replied, then kissed him so deeply that he could be in little doubt about my true feelings.

'This may sound corny,' I said, when we emerged for air, my fingers idly drawing circles on his chest, 'but I think I've found a lot more than my 'Amazing Alexis' here in Kefalonia.'

Alexis chuckled, the warmth of his laughter vibrating against my ear.

'Don't get me wrong, finding you is the cherry on top of the icing on the cake. But I've found out a whole lot of other wonderful things along the way in my journey to meeting you. Things and people. I've started to learn a new language. Just the basics, but I'm improving every day. I've made some wonderful friends. I've developed a serious *tzatziki* addiction. But I've met myself as well. I know that sounds ridiculous, but I feel much more comfortable in my own skin now and a lot happier about standing up for myself. I know what I want out of life, and how I'm going to go about achieving it. I never thought a dodgy tattoo would be the catalyst for that.'

Alexis smiled back at me and I felt my senses buzzing with joyful anticipation.

'I will always be very grateful for the tattoo,' I continued, 'but I think I am going to get it covered up, after all, rather than changed to Alexis. A tattoo of a name isn't really for me, however important to me the person whose name it is. The beach scene that Niko drew was gorgeous. I can't think of a better image to have to celebrate my new life.'

'Whatever you choose, I am sure it will look very beautiful on you.'

His fingers returned to their dancing exploration of my skin.

'Did you know, that in Greek we do not really say "I miss you?"' he murmured against my ear.

I had to concentrate hard to reply.

'No, I didn't know that.'

He traced his index finger along my collarbone inducing a delicious shiver through my body.

'We say *Mou leipeis,*' he continued. 'In English, I think that would literally translate as *You are missing from me.*'

'What are you trying to say?' I asked.

His hand moved up so he was gently massaging the nape of my neck. 'What I am trying to say, is that I think I missed you before I even knew you. Or rather, that you were missing from me before I knew you.'

His beautiful voice was steady, but his accent had grown stronger, something I noticed happened in moments of great emotion.

'I wish there was something as lovely that I could say back in English,' I said. I lowered my gaze and took a deep breath for courage, then looked back up at him. 'There is only this. I feel the same way too. I've fallen for you, Alexis.'

'And I have fallen for you too, Lydia,' he replied.

Somewhere in the distance a *bouzouki* was being played. We moved closer still and danced on into the night.

Epilogue

Three months later

'How are you getting on?' asked Alexis, leaning over and kissing my neck in a place which he knew was particularly sensitive. I shivered with delight, but pretended to wave him away.

'Don't distract me when I'm working. I need to finish reading through this final paragraph, and then I can send it off.'

'This is not what we agreed when I persuaded you to use the back room as your office,' said Alexis, peering over the top of his glasses at me and pretending to grumble.

'You, Amazing Alexis, are quite the distraction. I'll get my own back later when you're trying to sort through your deliveries.'

'I shall very much look forward to it.'

I blew a kiss in his direction and then re-read the final sentence of my blog post. It was a piece describing the facilities and food on offer at a new taverna which had opened in the town of Skala on the southern tip of the island. Not only was I being paid to write the post, but Alexis and I had been able to indulge in a very romantic date night there in the guise of research. The initial introduction to Andreas Rouvas and his commercial empire had led to other opportunities, and now I was building up quite the business writing English copy for hotel websites and tourist destinations around the island. So much so, that I'd had to cut my hours at the Helios, which was good, as the commute across town from the apartment I was now sharing with Alexis was less convenient first thing in the morning than it had been heading down the stairs from my staff quarters at the hotel. I was quietly confident that it wouldn't be long before I could afford to stop the cleaning job altogether. It had been the perfect stopgap, but now I was building my own business, I was excited to be able to concentrate on it full time. Yiota had already assured me that she had my replacement lined up to fill in until Eleni returned from her maternity leave.

I double-checked a final spelling, and then hit Send.

'*Poli kala,*' said Alexis.

'Yes, very good, indeed,' I replied. I was now attending classes at the local lyceum which had reopened for the autumn term, but Alexis was helping me by dropping in extra Greek vocabulary whenever possible. My conversational skills were still pretty stilted, but I would get there. And in the meantime, Alexis and I had English, and other, more interesting ways, in which we could communicate very well indeed.

Alexis checked his watch. 'Are you nearly ready to go? We should be leaving before much longer.'

'Give me two minutes to change my top and put some perfume on, then I'll be all yours.'

'You smell lovely as you are,' he said solemnly.

'That's very sweet of you, Alexis, but I want to make a good impression when I finally meet your brother.'

'Very sensible. You should keep your options open,' he replied with a grin, as confident in my love as I was in his.

'Absolutely. I hear he's pretty awesome, after all.' I winked at him.

When I descended the stairs a short while later, Alexis was waiting for me at the bottom.

'If you carry on looking at me like that, we really are going to be late for the picnic,' I said, my insides skipping at his expression.

'I am sure my brother wouldn't mind,' said Alexis, then gasped as I twirled round for him. 'The new tattoo looks wonderful.'

After thinking about it carefully, I'd finally decided to return to Niko to have the Awesome Andreas tattoo covered up. We'd slightly adapted his design, making it smaller, and adding one very important addition to the lounger, a book, in honour of Alexis's shop, and our shared love of reading.

It had taken a couple of sessions, during which I'd longed for the anaesthetic qualities of wine, but had resisted. The healing process thankfully had been more comfortable than for the original – perhaps something to do with the fact that I hadn't had to spend the first few days of it trying to keep the thing hidden – and today was going to be its first proper outing in its fully finished and healed glory. I'd chosen a cropped T-shirt to wear for the very purpose.

Alexis locked up the shop, and then we set off through town, waving at Niko on our way past his studio.

'It's looking good, Lydia,' he called after us. 'If you want another, I do it for a special price.'

'No thanks, Niko, I'm happy with the one. Your artwork has worked the magic it needed to,' I said cheerily. Although Kat had been convinced I'd get hooked on tattoos, I knew that one was more than enough for me.

'You must add that to your article when you write it for my website,' he insisted. 'Let me know when you are free to talk about that.'

I took Alexis's hand as we turned the corner.

'It sounds like you have acquired another customer,' he said proudly, nudging his hip against mine. I responded by looping my arm around his waist and giving it a squeeze.

Our progress through town was slow because friends kept on stopping us for a chat. I'd never felt so much part of a community before, and I was loving it. The people of Sami had welcomed me with open arms, and Alexis's bookshop had reaped the rewards of their curiosity to meet his new girlfriend, as they all stopped by to check me out, buying books as cover for their visit. Their warmth and friendliness were also helping tide me over until Kat and Amira could come out and stay again. They'd already made one flying visit to meet Alexis, or inspect him as Kat had termed it, and we were in constant FaceTime contact to plan their next trip. Thank goodness for budget airlines, that's all I could say.

We wandered along the coastal path, enjoying the sound of the waves washing up against the shore. The cicadas were chirping in the undergrowth and the scent of wildflowers filled the air. I wanted to dawdle and soak up every step, but there was an important meeting ahead of us. Even though I was excited to meet Alexis's brother, who was finally back on the island after spending the summer working on one of those super yachts I'd found so intimidating at Fiskardo, I was nervous too. I knew how much Andreas's opinion mattered to Alexis, and I hoped I would pass muster. I'd suggested several times we chat over video call, but Alexis had been keen for our first encounter to be in person. Even now he'd kept quiet about exactly where it was we were going.

'Nearly there,' said Alexis, as if he'd read my mind. We left the coast and started walking up through a residential street. I wondered if we were heading to a friend's house. I knew Andreas didn't bother renting a place because he was at sea so much. But then I spotted a sign, and felt a burst of excitement.

'The Melissani Lake? Are we finally going to visit?'

It was the one place I'd been longing to see ever since my return to Kefalonia. Everyone raved about how beautiful it was, but the girls and I hadn't been able to get tickets when we'd come on holiday, and somehow, I'd still not got round to going.

'Maybe,' said Alexis, his smile growing broader.

We rounded a corner, and there we were at the car park. I'd expected it to be heaving like the Drogarati Cave, but it was strangely quiet with only a couple of vehicles parked up.

'Goodness, it looks like we're going to have the place to ourselves, how lucky are we?' I said.

Alexis shrugged his shoulders. 'They are doing some maintenance work on the visitor centre. A friend of a friend works here and said that we could come down while they are officially closed for the day.' His tone changed. 'Ah, here is my brother.'

It was surreal seeing a mirror image of Alexis walking towards us, but once I'd got over the similarities of the brothers, I started to recognise the ways in which Andreas was obviously different.

'*Iassou* Andreas, we meet at last,' I said, giving him a warm hug. 'You have a very different stride from your brother. And I'd say your nose is slightly bigger than his.'

Andreas grinned. While Alexis's lips always quirked to the right when he smiled, I noticed that Andreas's went to the left.

'Very good, very good. Even our own father does not always notice that.' He leaned forward and kissed me on both cheeks. He smelled different to Alexis as well. 'I am so pleased to meet you at last. Alexis kept you such a secret from me, and now he can't stop talking about you. Welcome to the family.'

I felt my cheeks turn hot with happiness. Everything was going to be just fine.

A car door slammed, and Yiota emerged, closely followed by Angelo. They paused to help a couple out of the back seat.

'Eleni, have you brought the baby?' I asked with delight. After Stephano had rushed Eleni to hospital on the night of the party, mother and baby had had to stay in for a while following complications during the birth. Alexis and I had been among the first to visit them when they'd come back home, but so far they'd managed to keep very quiet about one important thing – what they were going to call their new son.

'Certainly, we thought this would be a good occasion to introduce him properly to everyone.'

'Does that mean we are finally going to hear the name? I can't believe you've taken so long deciding,' said Alexis.

'We wanted to try it out for a while to make sure it was the right fit for him. And it is. Everybody, this is A—'

'Not another Andreas?' said Alexis's twin.

Eleni and Stephano exchanged amused glances.

'No, we felt that there are quite enough Andreases on the island already,' replied Eleni. 'This is Achilles.'

'A good, strong, heroic name.' I smiled. 'This makes our picnic even more of a celebration.'

As we unloaded baskets of food from the car boot, Andreas drew me to one side.

'I wanted to say again how happy I am that Alexis and you have found each other. I think it's pretty awesome.'

'Stop trying to claim the credit,' said Alexis, marching past with the food, and playfully elbowing his brother. 'Just because it was your name on the tattoo, it doesn't mean that you played the role of cosmic matchmaker.'

'Ah but Cupid works in mysterious ways,' said Andreas, his eyes twinkling with amusement. 'And if you two are very nice to me, I might agree to do the hard work of rowing the boat so you love birds can sit back and enjoy the trip.'

'It's why we really invited you,' I said, deciding that I might as well jump straight into the bantering family dynamic. Andreas grinned broadly.

It took a while to assemble our group at the entrance to the lake, despite the small size of the party. It was amazing how much organising it took to get seven adults, a baby and about a ton of food into position. The entrance to the lake looked pretty non-descript, but after my experience at the Drogarati Cave, I wasn't going to let that deceive me. We walked down a concrete corridor to a jetty where a rickety wooden rowing boat was tied up waiting for us. I felt a moment of misgiving, remembering my adventure on Captain Andreas's ship, but then I reassured myself that it must be perfectly safe if little Achilles was going to be joining us.

All thoughts of fear quickly disappeared as Andreas rowed us through a narrow rocky passage, which at points was so low that we had to duck our heads, and out into the Melissani Lake itself. I gasped as I took in my surroundings. The lake was in a vast cave which was open in the centre of its roof. The sun was hovering nearly overhead, sending shards of light dancing over the surface of the water. Birds darted in and out, as if they were playing a game of tag, while beneath the water's surface, fish lazily explored the depths. Andreas set down the oars and let the boat gently drift around the lake.

Alexis checked his watch. 'Nearly midday,' he said, then started to hand out the food for our picnic.

There couldn't be many better places in the world to be. As we tucked into our feast, I looked around at the occupants of the boat, people who I would never have met if it hadn't been for that drunken, impulsive decision to get a tattoo. They were good friends who already felt like family. And then of course there was the one, even more special person for whom there was not a tattoo in the world eloquent enough to encapsulate my feelings. As Alexis's watch buzzed to mark midday, high overhead the sun's rays started shining straight down through the open cave roof and into the lake, illuminating the clear depths so it looked like our boat was floating in the air.

While the rest of the party were distracted by the spectacle, I turned to Alexis, needing to share this moment with him. I reached out and stroked my hand down the side of his face. He cupped the back of my neck and pulled me close for a heart-melting kiss.

'Happy?' he whispered in my ear, as I rested my head on his shoulder, the boat rocking gently beneath us.

'Very,' I replied.

Acknowledgments

Greece is one of my absolutely favourite countries to visit, and while travel has been challenging over the past couple of years, it's been such a joy to spend time there in my imagination while I've been writing this book. My first thank you has to be to my parents who took me to Greece when I was a child and sparked an enduring love. And I'd also like to send my heartfelt gratitude to those who have taught me the Greek language, both the ancient and modern variety.

It takes a team to bring a book into the world, and I'm very fortunate to have such a fabulous one on my side. Thank you to my lovely editor Jennie Rothwell and the rest of the wonderful One More Chapter team for all your enthusiasm, encouragement and expertise. From the gorgeous cover design and insightful editing to the eye-catching marketing and all else in between, I am truly lucky to work with you wonderful lot! And thank you also to my amazing agent Amanda Preston for your tireless support and belief in me, I don't know what I'd do without you!

To the powerhouse of talent that is the Book Camp squad – I really appreciate your friendship and cheerleading. It was great to catch up again in real life at last! I'm already looking forward to our next reunion.

And finally, thank you to you, the readers, for choosing this book. Your backing means the world to me. I really hope you've had as much fun travelling to Kefalonia with Lydia as I have.

Read on for a preview of _Duvet Day_, another uplifting and funny romcom from Emily Kerr...

Young lawyer Alexa Humphries's one true love is her precious duvet, yet she is torn from its comforting embrace every morning while the foxes are still scavenging the bins outside and doesn't get back until long after most normal people are already asleep.

Worn down by the endless demands of her suspicious boss and her competitive, high-flying housemate and fellow lawyer, Zara, Alexa barely recognises herself anymore.

But today is different. Today, Alexa just cannot get out of bed to face the world.

Everyone deserves a duvet day, don't they?

Duvet Day: Chapter One

Tuesday 23rd April

4.57 a.m.

There's nothing quite like snuggling in the warm embrace of my one true love. It's where I feel utterly content. Here I am safe, happy, and briefly able to remove the mask of sensible, Grown-Up Lawyer that I have to show to the rest of the world. Here, for a few blissful moments, I can finally feel like Alexa Humphries, actual human being, rather than Alexa Humphries, corporate drone. But the trouble is, that's all it ever is. A few blissful moments. For my darling, king-size, 13.5 tog duvet and I spend most of our time apart, cruelly separated by the ever-growing demands of my job, which has become more of a lifestyle choice than just a career. This is so not how I imagined my dream life in London would turn out.

Take today, for example. It's still dark outside. The foxes are scavenging by the bins on the street corner, and the noise of traffic has quietened to an occasional grumble from its usual constant roar. Anyone with any sense is deep in the land of nod, and according to my employment contract, I'm not expected at work for at least another four hours. But whereas lawyers are steely-eyed and detail-oriented in pretty much every other aspect of our business, when it comes to following the letter of our own working hours, we're expected to become forgetful and instead do what is necessary. And it turns out that my employers consider it necessary for me to be on call. Permanently. Which is why I didn't get to my beloved bed until nearly 1.30 a.m. and why I've been awake for the last half hour stressing about the day ahead and panic-reading obscure bits of contract law for a particularly complicated merger that's looming on the horizon.

It's not like I'm extremely senior and important either. When it comes to the food chain of office politics, I know I'm the pond life. But if I want to make it from plant to herbivore and beyond, I need to play the game. I'm just not sure I like this particular game that much any more.

Despite that old cliché of lawyers being bloodsuckers out to make as much money as possible, whatever the cost to others, I've always had a rosy-eyed view of the profession. It started when I was six and the local solicitor helped my grandma prevent developers from forcibly buying the family farm, and then was solidified by my addiction to the movie *Legally Blonde* during my formative years. Sure, the main character, Elle, went through tough times, being patronised by a pervy professor and being constantly underestimated because of her hair colour. But she triumphed as the underdog and rose to great heights, all while wearing killer heels and carrying her faithful pooch in her designer handbag. I would sit in my teenage bedroom, teeth aching from my latest trip to the orthodontist, face covered in bits of toothpaste in a vain attempt to dry out my spots, and promise myself that, one day, I would be like Elle: a confident, successful woman full of integrity, standing up for justice, and fighting for those without the power to fight for themselves.

The spots vanished (mostly), and the teeth were straightened, but somewhere between law school and venturing into the big, wide world, I got lost. It's been two years since I became the envy of my university buddies by joining Richmond Woods. But I didn't realise when I signed on the dotted line that I might as well have signed in blood. It's one of London's leading law firms, notable for having one of the biggest budgets for pro bono work in the city, which is why I was so desperate to get the job in the first place. Alas, while the people on the fifth floor get to make use of that philanthropic power and do some good in the world, I'm trapped on a treadmill on the second floor, charged with applying my skills to help a lot of rich, bossy men become even richer and bossier. The richer bit is from using my legal know-how to help them negotiate company mergers and takeovers, the bossier bit is from being a real-life Alexa who they can enjoy ordering around with the same lack of respect they use to operate their voice-activated devices. The only way it could be worse was if I was called Siri instead.

I stretch out my toes to take full advantage of the still-toasty hot-water bottle at my feet. My room in the house-share has beautiful big windows, making it a light and airy space, or so the girl moving out promised me when she showed me round. I unfortunately failed to consider the fact that the stately Victorian sash windows with their glorious view of the squat opposite were single-glazed. Add into the mix ill-fitting wooden frames which are suspiciously squishy, and it's a recipe for a permanent draught akin to a gale. Even during last summer's heatwave, there was only about one week where I didn't need some extra form of warmth to get me through the night. I suppose what I could really do with is a hot bedmate – in both senses of the word – but as I appear to have formed an unhealthy, all-encompassing relationship with my job, I can't see that happening any time soon.

Instead, I'm trying to keep warm with my current bed attire, an anything-but-sexy unicorn onesie. It's all the colours of the rainbow, fleece-lined, with a furry exterior, complete with tail and silver horn. Don't get me wrong, I love a cosy pair of PJs as much as the next girl, but a unicorn onesie is definitely at the extreme end of things, and when my twin brother Charlie handed it over to me for Christmas with a wicked grin on his face, I swore I'd never lower myself to actually wearing it. But what can I say? Needs must. My laundry pile has been growing its own ecosystem because I've been getting back from work late, and I'm too scared of incurring the wrath of my Queen Bee housemate Zara to turn on the washing machine after dark. In desperation last night, I'd dug out this little number from the back of my wardrobe, where it had been languishing in a cocoon of torn wrapping paper. I'm trying not to imagine the look of triumph on Charlie's face if he knew I was wearing it. He's always on at me to "Chill out and go with the flow", which is all well and good if you're content coasting your way through life by occasionally busking in the local market town back home, like he does, but it doesn't really cut it in the corporate world I've ended up stuck in.

The windows rattle as a lorry rumbles down the road, sending another chilly blast of morning air over my face, and making the curtains flutter. Shards of orange light from the streetlamps dance their way around the walls, sharpening the fuzzy details of my room. I gaze around, nostalgic thoughts of my childhood home making me see my current surroundings as if for the first time. I'm barely ever in here when I'm not sleeping, and I can't remember when I last actually paused and considered my surroundings. It's a depressing sight; wardrobe doors hanging open to reveal a row of identikit suits, the pile of dirty washing overflowing out of a bag in the corner, and stacks of musty legal tomes leaning precariously by the bed. It's more of a habitat than a bedroom, certainly not what someone would associate with a so-called professional woman in her mid-twenties. The only uplifting feature is the collection of pictures on my walls. They're bright abstract prints of some of the most famous London landmarks, images which adorned my student bedroom to inspire me during the long days of learning case law and wading through incomprehensible legal jargon.

When I first moved here, I had visions of changing the world during the week, and then ticking off each famous landmark during the weekends, but I'm always too knackered to be bothered. Most of my weekends are spent comatose, wrapped up in my duvet and trying to catch up on all the sleep I've missed out on during the weekdays of corporate kowtowing. The realisation saddens me. It's like I've blinked and suddenly two years have passed without me getting any closer to the dreams of making a difference that I'd once held so dear. How have I let things get to this position?

I turn onto my side, blocking out the too-cheery images, and try to ignore the crushing sense of failure which threatens to overwhelm me. I need to get a grip. Nobody likes a misery-guts and this one-person pity party needs to stop. Time to focus on the day ahead. Right on cue, my phone buzzes, warning me that yet another email has landed in my inbox. When I first started at Richmond Woods, being gifted a work phone and being told that I could also use it for my personal calls felt like a demonstration of trust and respect. However, after the thrill of being able to ring utility companies' premium-rate phone lines without having to worry about the cost had worn off, I realised the hard reality of the apparently generous gesture. I started to resent the fact that I was expected to carry a device akin to my own personal slave master in my pocket all the time. Even in my supposed downtime I find myself obsessively checking messages and feeling stressed if I don't reply to my seniors within half an hour. Sometimes it feels like my head might explode with the pressure of keeping on top of everything.

Despite my best efforts last night, my inbox is still at the higher end of double figures, and suddenly it seems impossible that I'll ever get through it all. Several of the emails have been sent with bright red exclamation marks in the subject line to denote them as extremely urgent, and just in case I haven't got the message, "SORT THIS NOW" has been added in shouty capital letters. I cringe as if I was actually being yelled at. Of course, no one at Richmond Woods would be so coarse as to raise their voice in person, but they've developed all kinds of passive-aggressive methods of creating the same horrible effect on us lowly minions.

I know I should start chipping away at my replies, but I'm desperate for just a few more minutes of peace. I find myself grabbing my own battered mobile and falling into my usual procrastination habit of scrolling through Instagram, trying to escape reality into a world of hashtags promising glossy positivity.

Pictures of cute animals and gorgeous holiday destinations normally do the trick in cheering me up, but today all I can notice are my friends' posts about their perfect lives. Instead of putting a smile on my face, they increase my sense of melancholy. I gaze at the shiny picture of my best friend from school, carefree and laughing with her fiancé on Sydney Harbour Bridge, and try to remember the last time I saw any of these people in real life.

When I make my weekly call to my parents, they always ask after my old school and uni mates, and the answers trip off my tongue. Laura's engaged, Michael's got another promotion and oh, did I tell you that Sara thought she bumped into Prince William at Waitrose the other day? But now I'm stopping and actually thinking about it, I realise my friends haven't told me these charming anecdotes personally. They've made general announcements to me and several hundred others of their closest online followers. I've double-tapped my appreciation and sometimes there's even been the briefest exchange in the comments along the lines of, "Congratulations lovely, we must meet for a proper catch up soon", but I can't remember the last time it actually translated into a real-life interaction. Have I allowed social media to paper over the cracks of where an actual social life should be? I always assumed everyone was too busy, but a growing fear is telling me that maybe I'm the only one struggling, while everyone else really has got it sorted so that they're #livingthedream.

Suddenly my body jerks and the sick sensation of being about to fall off a cliff jolts me back to full consciousness. That was close. Much as I need the sleep, I can't afford to drift off again. Regretfully, I push the hot-water bottle out of reach so I don't get too comfortable. I know I should be getting on with work. The senior partner I report to has flown out to Japan to help a client finalise a deal, and her flight is due to land in Tokyo at any moment. I'd be prepared to bet next month's rent money that she'll ping a dozen missives my way as soon as she does. Genevieve's notorious for expecting an instant acknowledgement and I daren't let her down. Besides, she's on the appointments board for the pro bono department and maybe, just maybe, one day she'll recognise my hard work and reward me for it with a position there, and then all this will have been worth it. Or that's what I keep telling myself, anyway.

My work phone buzzes once again as the expected emails arrive. My fingers hover over the screen, but just the thought of sending even one more reply makes me feel like a steel band is tightening around my head, and I find myself pushing the phone away. Despite my good intentions, I shuffle back down my mattress, burrowing myself into my duvet like a hibernating animal. If I can't see the emails, maybe I can pretend they don't exist, I tell myself, much like a small child playing hide and seek by merely covering their eyes.

The phone's buzzing continues, and through the thin party wall, I hear the distinctive thumps of Zara jumping out of bed and switching her light on. It's a badge of pride among us junior lawyers if we can count the number of hours of sleep we've had on one hand. Zara claims to thrive on this, but anything less than six hours and I find my brain becoming sluggish and my reactions slowing until I feel like

I have jet lag. Sometimes, I'll have a whole conversation with someone and feel like they're talking to me on a time delay, so it takes me several seconds to be able to process what they're saying and be able to respond appropriately.

Now she's in circulation, I know I should look at my emails. Zara and I work for the same firm and in the same department – another reason why I feel I can't even switch off when I get home. When I first moved to London, it seemed like the easiest solution to share a house with a colleague. Yes, I know, what was I thinking? But by the time I'd realised quite how ruthlessly competitive Zara is, I'd already signed a six-month lease. Somehow, it's gone on a lot longer than that initial agreement, but I'll just add that to my long list of things that I've let slip. I barely have time to buy a pint of milk, let alone look into moving house. And on the plus side, our other housemate Sam is no bother. In fact, she's no bother to the point that we've only ever communicated through the house WhatsApp group. She moved in at Christmas when I was home visiting my family for a brief forty-eight hours, and she appears to work weird shifts too. Or maybe the reason we've never met is that she's got a much better social life than me. Most people have, after all.

Now the clattering sound of Zara typing on her laptop punches its way into my room. She's attacking the keys as if they are promotion rivals. Even when I pull a pillow over my head, I can still hear her tapping away, each jab nagging at my growing sense of anxiety. It's like she's doing it deliberately, making sure I know she's already hard at work while I'm being a lazy layabout. I know I should pick up the work phone again, send out my own replies and signal that my working day has begun. But somehow today it seems impossible. The very thought of rolling out of bed, getting dressed and dragging myself into the office for yet another day of thrashing myself to the limit is enough to make me groan out loud. I wish I could carry on pretending to myself that everything is OK, but this morning, I just don't have the energy to even try.

I poke my nose out of my duvet and stare wistfully at the family picture teetering precariously on what was meant to be my dressing table, but which I use instead as a makeshift desk. It's a classic Humphries image, illustrating the family pecking order perfectly, with me the default target for teasing. My older brothers are cracking up, my mum and dad are hiding their amusement with mock outrage, while I'm rolling my eyes at Charlie who was taking the picture. I can remember the suggestion he made to elicit such a response. I'd been in a hurry to make my train back to London, and being delayed for a family snap was not helping my stress levels. After dragging me back to the doorstep and plonking me in position, Charlie had peeked above the lens of the ancient camera and fixed me with a stern stare as I protested my urgent need to get going, right now.

"Lighten up, sis. Just throw a sickie. What's the worst that can happen?"

His words echo around my mind.

Throw a sickie...

I can't.

Charlie wouldn't think twice about it. But I'm the sensible twin. It would be completely out of character for me to do something so spontaneous and rebellious. I'm expected at work. I've got deadlines to meet, clients to appease, bosses to impress. I can't let my colleagues down. But Charlie's voice in my head is insistent.

What's the worst that can happen?

I know the answer to this. A day out of the loop could leave me on the back foot for weeks. I could lose the respect and trust of my colleagues, my job even, were I to get found out. I can't do it. It would be foolhardy.

But even as I try to bully myself into getting up and getting on with what needs to be done, my gaze travels back to those pictures of London, images which used to stand for hope and now represent nothing but personal failure. How long can I keep lying to myself that things are going to get better? I realise I've had enough. I am done with feeling like this. I need to do something about it.

Before I lose courage, I reach out, pick up my phone and find myself typing an email I never imagined I would dare to write. It's time I took my destiny into my own hands.

Don't forget to order your copy of *Duvet Day* to find out what happens next...

ONE MORE CHAPTER

One More Chapter is an
award-winning global
division of HarperCollins.

Sign up to our newsletter to get our
latest eBook deals and stay up to date
with our weekly Book Club!
<u>Subscribe here.</u>

Meet the team at
<u>www.onemorechapter.com</u>

Follow us!
 @OneMoreChapter_
 @OneMoreChapter
 @onemorechapterhc

Do you write unputdownable fiction?
We love to hear from new voices.
Find out how to submit your novel at
<u>www.onemorechapter.com/submissions</u>